W9-CSU-689

SPAWNING THE FOURTH REICH . . .

The Phoenix felt the blood rush to her head and she was on the verge of screaming into the phone but the caller continued.

"We'll finish them off either before they get there or once all three of them are together.

"I'm truly sorry we've had this little delay but I assure you things will all be in order again by the end of the day."

She was tempted to say *they better be* but instead simply hung up the phone. She moved out of the telephone booth and stood for a moment in the bright morning sun.

She raised her arm above her head and immediately attracted the attention of a taxi. She could hardly wait until the White House reception this evening to hear all the small talk about the accident that the President's press aide and his girl friend were to be involved in. It had to be an accident. It always was. For an instant she wondered if the F.B.I. man would be part of the same accident or whether the Organization would find a separate way to be rid of him. No matter, his death certainly would not cause the kind of alarm the death of a White House aide would.

The cab pulled up and she entered the back, turning on her most attractive smile to the driver who was looking at her through his mirror. Filthy slob, she thought.

BLOCKBUSTER FICTION FROM PINNACLE BOOKS!

THE FINAL VOYAGE OF THE S.S.N. SKATE   (17-157, $3.95)
by Stephen Cassell
The "leper" of the U.S. Pacific Fleet, SSN 578 nuclear attack sub SKATE, has one final mission to perform—an impossible act of piracy that will pit the underwater deathtrap and its inexperienced crew against the combined might of the Soviet Navy's finest!

QUEENS GATE RECKONING   (17-164, $3.95)
by Lewis Purdue
Only a wounded CIA operative and a defecting Soviet ballerina stand in the way of a vast consortium of treason that speeds toward the hour of mankind's ultimate reckoning! From the bestselling author of THE LINZ TESTAMENT.

FAREWELL TO RUSSIA   (17-165, $4.50)
by Richard Hugo
A KGB agent must race against time to infiltrate the confines of U.S. nuclear technology after a terrifying accident threatens to unleash unmitigated devastation!

THE NICODEMUS CODE   (17-133, $3.95)
by Graham N. Smith and Donna Smith
A two-thousand-year-old parchment has been unearthed, unleashing a terrifying conspiracy unlike any the world has previously known, one that threatens the life of the Pope himself, and the ultimate destruction of Christianity!

Available wherever paperbacks are sold, or order direct from the Publisher. Send cover price plus 50¢ per copy for mailing and handling to Pinnacle Books, Dept.17-235, 475 Park Avenue South, New York, N.Y. 10016. Residents of New York, New Jersey and Pennsylvania must include sales tax. DO NOT SEND CASH.

HITLER'S DAUGHTER

TIMOTHY B. BENFORD

PINNACLE BOOKS
WINDSOR PUBLISHING CORP.

PINNACLE BOOKS

are published by

Windsor Publishing Corp.
475 Park Avenue South
New York, NY 10016

Copyright © 1983 Timothy B. Benford

All rights reserved. No part of this book may be reproduced in any form or by any means without the prior written consent of the Publisher, excepting brief quotes used in
reviews.

Second printing: October, 1989

Printed in the United States of America

HITLER'S DAUGHTER

Prologue

The ambulance driver watched the two escort motorcycles rise slightly and shudder as they landed on the moonlit road that wended before him. He instinctively moved his foot from the accelerator and eased it halfway down on the brake, hoping to lessen the shock as his vehicle began the same incline.

Silently he cursed the SS Gross Deutschland Division cyclists he was following. The ambulance bucked over the hump and crunched against the ground.

The Wehrmacht sergeant had driven from the airport to St. Nazaire on the French coast many times before but never at such speeds. He accelerated again to close the distance and at once heard the increased whine of the rear escort motorcycles also picking up the pace.

The impact had jolted SS Standartenfuhrer Dr. Helmut Wolf from the twilight sleep he had drifted into only minutes before. He gazed at the trees blurring by the passenger window of the camouflage-painted ambulance.

"A little slower, sergeant," he ordered. "There's no need to risk an accident—I assure you the U-boat will

1

be waiting at the quay." He slouched his small frame deeper into the seat and once again closed his eyes.

"Yes sir," the driver responded softly while letting up on the accelerator. "I was just trying to keep up with the escort," he added.

His hands, warm and moist from tightly gripping the steering wheel, were almost at eye level. Relaxing his grip, he flexed his fingers and slid his palms lower to cooler positions on each side.

Almost instantly the rear motorcycles pulled abreast. He wondered what was going through the minds of the heavily-armed SS men bouncing violently in the sidecars. Fearing a collision, he disregarded Wolf's order and accelerated to pull away.

"How much farther to St. Nazaire?" Wolf asked.

"Ten . . . maybe fifteen minutes, sir," the driver answered. "The town limits begin soon, but the quay is fifteen minutes away at most."

Wolf didn't respond. He pulled himself into an upright position and half turned to look at his patient sleeping in the rear of the ambulance.

An almost gentle smile creased the corners of his pale lips. His eyes locked on the stomach of the prostrate woman secured to the stretcher and a surge of pride swelled up within him.

He contemplated the embryo in her womb and the destiny that awaited it . . . and him. He permitted his thoughts to linger for a few moments and then he turned away. The smile on his face had grown into a full grin.

"Good," he said as he looked ahead at the asphalt ribbon rushing beneath the ambulance's headlights. "Very good."

The driver nodded, understanding the comment to be approval of the journey's termination.

In fact it wasn't.

Wolf's mind was creating images of other journeys yet to come. Journeys after he and the patient had safely arrived in the United States and the child she was carrying had matured into an adult. He orchestrated these fantasies with precise detail for several minutes. Finally his attention returned to the road before him.

Contented, the twenty-five-year-old doctor with the rank of colonel in the SS once again slid deep into his seat.

He watched the moon glide behind an irregular cluster of small clouds in the sky ahead. Its filtering light broke through in short, rapid bursts.

***

A sailor on the U-boat rocking gently in St. Nazaire harbor had also watched the moon succumb to the phalanx of clouds. He was now scanning the semidarkness of the village before him.

His eyes traced the outline of the rooftops of once-grand nineteenth-century homes nestled on the hillside beyond the double-spired clapboard church.

Turning toward the southern extremity of the wharf he wondered if this quaint town was always so quiet or if special precautions had been ordered because of the extraordinary visit of the U-boat. If Wehrmacht or SS troops were enforcing the curfew, he thought, it was certainly absolute. He could recall not one sound, human or otherwise, disturbing the almost eerie silence during the two hours he had been on watch.

Only the sound of the sea as it lapped the boat's hull and crashed into the barnacle-encrusted struts of the quay kept his mind alert.

Faint but rapid footfalls on the boat's ladder warned him someone was coming topside.

"Anything yet?" There was a slight trace of tension in the lieutenant's voice.

"Nothing, sir. It's almost too quiet. I'd feel a lot better if we weren't sitting here on the surface."

"So would we all," the lieutenant snapped.

He turned and ran his eyes across the mouth of the harbor and stopped where he thought the sun would be rising over the cobalt-blue sea in less than an hour.

"We've been here too long already," he added, "but the captain says there is no question about leaving before the convoy arrives."

"Sir?"

The sailor strained his eyes in the direction of the long street that ran almost directly in front of the quay.

"Something is moving out there, sir. I'm sure I just saw lights."

Both men peered down the street and as the moon drifted behind a heavy cloud cover the brightness of the headlights on the escort motorcycles was unmistakable. Now they could also hear the rumbling sounds of the vehicles as they approached.

The lights continued to grow closer.

"Go below and tell the captain the convoy is here . . . hurry!"

The captain arrived on the bridge before anyone else. He was followed by the executive officer leading six sailors armed with submachine guns.

As they spread out along the length of the U-boat the captain joined the lieutenant and fixed his gaze on the traffic rapidly approaching the quay.

Though his pulse rate had quickened with anticipation there was no trace of excitement as he addressed the lieutenant.

"What do you think, Lieutenant? Is it the convoy or the Allies?

The young officer frowned but continued to stare at the bobbing shafts of light. It was still impossible to identify the vehicles.

"It's the convoy, sir," he wanted to add *I'm certain of it*, but choked the words in his throat. His confident tone belied the flash of doubt the captain's comment raised.

St. Nazaire was only one of two French ports still in German hands. The Allies, in their rapid advance through France after the Normandy breakout at St. Lo, by-passed many occupied towns and villages as they fought to push the Germans back to the Rhine. For Germans in isolated areas such as this the spectre of Armageddon hung over them daily.

The ambulance and its motorcycle escort swept onto the quay and came to an abrupt halt hardly ten yards from the men on the U-boat who silently watched.

The clouds had gone and the wharf was bathed in brilliant moonlight.

The guards in the sidecars had their guns trained on the U-boat from the moment it had come into sight. Now the motorcycle drivers quickly dismounted and they too aimed their strapped-on weapons at the captain and his men.

For what seemed like several long moments neither side moved. It was a deadly standoff. If shooting broke out, the captain thought, there would be wholesale massacre. Nobody would survive.

He broke the silence with a calm, but authoritative question in his clipped Bavarian accent.

"Who is the commanding officer of this convoy?"

The SS man who had driven the left lead motorcycle snapped his heels together and brought his body to rigid attention.

"SS Standartenfuhrer Wolf!" he barked, then smartly moved to open the passenger side door of the ambulance for the young SS doctor.

Wolf slowly lifted his right leg to the ground and then brought his left limb out with no difficulty. The man who had opened the door extended a hand and Wolf pulled himself out of the vehicle. He reached back and retrieved an ornate, gold-topped cane.

Favoring his right leg, he limped a few steps closer to the U-boat.

"I am Standartenfuhrer Wolf . . . and your name, Captain?"

In a flat monotone that seemed to reverberate off the buildings several yards away the captain answered in the prearranged code that substituted for his own name: "Phoenix."

Wolf gave him a broad smile and, half turning to the armed men behind him, made a broad sweeping move in the air with his cane. They immediately brought down their guns.

The captain responded by thrusting his arm out forward and dropping it. Now the U-boat men's guns came down.

"Prepare to bring the patient aboard," Wolf ordered and then slowly began to make his way toward the improvised gangplank. The captain and lieutenant reached out and assisted him as he got closer.

"Thank you, Captain. I think we should have a few words while your men go below." It was more of an order than a suggestion. "The SS will attend to our passenger."

Now that Wolf was standing before the captain the U-boat officer took full measure of him.

Wolf did not fill the image the captain and other members of the Kriegsmarine had of the supermen in the SS. His slight build, his limp and dark Mediterranean features were at odds with the athletic, blond giants Propaganda Minister Joseph Goebbels had advertised on posters across Fortress Europe.

Nonetheless, the captain was not prepared to challenge the man's authority. Seventy-two hours earlier he had received a personal coded message from Admiral Karl Doenitz that clearly spelled out his subbordination:

"RENDEZVOUS BETWEEN 0100 AND 0500 HOURS WITH SS STANDARTENFUHRER DR. HELMUT WOLF IN THE FRENCH PORT OF ST. NAZAIRE. UNDER NO CIRCUMSTANCES ARE YOU TO DEPART BEFORE THE ARRIVAL OF HIS CONVOY. REPEAT. REMAIN IN PORT UNTIL YOU HAVE BOARDED STANDARTENFUHRER WOLF AND A CIVILIAN FEMALE. PREPARE YOUR BOAT FOR A VOYAGE OF CONSIDERABLE DURATION. ONCE CONTACT IS MADE WITH STANDAR-TENFUHRER WOLF YOU AND YOUR BOAT'S COMPLEMENT ARE UNEQUIVOCALLY UNDER HIS COMMAND BY DIRECT ORDER OF THE FUHRER. IDENTIFY YOURSELF TO HIM ONLY AS PER CYPHER SELECTION 3:OBW 202 5/1/45. NO RE-PLY THIS MESSAGE, ACKNOWLEDGE ONLY."

The captain ordered his men below and with Wolf watched the SS men on the quay begin to remove the stretcher from the ambulance.

The Wehrmacht sergeant who drove the ambulance deposited Wolf's satchel and a black briefcase on the deck and returned to the vehicle.

"Captain," Wolf turned toward him and locked his ebony eyes directly on the naval officer, "I suggest you too go below and read these orders."

He proffered an envelope that even in the limited light the captain saw bore the personal monogram of Adolf Hitler.

"They only concern our departure. Once we are at sea I will instruct you further." Without waiting for a reply Wolf turned away and again watched the transfer of the patient.

"As you wish, Standartenfuhrer." The captain hesi-tated for an instant then quickly turned and made his way below. He was eager to read the orders written on Hitler's personal stationery in the privacy of his cabin.

Wolf was back on the quay when the captain, his executive officer and two sailors who would handle the mooring lines reappeared on deck.

The SS men were at attention in front of the ambulance, parallel to the U-boat, having completed the transfer of the patient. Wolf was addressing them but as he noticed the captain and the others moving on deck he concluded his remarks.

". . . So now I must leave here. I would prefer to have remained in Berlin or even be returning now with you to German soil. We of Gross Deutschland SS Division have had the honor to carry out one of the Fuhrer's final orders. Remember this day, cherish it."

He turned away from them and, leaning on his cane, made his way once again up the gangplank assisted by the captain.

The SS men remained at rigid attention, savoring this unusually profuse praise Hitler himself had asked the Standartenfuhrer to convey. They watched him reach the deck of the U-boat, turn toward them and shoot his arm skyward in a final "Heil Hitler!"

Their attempts to return the Nazi salute were lost in the ear-splitting staccato as the U-boat's executive officer fired the forward machine gun at them from point-blank range.

Its bullets seemed to raise their bodies in a grotesque, tumbling ballet, chopping some in half, ripping limbs off others and exploding their heads.

It was over in under 15 seconds.

There, illuminated by the flames from one of the motorcycle gas tanks, lay the mute and forever silent hand-picked members of Hitler's elite bodyguard. They had paid the supreme sacrifice for their devotion.

***

Nearly three weeks later, in U.S. coastal waters, civilian-dressed Standartenfuhrer Helmut Wolf and the pregnant woman with him transferred to a private yacht and bid farewell to the U-boat.

Several hours later, as the U-boat silently glided toward a haven in South America, and as its crew prepared to celebrate their successful mission, the captain executed the last order he had received from Wolf. He opened the black briefcase.

The explosion created an underwater flash nearly one hundred yards in diameter. On the surface the usually cold Atlantic boiled briefly.

Chapter 1

Washington D.C. 1984

Although it was 10:30 PM the Secretary of State's cocktail party was just starting to come alive. By Washington standards this Friday night was very young.

White House press aide Ted Scott had looked at his watch twice now within the past five minutes. He was tired and bored. The door opened and several more guests arrived at the rapidly filling Georgetown apartment.

For the last twenty minutes Ted found himself cornered as the uninterested third party in a lengthy discussion about *USS Nimitz* class nuclear-powered aircraft carriers. The Pentagon's Chief of Naval Operations and the senior Southern Senator on the Appropriations Committee were spheres apart.

"Let me tell you something, Admiral," the portly senator drawled, "Those suckers priced out at $3.5-billion good old American dollars each in 1984 money. Be happy you got four of 'em."

He paused and shook his head then added, "Gawd, then we've gotta fill 'em up with F-14s at over a million dollars apiece!"

"But Senator," the admiral retorted, "the other eight

11

carriers in our flattop fleet are floating relics . . . and furthermore . . ."

Ted excused himself and wedged his way between the two men. He began to weave toward the portable bar tucked against the open French doors leading to the plant-covered sundeck.

As he deftly maneuvered his glass between several reaching arms and onto the bar's hammered copper surface he was tapped on the back by Jim Hanlon, administrative aide to Congresswoman Leona Crawford Gordon.

"Ted, your boss wants to see you," Hanlon said, pointing in a general direction across the room. "He's over there in a group paying homage to Miss Television America."

Hanlon's eyes widened and he lunged past Ted for a narrow space that had opened at the bar. Ted's low "Thanks" was smothered by the rising din around the bar.

Ted began backtracking across the room, occasionally smiling or nodding in recognition as he passed the acolytes of power in this capital city.

The senator was tapping his chubby index finger on the admiral's chest. "But if *my* state had some of those fat Navy weapons' contracts I just might be inclined to reconsider my vote on giving you people another aircraft carrier or two . . ."

White House Communications Director and Press Secretary David Holland, raised his hand above his head in a circular motion. Ted acknowledged it and moved his six-foot frame closer to the group.

It was obvious that Sharon Franklin was the center of attention. Strikingly beautiful, and with a near-perfect Grecian figure, her sharply chiseled features were accented by long chestnut brown hair that matched her seductive eyes.

In addition to being a first-rate journalist, her looks were thought to be equally responsible for the continually high ratings her nightly *Washington Report* television show generated.

As Ted reached the perimeter of the group her resonant voice carried to him.

"I called that gutless twerp who's responsible for the network's distribution to affiliate stations and told him if he ever again cut time from my slot for such dribble, such garbage, they could go out and find themselves another anchorwoman." She paused and took a healthy swallow of her drink.

Ted slipped alongside David Holland, about halfway around the select group waiting for Sharon to continue.

"Good evening Miss Franklin, David, everybody."

His greeting was returned by bobbing heads and all eyes once again focused on the woman her detractors mockingly called "Miss Television America."

Sharon Franklin gave Ted a weak smile and picked up her dialogue.

"Those airheads in New York think they're still back in the 1930s or 40s! Who cares if a bunch of silly roughnecks want to dress up in uniforms and hold parades? It's utterly ridiculous." She paused again and sipped her drink.

David Holland fixed an artificial smile on his face and feigned sympathetic concern.

"Sharon, the White House is just as disturbed as you are. Your profile on the Vice President is something we've been looking forward to. I hear it was a fantastic piece of electronic journalism. It will be scheduled again, won't it . . . I mean we'll have an opportunity see it this week, don't you think?"

She looked directly at Holland and her piercing eyes told him she had seen through his veiled concern. But

Sharon Franklin had her own reasons for wanting the profile of Elliot Benedict to appear as soon as possible.

Softening her eyes, she permitted an ever so slight smile to betray itself on her lips. As she brushed a lock of hair behind her ear she answered in a low, more feminine voice than before.

"Yes, David, it will appear . . . and soon."

Then briefly looking at each person in the small group her tone changed to conspiratorial.

"I want you to know I have a proposal for the network concerning a five-part series on the front-runners in both parties before the national conventions in August. The profile I've just done on the Vice President is just what I need to sell the idea. Naturally, I expect to host and produce it and you can be sure Elliott Benedict's segment will be even better than the profile!"

There were laughs and chuckles from those around her.

It was common knowledge in high Washington circles that despite her supposedly impartial reporting of national political events, Sharon Franklin was actually a staunch supporter of the incumbent Administration.

Almost as well known was her discreet but continuing affair with the bachelor Secretary of State, Chester A. Manning. Some went so far as to suggest that the Secretary only invited people to his frequent parties whom she had favorably passed approval on.

"Sharon," it was an Under-Secretary of Labor venturing to change the conversation, "speaking of the conventions, would . . ."

David Holland caught Sharon's eye and quietly excused himself. Touching Ted's elbow, the two men eased themselves away. As they moved in the direction of the door, Ted asked:

"What the hell was that all about?"

"You mean her How-Dare-They-Do-That-To-Me

speech? Oh, the network preempted the last thirteen minutes or so of the *Washington Report* tonight to show some video tape of a pro-Nazi demonstration in New Jersey this afternoon. It was nothing more than a bunch of kooks performing for the TV cameras until some hecklers in the crowd broke through police lines and turned it into a pretty good brawl. Didn't you catch it?"

"No. I was working on the endorsement the President may or may not give to Leona Gordon's immigration bill. I had the video recorders set and plan to catch up on tonight's news tomorrow."

Holland raised his eyebrows and patted Ted on the back.

"Working another Saturday? My, my, you are the devoted aide."

Ted gave him an annoyed look as they reached the door.

"Not really, David. Jil is due back Sunday from the D.C.—Paris run and I thought I'd spend the day catching up on some things so I wouldn't have to come in Sunday!"

Holland laughed and shook his head. "You're a card, Ted, a real card. Anyway, give my regards to that lovely lady of yours. You young people certainly live an unusual life. What a romance! You, a workaholic for a lame-duck President and her, spending half her time in foreign cities when she's not serving drinks at thirty-five thousand feet."

Ted let the unkind reference to President William Chandler being a "lame-duck" slide. He also controlled an urge to say that if the President's Press Secretary spent less time aligning himself with the Vice President, others on the press staff would be able to work relatively normal hours. Instead, he changed the subject.

"David, Jim Hanlon said you wanted to see me."

At that moment Hanlon reappeared. "Hey Ted, if you're leaving could I catch a ride?"

He opened his jacket, exposing a beeper. "The Congresswoman beckons." Hanlon knew Ted lived a short distance from Leona Crawford Gordon.

Holland looked from Hanlon to Ted and slowly shook his head. "It's nothing that can't wait. But if you *do* go in tomorrow, I've left something in your box. After you read it call me."

***

The flashing red light on the phone was the first thing Ted noticed as he entered the darkened office. He flicked the wall switch to light the office and then casually positioned himself on the corner of his desk while tapping out the three digits that would connect him to the message center.

"This is Ted Scott; you have a message?"

"Yes Mr. Scott." The operator took only a few seconds to locate it. "A Dr. Bauman, Aaron Bauman, in New York City called this evening. He wanted your home number. I couldn't give it to him, naturally. But he did leave a message.

"He said you'd recognize his name and that it was urgent that you called him back. He left a number and said not to worry about the hour if I could reach you. He was *very* insistent."

Ted was confused. "What made you think I'd be back here tonight?"

"Oh I didn't expect you, not until Mr. Holland called to tell security he thought you might stop by. I had left a message to be put in your box but decided to use the light," she replied cheerfully.

"Thank you," Ted answered with a trace of annoyance. Holland had known he'd come by to pick up the information tonight! It bothered Ted that Holland could predict his actions so well. He took down the number the operator gave him and this time gave her a civil "Thank you."

Ted searched his brain to place Dr. Bauman with a face or incident that he should remember. It didn't take long.

He remembered interviewing Bauman nearly a decade earlier while on the staff of *The Bayonne Times*, a New Jersey daily newspaper in the southern part of Hudson County.

Bauman was a survivor of the concentration camps and since arriving in the United States after the war had spent his life lecturing about the Holocaust and hunting down Nazis. Ted remembered that Bauman had come to Bayonne to address a gathering in the Jewish Community Center on the subject of Adolf Hitler having fathered children.

Bauman proffered a theory that the Fuhrer had at least one son and one daughter. He had made interesting copy, Ted thought, but why would he be calling now, after all these years? Ted also wondered how Bauman had located him.

Though he still wanted to view the news tapes he decided to first make the call. Bauman had said call, no matter how late and that was exactly what Ted would do rather than put it off till tomorrow.

The phone rang three times before a crisp, sharp voice answered. "Hello? Who is this?"

"Dr. Bauman? This is Ted Scott returning your call. You told the operator it didn't matter what time . . ."

"Oh, yes, Mr. Scott, no matter the hour. Thank you for calling back. I hoped you would remember me; it's been so long."

"Yes, I remember you, Doctor. You spoke to a full house at the Community Center in Bayonne and then spent some time educating me and another reporter on the Nazis." Ted thought instantly of the demonstration earlier in the day that Sharon Franklin was so furious about.

"Yes, yes, you do remember. I spoke about Hitler's children, a subject that has haunted me but one, unfortunately, that I had little evidence to support. That's why I'm calling you now."

For the second time in the last fifteen minutes Ted felt a wave of confusion engulf him. But Bauman quickly put it aside.

"I now have proof that Hitler's daughter not only lives but is involved with the government in Washington. That's why I thought of you. With your help she can be exposed."

Ted wanted to interrupt and remind Bauman that he was now on the White House staff, not a reporter, but the old man hardly left a breath between sentences.

"She is there, close to the White House, Mr. Scott, and I fear that she is trying to work her way in. She is as dangerous as her father ever was. Twice already she has tried to have me killed to stop me. I want . . ."

Ted cut in abruptly.

"Dr. Bauman, if someone tried to kill you why don't you go to the police and give them their name?" He wanted to terminate the conversation. Bauman was apparently paranoid and chasing phantoms, he thought.

"I can't, Mr. Scott. She is powerful and is surrounded by others also with great power. This I know. There are enough of them, and they have the facilities to silence me. They've killed three people who've cooperated with me and the police have done nothing. They list the deaths as accidents.

"I can show you the proof. I can bring it to Washington and we can take it to the FBI. They'll at least look at it if you help me. Once they begin to check what I've uncovered then they will believe for themselves. Alone

I am only another crazy old Jew who sees Nazis around every corner. They'd laugh at me."

Bauman's voice had been very somber toward the end and Ted picked up the overpowering rejection it conveyed. He wanted to again suggest Bauman take his charges and story to the police but thought he might be able to get that message across in another way.

"Dr. Bauman, you must realize that my obligations with the White House keep me very busy and no matter what my personal feelings are, I'd find it difficult to make the time necessary to get involved in this. If you're certain that . . ."

"If I'm certain? Good God, man! Haven't you heard what I've been saying? They, she, has had three people killed and would kill me too if they knew where I was! The threat of a new generation of Nazis in America is greater than the threat that existed in Germany in 1931. She leads a bold, dedicated and well-financed organization. They are Americans, born here.

"Oh, there are still some of the World War II crowd. They are the teachers, but they no longer pull the strings. The torch has been passed to the *kinder*. And Adolf Hitler's daughter is at the center, like a queen bee . . ."

Ted glanced at his watch, again waiting for a pause that would enable him to cut in. He decided he would have to be firm.

". . . with enough money and seeking the power to make their perverted dreams come true. Those marches by the American Nazi Party, like the one today, the crazies goose-stepping around in brownshirts, they're nothing more than exhibitionists and bullies. No, the ones we have to fear, really fear, are the ones working quietly." Bauman paused to catch a breath and Ted moved in.

"Doctor, you must understand that I can't permit my

position here to be used unless you first give me something concrete to digest. Give me something I can evaluate and, if necessary, present to people in government who can objectively examine it."

Ted was sure this ploy would deter Bauman. It was a polite kiss-off.

"Mr. Scott," Bauman's voice was firm and clipped. "If I send you documentation and, if after reading it you believe that there is even a *possibility* that what I've uncovered could be true, then, Mr. Scott, will you listen and take me to the director of the FBI?"

Ted was stunned. Bauman wanted to go to the director! There was a limit to how far he could humor the old man, Ted thought. He had no intention of doing anything more than reading any "proof" Bauman sent him hoping he could find enough loopholes to reject it or at least explain that it wasn't strong enough for Ted to take any further.

The suggestion of going to the director was unbelievable. Before Ted could answer, Bauman continued.

"I'm sorry, Mr. Scott. I shouldn't put you into such a difficult situation before you have seen what you call 'something concrete to digest.' I think you'll be able to make up your mind after I've given you a few things. This isn't what I intended to do. I wanted to be there with you to answer your questions as you read. I also have a journal that I've kept for all these years. But that I'll show you when we meet, and I'm sure we will. For, now I'll send you copies of other things, including translations of sworn statements taken in Germany and France." Bauman's voice had grown tired.

"That will be fine, Doctor. I don't want to sound uninterested or official but I think you can understand how sensitive my job here is. I can't afford to do anything that would leave the Administration open to ridicule. I promise you I will read whatever you send and get back to you to discuss what further action might be appropriate. By the way, how did you locate me?"

"That was easy. *The Bayonne Times* mentions that you were once a staffer whenever the opportunity arises in a story that has your name in it. I have some friends there, still. People whom I've kept in contact with since my first visit. They tell me."

For a brief instant Ted felt a mixture of emotions. He felt sorry for the old man who had dedicated his life to this tortured search. He didn't want to be responsible for destroying a dream, no matter how fantastic it seemed.

He also had a difficult time accepting the fact that Bauman considered him so crucial in it all. To Aaron Bauman, concentration camp survivor, Ted Scott represented a hope to prevent the horrors of the Nazis from happening again.

Fact or fiction, the responsibility made Ted uncomfortable.

Chapter 2

After the call to Bauman, Ted turned his attention to the envelope that David Holland had left earlier. Opening it he again felt annoyance that his actions were so predictable to the White House Press Secretary.

When he'd finished reading, Ted carefully folded the two-page memo and replaced it in the envelope. Tapping it on the desk top unconsciously he turned around to face the bank of three small television sets, each connected to a video recorder, and selected the one which contained the tape of Sharon Franklin's *Washington Report*.

Using the remote switch on his desk he turned it on, staring blankly at the fading image of the network logo as the scene cut to the nation's favorite anchorwoman. He was again fingering the envelope from David Holland and trying to decide how best to respond to the unorthodox request his one-time mentor had just made.

Minutes passed and Sharon Franklin's lovely face had been replaced by a young, obviously excited reporter who kept looking over his shoulder at the melee taking place behind him. Ted's eyes were viewing the events on the screen but his mind continued to wrestle with the message in the envelope.

Police were dragging away a kicking young girl while

all around civilians and a small group of men wearing pseudo-German military uniforms were pushing and shoving with an occasional exchange of blows.

The camera again closed in on the reporter now interviewing an old man who was pounding his right fist into the palm of his left and carrying on an extremely animated diatribe.

Ted Scott heard none of it. He had not turned up the volume. As the silent images before him played out the events which had taken place earlier that day and then gave way to a series of commercials he switched off the set and slowly left the office.

The message he had received from David Holland had upset him so that it never occurred to him to put it into his pocket. It wasn't until he started the Corvette that Ted realized the envelope was still in his left hand. He stuffed it into his jacket pocket and pulled the car slowly away from his parking space for the drive to his apartment.

***

The room was bathed in darkness except for the slight glow of a nightlight slicing across the floor from the bathroom.

The hum of the air conditioner prevented Ted from hearing the click as the front door tumbler gave way.

There was no reason for him to be aware that someone had entered the apartment but he was. Since childhood he had always been able to sense movement around him when asleep. He was awake now, but didn't move.

Straining, he could hear the quiet movement in the apartment and then he knew the bathroom door had been pushed open even before the soft orange light moved across his face. He opened one eye.

"Hi, flygirl," his voice was heavy with sleep. A tired smile wrinkled his face.

"Shhh, stay asleep, love. I'll be back in a minute." Jil

Baker gently bent over and planted a soft kiss on his cheek and then went into the bathroom to prepare for bed.

Ted promised himself he would stay awake and make love to her. Yet as quickly as he had slipped out of sleep he fell back into it.

His senses were aroused again several hours later by the rich aroma of freshly brewed coffee. This time when he awoke the room was filling with sunlight and the sounds of Jil preparing breakfast in the tiny kitchen. It was 7:15 AM Monday morning.

Ted came to the table several minutes later. Jil was surprised to see that he had already shaved.

"Good morning," her perky smile and cheerful tone brightened the room.

"Good morning yourself," he answered in a playful way.

She walked over and threw her arms around his neck. He let his hands take in the graceful arc of her back and enjoyed the pressure as her full breasts pressed against his chest.

They kissed slowly several times before any other words were spoken, breaking only at the sizzling command of coffee perking over.

"Paris must have been pretty good. You're half a day late."

"Sorry, love. Equipment problem. We had a six hour layover until they flew another plane in from Shannon. You didn't go to the airport, did you? You called first, I hope?"

"Naturally. And they told me your airline didn't even *have* service between D.C. and Paris. You're a fraud," he teased.

"Oh, darn," she exaggerated a pout, "You will forgive me. I just can't help myself. I'm really a courier for the

CIA and now you've blown my cover." She giggled and returned to the table with two cups of coffee.

"How was Paris? Did you get to see anything new this time?"

"Lonely without you. Spent most of my time at the Louvre . . . didn't accept any invitations for dinner . . . found the prices higher, fashions ridiculous and weather marvelous."

"Terrific. When are you going to get me on a free-ride? That's the only reason I bother with you. Hell, pretty girls are a dime a dozen in this town." Ted was in exceptionally good spirits despite the moody weekend he had spent thinking about David's memo.

"You know the rules, Mr. Scott, only spouses and immediate family fly free. Live-in boyfriends don't."

"So, let's get married. There . . . I'm asking you again."

Jil looked at him with hungering eyes and then repeated the same sentiment they both knew so well.

"Oh Ted I want that very much, you know that. But I'm not ready yet for the suburban life. You have an exciting job working with the President of the United States . . ."

"Only until his term ends, I've told you that."

"Yes, but then what? Will you go back to being a newspaperman? Will you want to work in Washington or find a small weekly that you can buy somewhere? It's a choice you have to make without pressure from me."

She paused briefly and added. "I'm still enjoying myself. How else could someone with a middle-class background see the world and get paid for doing it? I'm only twenty-five, Ted. Let's not rush into marriage and then hate each other for the opportunities we both will have missed a few years later."

Ted put up his hands, "OK, OK, you win. But the offer still stands. Just name the date."

Jil wanted to get the morning banter back on a light note. She rose from the table and headed for the stove.

"Well, darling, you must admit that this kind of arangement beats paying rent! Can I be blamed if you're a chauvinist and won't permit me to kick in for room and board? Come to think of it, you're a bit daffy."

She was bringing the hot pot of coffee to the table and did a fast sidestep as Ted rose from his chair and made a playfully agressive move toward her.

"C'mon, c'mon. Save that energy for later, one of us could get burnt. Get the newspaper while I butter up some toast."

Ted smiled and managed to peck her cheek before going to retrieve the *Washington Post* from the hall.

During the light breakfast Jil told Ted about a restaurant she and some other flight attendants had discovered.

He told her about his lazy weekend, including the fact that he had managed to stay completely away from the office. He avoided the memo from David Holland and instead told her about the strange call from Aaron Bauman.

"What's amazing, honey, is that this old guy believes Hitler had children, or a daughter at least. And he wants me to hold his hand and take him to the FBI. Christ! Wouldn't I look like a jerk?"

"When you met him in Bayonne, years ago, did he act crazy then?"

"No. That's just it. He doesn't come off like a crackpot. A little excited, yes, but not a first-class screwball. But the premise of Hitler's daughter preparing to take over this country seems a bit much."

Jil was watching Ted over the rim of her cup. She finished her swallow and shrugged her shoulders.

"Oh, don't take me wrong, I'm not saying I believe it," she said, "but in the last quarter of a century we've had a President killed in a motorcade, a President and

Vice President forced to resign, and a Congressman who was appointed Vice President actually become President, plus a movie actor elected to the White House. We've also had a Senator murdered after winning a primary and a former governor shot and crippled while they were running for President. Who's to say what's normal anymore?"

Ted thought about what Jil said for a few moments before responding.

"Well, nonetheless, it's weird. You'd think a person who lived through that horror in the camps would do anything to forget it, not force himself to keep the memories fresh by spending his life on a crusade."

Jil frowned and a trace of resentment slipped into her tone. "Ted, a little while ago I got the feeling you felt sorry for him. How can you turn around now and dismiss him as a fanatic or something?"

"Look, hon, I'm not being cruel. I think that maybe when a person wants to believe something enough, and spends their life trying to prove it, then maybe they are able to make the evidence fit the patterns they want, know what I mean? Anyway once he sends me the stuff, if he sends it, I'll look at it and give it to Reynolds. Dick can handle this much better than I can. Furthermore, he's due to retire from the Bureau in a few months. He'll have the time to listen to Nazi stories. It'll be good for them both, him and Bauman."

Ted glanced at the sunburst wall clock and quickly stuffed the last chunk of toast in his mouth.

"Hey babe, great breakfast. You do wonders with coffee beans and bread. Can you clean up this mess? I'm running late. Meet me at Enrico's for lunch? I'll try to be there for twelvish and steal some time from the office. I've got it coming."

He slid out of the booth seat and pressed a hard kiss

on Jil's cheek, then bolted into the alcove bedroom to dress. She hadn't had a chance to get a word in edgewise.

"Sure, sure, run off and play games at The Powerhouse and leave me with cups and dishes." She shook her head and mumbled "At least I get paid for doing this when I'm flying!" Then, louder, "You're lucky I'm off for two days. That hamper is starting to let off vapors, champ."

"Sorry."

"Mr. Scott, didn't your mother teach you anything about taking care of yourself and cleaning up?"

"Never had the time, Ms. Baker, mam. Besides it always seemed too domestic!"

Jil smiled at his glib remarks and picked up the newspaper to glance at while finishing her coffee. There was an editorial on the inside about the Nazi demonstration in New Jersey and, because of the conversation she and Ted just had, she began to read it.

Ted was busy rushing to get dressed. He continued to call out to her from the other room.

"Holland asked me to spend next weekend at Camp David with him and the Benedicts. Chandler is letting them use the place, but I'm really not interested in going. Why don't you swing some time off and we'll go into the mountains and grab a cabin. Make like the rabbits, how's that?"

He was sitting on the bed and forcing a shoe on.

"Sound like a good idea to you? You can pull the time, can't you? Where's that other damned shoe?"

He was on the floor on all fours hunting and looking under the bed. He could see Jil now standing in the doorway. He gave her a quick glance and a smile and returned to his search.

"Ah ha!" He stabbed an arm out to retrieve it. "There's the little bastard. Must have crawled away."

Jil's trembling voice made him turn and look up at her.

"Ted? His name was Aaron Bauman, wasn't it, the old doctor?"

"Yeah, sure, that's it. So?"

She dropped the newspaper on the bed. Below the editorial about the Nazi demonstration in New Jersey was an obituary.

"He's dead," Jil said. "The police found his body yesterday at an amusement park in New Jersey. They say it was a freak accident."

Chapter 3

Ted sat on the edge of the bed in near shock as he read the newspaper article.

"I just can't believe it," he mumbled. He shook his head and began reading the short wire service story about Aaron Bauman's accidental death once again, slower this time.

Jil had moved into the room from the doorway and was now seated next to him. She draped her right arm around his shoulder and rested her head against his chest.

"It's so eerie . . . it's just weird. He calls you and says somebody is trying to kill him and then he really *is* dead. Ted, do you think he was murdered?"

"Murdered? You can't be serious. Who would have killed him? Hitler's daughter or some other Nazis? No, hon . . . it's just an unfortunate coincidence or something. You read the story. He was drowned in an accident at an amusement park. I just feel lousy about it because I didn't take the time to be more considerate when he called . . . and it is a funny feeling to talk to someone one day and then read about their death a few days later."

"But Ted, aren't you at all curious as to why an old man would be in an amusement park late on a Saturday night? Could he have gone there to meet somebody, the person who killed him maybe and . . ."

"Wait a minute, Jil. You are really caught up in this, aren't you? Don't try to make something out of nothing. People die all the time and people also visit amusement parks all the time. The story says he was the last passenger to ride on the log flume ride before it closed. He apparently fell out somehow. Things like that happen. It was an unfortunate accident, Jil, nothing more."

Jil rose from the bed. She had a slight frown on her face as she extended her hand to Ted.

"You're probably right. Or at least I hope you're right. But I wonder if he actually mailed anything to you. According to the newspaper the accident occurred late Saturday night."

Using a minimal amount of support from Jil's hand Ted pulled himself up from the bed. "And I spoke to him late Friday night. He could have mailed something to me Saturday before going to the park, I guess. We'll see."

They were moving back toward the kitchen again and Ted shot a fast look at the clock.

"Damn it. Look at the time fly. I've got to be moving!" He spun Jil toward him and gave her a quick but tender kiss.

"Enrico's, noonish, right?" He paused briefly for her answer.

"Enrico's it is. Now be gone." She slapped his back-side firmly.

Ted had been gone hardly more than an hour when Jil answered the door to accept the large, bulky Express Mail package.

Dr. Aaron Bauman had done what he promised, Jil thought. She couldn't resist the temptation to open it and read whatever it was the old man believed was proof that Adolf Hitler had a daughter and that daughter was now alive and dangerous in Washington, D.C.

***

Less than a mile from Ted and Jil's apartment an attractive, well dressed woman in her mid-thirties had positioned herself at a particular pay telephone outside a florist shop on Pennsylvania Avenue. She had never used this phone before and would never use it again. It was simply one of a long list that had been pre-selected for her to receive messages of the most sensitive nature. When she answered it she would only identify herself with a one word code and say nothing else. The caller would do all the talking. She checked her expensive wrist watch and at the same instant the phone rang.

"Phoenix," was her immediate and only utterance.

"Good morning Phoenix. The good doctor will no longer be a problem. He suffered a fatal accident Saturday night.

"However, we believe he contacted someone in Washington by phone and may have sent a parcel to them Saturday morning. We found a piece of paper in his wallet with the phone number of the New York City Post Office and the words "Express Mail to Washington" scribled. Underneath it was a name, T. Scott, and a phone number with the initials "W.H." after it.

"So far we have been unable to locate where he lived. The driver's license he carried showed an address that is almost two years old. He had no car, incidentally, that we're sure of.

"Once we locate this T. Scott we may discover if he sent him the journal or other information. We are checking government directories now to see if a T. Scott is listed in any of them.

"Scott, even if he doesn't have the journal, could lead us to where Bauman lived we think, so we are working on . . ."

"That won't be necessary," Phoenix cut in. "Ted Scott is on the White House Press Staff! Do whatever is necessary to retrieve any and all information the doctor sent to him, *at once!*"

She clicked the phone down and stepped from the booth without a hint of anxiety visible to any passersby. She appeared calm and quite innocent as she stepped to the corner and hailed a cab to take her to the garage where she had parked her car. Inwardly she was furious with the Organization for fumbling this assignment at the very last moment. She was also annoyed with herself for having broken her code of not speaking to callers when these messages came. But this was an extraordinary circumstance, she thought as she smiled at the cab driver and automatically gave him the address she wanted.

Why would Bauman contact Ted Scott, she wondered. What possible connection could the old Jew have with someone on the White House Press Staff. Whatever it was it was unfortunate for Mr. Scott, possibly even fatal, she thought.

As the cab slowly moved through the heavy Monday morning Washington traffic Phoenix became more relaxed. At least whatever it was Bauman had sent would be easier to retrieve from Scott than if it had been sent to someone in the Justice Department.

***

Jil Baker waved off the waiter for the third time. She was slowly sipping what was now a cold second cup of coffee. Ted was late, as usual, she sulked, but then she had been a full fifteen minutes early for their lunch meeting at Enrico's. It was now 12:15.

Ted gave her a big wave from the entrance and swiftly moved between the rapidly filling tables. He wore a smile almost as broad as his ruggedly masculine face.

"Hi darling." He bent over and gave her a quick peck

on the cheek, then stood upright and dramatically checked his watch.

"Right on time. Enrico's at noonish!" he boasted.

"Noonish, Teddy dear, means twelve o'clock, not 12:15 but who's counting," she teased half-heartedly as Ted seated himself across from her. The waiter instantly appeared and asked if they would care for drinks before lunch, giving Jil's coffee cup a slight scowl. Ted ordered two Bloody Marys and quickly added a chef's salad for himself and turned to Jil with an urgency that told her this would be a quick lunch. She ordered a tuna salad. The waiter departed less than impressed with the order.

"You seem to be in a hurry," she said in an annoyed tone.

"I'm sorry, honey, it's just that the pace is so fast at the office—everything rush, rush, that it tends to creep into my actions even when I'm away from the place." Ted slouched into the leather-tufted chair and let his arms hang down almost touching the floor. "And what kind of morning have you had?"

"Frightening."

"Frightening? What kind of morning is that?"

"I'll tell you what kind. An Express Mail package came from Dr. Bauman a few hours ago and it was full of photo copies of papers and documents in English, German and French. The old man really did his homework, Ted. There is a pile of stuff here that makes a pretty strong case about someone killing people who have helped him, and some of the facts he has uncovered, well . . ."

"Wait a minute. I thought this was going to be a lunch for just the two of us, not a wake. Don't tell me you brought that material with you?"

"I did. It's right here." Jil reached down and slightly lifted the shopping bag resting on the floor next to her.

"Holly cow, babe," Ted was shaking his head and getting ready to tell Jil he didn't want to hear anything more about Bauman or Nazis today when she interrupted. Jil raised her voice and Ted could clearly detect the strain in it.

"Ted, we've had four phoney phone calls this morning. I'm sure it was the same man each time but he gave a different excuse for calling. First it was a wrong number, then he said he was canvassing for *Washington Post* subscriptions, then it was an insurance company offering a whole life or something plan and the final call, just before I left to come here was just a dead phone after I said hello.

"Doesn't that sound as if someone is trying to find out if anybody's home? I think somebody knows Dr. Bauman sent this package to you and now they want it. I think they are trying to find out if you are home or not so they can break in and search the apartment."

Ted was less defensive now and a little concerned over Jil's reactions to the phone calls.

"Okay, honey. Calm down." He paused to regroup his thoughts then continued. "So you scooped up the package and brought it with you. Good thinking. If anybody is after it they'll come up with zeros. But the important thing is you got out of the apartment." Before he could continue the waiter appeared with their drink orders.

"Ted, take this material and keep it in your office or somewhere for now, until we find out what this is about." She slid the bag across the floor to him.

"Good idea. That way I'll also have a chance to look at it and pass it off to Reynolds."

"Reynolds? Why him? I thought you were only going to give it to him in order to get Dr. Bauman off your back. That hardly seems necessary now. If Bauman was murdered don't you think this is now something for the police?"

"Sure, if he *was* murdered. We really don't know that. But if some subversive group is planning to break into our apartment *that's* a job for the FBI. Furthermore, Reynolds can ask questions and get answers from the New Jersey police that I can't." He paused as the lunch orders arrived. "Trust me. Reynolds will be able to put this thing into its proper perspective."

Jil sunk her fork into the tuna salad and couldn't help feeling that despite his apparent concern Ted was patronizing her.

The remainder of lunch was spent on small talk and after the bill was paid Jil noticed Ted glance at his watch a few times. "Do you have time to drop me off near Marbury Place? I want to do some window shopping and I can't afford to keep hailing cabs." The area she mentioned was a short walk from their apartment and Ted quickly said he would. Jil wasn't surprised that Ted didn't offer to go back to the apartment with her just to be sure everything was safe. It confirmed her earlier feelings that he took the phone calls less seriously than she did.

They kissed hurriedly as Ted wheeled the sleek Corvette into the corner and Jil got out. As he sped off toward the White House she suddenly no longer had an urge to go shopping but turned instead and began slowly walking back to their apartment.

Something was bothering Ted as he skillfully glided in and out of the mid-day traffic on Pennsylvania Avenue. Something Jil had said about the phone calls, but he couldn't put his finger on it.

Jil began hunting in her purse for her keys as she turned the corner and began heading toward the old brownstone that they shared. Why is Ted so impossible at times, she thought. How could a person look straight ahead at facts and yet fail to admit the possibility that they presented an alternative view? She was walking slowly, tumbling the ring of keys around her finger. The ornate stone and wrought iron steps going up to the apartment were in view now. They were less than one hundred yards away.

Ted found himself trapped against a corner curb behind a smoking bus and next to a moving van. When the traffic light changed, clouds of noxious fumes from the bus engulfed the Corvette and he silently cursed for letting himself get caught in such a bind. The bus was barely crawling and what seemed like an eternity passed before he was able to cut out from behind it, only to find himself now slowly following the moving van.

Jil reached the outside stairs to the apartment and began climbing them to the building's front door. As she turned the heavy brass doornob and pushed the richly carved wood and glass entrance door she paused and once again thought about shopping. She was in no mood now, she admitted and decided to simply spend the rest of the day cleaning up around the apartment.

Ted found an opening and took advantage of it, quickly pushing the Corvette around the van and into clear road ahead. The entrance to the parking area for the Executive Office Building was less than a half a block away but another bus was taking its time just up ahead. Ted was a bit on edge. He had no patience for city driving but the tension he was feeling now was something more. What was it that Jil had said that had set off an alarm in his head and why couldn't he recall it?

As he prepared to swing into the EOB parking area he shot a final glance at the back of the bus. The rear panel, just below the window, carried a poster advertisement for *The Washington Post* and included the paper's circulation phone number for new subscribers.

That's it, he thought. *The Washington Post* doesn't solicit new subscribers over the phone! Jil was right. Someone was calling the apartment to see if anyone was home!

He screeched to a halt in front of the parking lot guard box and ignored the cheerful smile from the uniformed officer who immediately recognized him. Ted looked at his watch. He had dropped Jil off nearly ten minutes ago. He hoped she was taking her time window shopping otherwise by now she could be back at the apartment. He prayed that if she was she wouldn't be walking in on someone there to search the place.

Ted shifted the car into reverse and quickly backed out of the entranceway. Slamming the shift into first he screeched away.

Jil inserted the key into the door and turned the knob, pushing the door open with her shoulder. She had hardly taken two steps into the room when someone grabbed her around the throat from behind.

As Ted broke every local speed and traffic law in metropolitan Washington, his mind raced through the lunchtime conversation he and Jil had had. Now, replaying it over again in his mind, he was able to notice for the first time her real concern. What a fool he had been, he thought. At lunch he treated most of what she had told him with a grain of salt but pretended to be more concerned than he actually was. The whole thing was just so incredible he believed her overactive imagination had gotten carried away. He cursed himself and he cursed Aaron Bauman for getting them involved in this.

Though Ted felt the trip back to the apartment was taking a long time he was actually doing it in less than half the time it usually took. His reckless driving caught the attention of a police car which was pursuing him but still more than a block behind. He turned the corner near Marbury Place and floored the Corvette for the last few hundred yards to their apartment.

Ted vaulted up the outside steps two at a time and then did the same thing once inside the building. Behind him he could hear the police car siren and the rapid slamming of doors as the police came running after him.

The apartment door was slightly opened and Ted hardly slowed down as he pushed it and ran into the apartment.

There was nobody there. His eyes raced around the room and noticed several signs that indicated a scuffle had taken place. A table lamp had been knocked over, his comfortable recliner chair sat in a new position, slightly turned as if bumped into and the window leading to the fire escape was open.

"Jil!" he called out as he ran to the window. "Jil, are you here?" He stuck his head out the window and caught a glimpse of a figure as it rapidly moved out of his line of vision in a neighboring yard.

"O.K. buddy, the race is over."

Ted turned and faced two policemen with guns drawn and at the same instant he noticed Jil's purse on the floor near the bathroom door, which was closed.

"In there!" he shouted and bolted toward the bathroom before the police could react. Ted opened the door just as the two officers caught and restrained him.

As the door opened Ted and the police saw the pile of woman's clothes scattered on the floor. In the tub, which was rapidly filling with water, was the unconscious body of Jil.

Chapter 4

Jil insisted on sitting up on the couch in the living room while Ted related the story to Dick Reynolds. Ted had tried to get her to remain in bed after they returned home from the visit to the doctor. The police had called the emergency unit to the apartment to administer treatment to her but after that was done Ted convinced her that they should visit his regular doctor.

Now Dick was sipping a cup of coffee while Ted, sitting on the same couch with Jil, told the F.B.I. agent of the afternoon's events.

"After the guy grabbed Jil from behind and tried to strangle her she managed to sink her high heel into his foot, which made him let go for an instant and she broke loose, but he quickly spun her around and landed a nasty shot across the face." Ted looked at Jil's puffed cheek and blackened eye for an instant, then turned back to Dick.

"That's all I remember . . . until I heard Ted's voice . . ." she was in too much pain to continue.

"Take it easy, honey, rest. I'll tell Dick." Ted paused and cleared a lump in his throat. "Christ, I feel like such a jerk. If only I had come back to the apartment with you."

Dick Reynolds cut in, aware that Ted and Jil were

both in a low mood and wanting to get the conversation back onto the facts and away from personal feelings.

"Look, kids, this is one of those unfortunate things that is full of 'ifs' and we are going to get nowhere fast if we keep sitting here blaming what happened on all sorts of mistakes. If somebody wanted to break into this place and get their hands on those documents there was no way you could stop them. Too bad Jil had to walk in on them, I agree, but look at the bright side. You got here before anything happened, anything more serious that is, and the documents weren't in the apartment."

"Maybe it would have been better if they were," Ted volunteered. "Then this thing would be over and we wouldn't have anything else to worry about. I'm just afraid that they'll come back again."

Jil interrupted Ted. There was anger in her voice. "Ted, no, no, no! A man was killed, Dr. Bauman, and he told you others were killed also for the information he sent you. Dick is right, what happened here to us could have been worse. By asking Dick to come here tonight and telling him the story we are doing exactly what you promised Dr. Bauman you would do before they killed him."

Ted looked at Jil with a sad understanding in his eyes.

"You know, earlier today when you kept mentioning that someone had killed him, I had reservations . . . it just seemed too fantastic. But after what happened today I'm starting to believe it."

Jil couldn't conceal the shock on her face or in her voice.

"*Starting* to believe it? Ted, someone tried to kill me: They filled the tub with water and dropped me in after knocking me out. I saw the man's face, how he was dressed. This wasn't some crazed drug addict in dirty clothes who happened to break into our apartment.

This was a man wearing a business suit, a big man, between thirty-five and forty years old. He had cold blue eyes and a sinister grin. I actually think he was enjoying the fact that I came back and surprised him."

Reynolds cut in.

"Jil, I think what Ted is trying to say is that Dr. Bauman's story about Hitler's daughter actually being alive and here in Washington seemed a bit much before any of this happened. Now that you've received the package of documents and somebody broke into the apartment the same day it all seems to be related. Of course the possibility of coincidence does exist but I think Ted was trying to say that he believes that less now, right Ted?"

Jil's lips were pressed tightly together and she shot a hard look directly at Ted. He realized he was having a difficult time explaining what he meant but he had to try again and clear the air. Right now, he thought, she thinks I'm an inconsiderate bastard.

"Yes, Dick, you're partly right." Ted turned to Jil and in a tender, soft voice continued.

"Honey, I don't care about whether Bauman was right and Hitler had a daughter or not, that's what I meant. But it seems as if there are people out there who may have hated him enough to kill him. They may also believe that they have to get their hands on the documents he sent me at any cost, and that's what scares me. I'm convinced it was one of them that broke in here and tried to kill you, not a local burglar or some kid who needed money for drugs. Whether or not there is a Nazi empire right under our noses and whether or not it is headed by Adolf Hitler's daughter is besides the point. Someone *thinks* we now have information that can threaten their cause or organization, or whatever."

"And maybe you do, Ted." Reynolds placed his coffee cup on an end table and lifted himself out of the overstuffed chair. "I think we all agree that what Jil experienced here this afternoon was an effort to retrieve Dr. Bauman's package. What did you tell the police?"

Ted also got up and following Reynolds lead began walking toward the door with him.

"Oh nothing about a Nazi plot, just that Jil had told me about the mysterious phone calls over lunch and then as I was about to go back to work I remembered that *The Washington Post* didn't solicit subscribers over the phone. That explained my wild driving. They were here themselves to see the rest and treated it as a break and entry that resulted in an assault. Naturally they called the White House and checked me out with David Holland and he convinced them it would be better to forget about the reckless driving charges."

Reynolds was at the door and Ted opened it for him. "You mentioned that David said he would stop by tonight."

"That's right." Ted glanced at his watch. "In fact he should be getting here any minute."

"Then I'd better go. I'd prefer not to run into him and it might be better if you two didn't mention that I was here at all or that you are giving me the documents to read tomorrow."

As Reynolds was leaving he turned once again to Ted.

"You still haven't had an opportunity to read the material the way Jil already has, have you?"

"No, Dick. On the way back from the doctor's office we stopped at a hardware store and I bought these." Ted pointed to three new security locks he had installed on their front door.

Once Reynolds was gone Ted joined Jil on the couch again. "Hon, I think we should keep this quiet for a while yet. I mean I don't want to tell David about the phone call from Bauman or the package or any of that right now, understand?"

"Yes, dear." Jil's eyes were heavy and she was drifting off to sleep.

"C'mon. Let's get you into bed. I'll spend some time with David and tell him I'm taking a few days off, until you are back to being yourself."

Ted no sooner tucked Jil into bed when David Holland arrived, replete with a large bouquet of flowers and a humorous get-well card. Ted went through the story once again in a convincing fashion and did not leave Holland with anything but the impression that Jil had been assaulted by a burglar she happened to walk in on.

It took a bit of effort to convince Holland that Ted needed a few days off from his job. As a concession Ted agreed to stop by the EOB in the morning and pick up some work he could do at home, including the draft of President Chandler's statement on Leona Crawford Gordon's immigration bill.

After Holland had left and Ted had looked in to check on Jil he went to the trunk of his car and retrieved the package with the documents Dr. Bauman had sent.

Ted made himself comfortable in his recliner and began to sort through the various papers. It was going to be a while before he got to bed.

A Washington D.C. police car slowly passed the building and cruised to the corner, making a right turn and continuing its nightly patrol. It had passed a dark Mercedes parked approximately fifty feet from the corner but the police officer failed to notice the two men sitting in the shadows of the car.

"So he had the package in his car all the time, damn it."

"Should we go back up there now and take it?"

"No. That wouldn't be wise. Let him read it. Let him read whatever the old bastard sent him. We'll take

him out, along with the girl, when they deliver it to
Reynolds tomorrow."

The man who had just spoken picked up a walkie
talkie.

"Base to Observer. We're calling it a night here. Wait
till you see the lights go out in the window and then
pack up the equipment. We'll relieve you around 8:30.
Got it?"

From a van parked at the other end of the street came
a terse reply: "Yes, sir."

The Mercedes slowly pulled away from the curb and
left its vigil but inside the van two other men sat with
an infra-red camera and a parabolic microphone ready,
if necessary, to record any more conversations in Ted
Scott's apartment or to photograph people arriving or
departing from the building.

***

Phoenix was in a very bad mood. This was the
second time in as many days that she was using a pay
telephone to get a report on the Bauman problem. The
attempt to locate the documents in Ted Scott's apartment apparently failed yesterday, otherwise she would
not have received the establishing call with its coded
message that told her it was urgent to be at this phone
this morning.

Damn. Scott should have been eliminated if necessary, along with anyone else who was also in the way.
There was no excuse for this kind of error. The phone
rang. It was exactly 8:30 A.M.

"Phoenix." Her voice was crisp and obviously annoyed but if the caller on the other end noticed it he
didn't let it show.

"Good morning, Phoenix. We had a little problem
yesterday but we are in the process of correcting it this
morning. Our man was unable to locate the package at

the apartment since it was in our young friend's car all
the while.

"Last evening, however, we were able to learn quite a
bit by listening with electronic ears to some interesting
conversations our young friend had with another government employe, a Mr. Reynolds of the F.B.I."

Phoenix felt the blood rush to her head and she was
on the verge of screaming into the phone but the caller
continued.

"Besides our young friend and his girlfriend, Mr.
Reynolds is the only other person who is aware of the
contents of the package. Scott is planning to give the
package to Reynolds this morning and we have arranged
it so that both Scott and the girl will have to drive out
to Reynolds house. We'll finish them off either before
they get there or once all three of them are together.

"By the way, Scott had another visitor last evening.
David Holland. But he didn't tell Holland anything
about what has been going on.

"I'm truly sorry we've had this little delay but I
assure you things will all be in order again by the end of
the day."

She was tempted to say *they better be* but instead
simply hung up the phone. She moved out of the telephone booth and stood for a moment in the bright
morning sun. It was a beautiful day, a day that would
become even better once the Organization had the package that Bauman had sent.

She raised her arm above her head and immediately
attracted the attention of a taxi. She had a busy schedule ahead of her and decided she could hardly wait until
the White House reception this evening to hear all the
small talk about the accident the President's press aide
and his girl friend were to be involved in. It had to be
an accident. It always was. For an instant she wondered
if the F.B.I. man would be part of the same accident or

whether the Organization would find a separate way to be rid of him. No matter, his death certainly would not cause the kind of alarm the death of a White House aide would.

The cab pulled up and she entered the back, turning on her most attractive smile to the driver who was looking at her through his mirror. Filthy slob, she thought.

Some twenty-six miles away in the Virginia country-side Dick Reynolds walked around his car and muttered some choice curses. If only he had locked the damn car in the garage last night instead of leaving it here in the driveway those friggin' punks wouldn't have been able to cover it with spray paint.

Reynolds again walked down his short driveway and surveyed the scene along the rest of the street. He could see wild paint designs on at least three of his neighbors' cars. He shook his head and decided to go inside and call the Bureau to tell them he would be in late today. Then, he thought, he'd better call his insurance agent and get a claims man down. As an afterthought he also decided it would be a good idea to call Ted and ask him to bring the package of documents here to the house instead of meeting in his office as they originally planned.

Look at that windshield, he grunted to himself. It would take a couple of hours to get the paint off just so he could drive the car.

Chapter 5

Ted got to the phone before it began its second ring.

"Whoever you are, I think you're a gutless coward. Why don't you come by now, eh? I'm home. Try your strong-man stuff with me instead of a woman. . . ."

"Ted? Is that you?"

"Huh?" Ted was surprised to hear a voice at the other end. He recognized it immediately as Reynolds.

"Oh, Dick, hi. Good morning. I thought it was another silent phone call. It seems the clown who was here yesterday is getting his jollies calling us and then not saying anything when we pick up the phone. We've had four calls in the last hour."

"It sounds like somebody wants you to leave the apartment again so they can finish searching it, Ted. And I'm calling to tell you you can oblige them."

"What's up, Dick? Are you saying we're getting together earlier than we agreed last night?"

"Yeah. We had some mischief in the suburbs last night. Some screwballs went on a rampage with spray paint and did up the whole neighborhood. My car is covered with the stuff. Any chance you can make your way out here with the package?"

"Sure, Dick. We'll *both* be there in about a half an hour. I'm not leaving Jil home alone in this place. But before we go out I'm calling the cops and telling them about the calls. Maybe they can keep an eye on the place and nail the son-of-a-bitch when he breaks in."

Downstairs in the van parked on the street the two men monitoring the call relaxed. One let out a deep breath of satisfaction while the other smiled and lit a cigarette.

"Let's pack this gear away. I'll raise Lupo and let him know it is going off perfectly. I don't think we'll have to spend anymore time in this hotbox."

In midtown Washington a receptionist answered the phone in the richly decorated office of Dr. Harold Lupo and regretted to tell the caller that the doctor was not in but would get back to her when he returned.

Less than fifteen feet away, behind the closed door of his private office, Dr. Harold Lupo slowly rocked back and forth in his heavy leather chair. He was indeed in his office but not for calls that came in on any phone other than the private one which he was now using to talk directly to the Phoenix. As he spoke he played with the gold knob on his cane. The same cane he had brought with him after the submarine voyage across the Atlantic some thirty-seven years ago.

"I'm very happy that you are now calm. You shouldn't get yourself excited about these things, they always work out. We *do* have an efficient organization, my dear. I know. I built it while you were growing up. Just go about your usual business today and I'll call you before you have to go to the reception tonight. We are too close to our goal now for anything such as this unfortunate incident to stop us."

She felt better just hearing his voice. He was so confident, so sure of everything all the time. Even though he was the only person she had ever really gotten close to she still could not call him anything but "Doctor." He had been her surrogate father and mother while she was growing up. He had been the one who over the years carefully explained everything about her real father to her. How much he had loved her and how his wish was for the doctor to escape from Germany with her and bring her to America where there was already a newly formed Organization. The Doctor did this and the Organization provided the money for her education and now here she was on the brink of great power. On the brink of being at the very heart of all the power in the White House.

The Doctor had spent his whole life preparing her for the days which were just ahead. Sometimes she wanted to throw her arms around him and hug him and tell him she loved him and without being disrespectful to the memory of her real father she wanted to call the Doctor "father" just once.

But she knew she couldn't and she never would. The Doctor had been selected to care for her and raise her to this moment of greatness because he was trusted and one hundred percent loyal to her father. Now that loyalty was fully transmitted to her. And even though it sometimes pained her, she had to remember who she was and that the Doctor was only an obedient servant, not her father.

Her father was Adolf Hitler.

***

As soon as Ted and Jil crossed the Potomac and the car began to swallow up the beauty of the Virginia hills Ted let off on the accelerator and began to drive more leisurely. The roadway before them was a series of slight hills and soft, rounding curves nestled among rich green foliage. The road they were on was relatively empty at this time of day and would not again be heavily used until later that evening when the commuters began their trek homeward.

"What time is it?" Jil asked.

Ted checked the digital clock on the dashboard and answered, "Nine-fifteen. We are running later than I expected but I'm in no hurry. How about you?"

"No hurry either. I'm just relaxing and enjoying this great scenery."

"Great. You relax because it gets even better. About a mile or so down the road we turn off and take a *real* country road that goes on for almost six miles and you'll see nothing but chickens, cows, and a rickety old house or two here and there. It's a short cut, on the way to Dick's and I love it."

"Sounds super and still in screaming distance to Washington!"

"Yeah, that's why Dick loves it out here. He calls it the 'best of both worlds.' "

"Not too original."

"Who said F.B.I. guys were supposed to be original?" Jill laughed. It was more of a short giggle and sounded rather funny. Ted gave her a sideways look and burst out laughing. This in turn made Jil giggle again and now the two of them were in a silly mood adults sometimes lapse into for no apparent reason. They were both laughing uncontrollably now and Ted had to slow the car down in order to keep it under control.

A short time later Ted made the turnoff he had mentioned to Jil. They had both calmed down and were driving along quietly.

"Ted, I didn't know you had a gun." She let her eyes fall on the Walther PPK automatic tucked into Ted's pants and partially covered by his jacket.

"Oh, this." He made a quick nod with his head in the general direction where the gun was stuffed. "It's something I picked up in Nam. Lots of guys had a handgun as extra insurance. I thought it might not be a bad idea to keep it handy after what's been going on."

"Guns make me uneasy, Ted. I wish you wouldn't carry it. Besides, it's against the law. You could get in serious trouble."

"I know, but under the circumstances I'll risk it. I

just feel a bit more secure having it with me until this thing blows over."

Ted wanted to change the subject and was just starting to point out an old farmhouse several hundred yards back from the road.

"Look at that old place. It must be . . . what the hell??"

The big Mercedes had come up from behind them seemingly out of nowhere and when it was abreast of the Corvette, nudged it hard.

"Ted!" Jil screamed and braced herself against the dashboard with one arm, the other draped around the back of her seat. The car swerved wildly for a few seconds until Ted could gain control.

But almost as fast the Mercedes again connected with the smaller car, this time harder.

"Shit! That guy must be crazy or drunk." Ted was startled. He again fought the wheel to avoid going into a drainage ditch that ran alongside the road. The powerful Mercedes bumped their car twice more rapidly.

"What the hell is going on? Who is that nut?" Ted accelerated and pulled slightly ahead. He tried to get a look at the other driver but the glare from the sun created a shield.

"Ted! It's probably one of them. They'll kill us both for the package!" Jil's voice was on the verge of hysteria.

"No chance. This baby will outrun him any day of the week. Try to get a look at his face. See if it is the guy who worked you over yesterday."

"It's hard to see his face . . . the sun . . . Ted! He's coming up again, fast!"

The Mercedes caught the rear end of the Corvette with a vicious blow that sent the smaller car into a half spin which Ted almost wasn't able to correct. Now the larger car was abreast of him again and slammed into the Corvette's side with tremendous force. Jil could feel the car rocking almost to the point of turning over on its side. She was now too terrified to scream. The instant the car righted itself Ted put his foot to the floorboard and the sports car lurched ahead. He put nearly two car lengths between them before he caught the increasing reflection of the Mercedes in his sideview mirror, what was left of it. "That's got to be a souped-up model. No way he could stay with us at these speeds otherwise."

Ted darted his eyes from the road ahead to the image of the big car which was closing the gap on them fast. As the trees blocked the sun, creating fractions of shade, he could see the other driver's teeth locked into a wild grin. The bastard must be mad, Ted thought.

The Mercedes caught up with the Corvette easily and smashed against it three more times in quick order. It was all Ted could do to keep the speeding car from being bounced off the road. There was a turn up ahead and Ted hoped another car would be heading in the opposite direction. Somehow he managed to get slightly ahead as both cars screeched into the turn. His heart sank. The road ahead was empty of traffic but he noticed that the drainage ditch was less severe along this stretch.

He again floored the Corvette as he was still in the turn and could feel the power of the engine straining as the car fish-tailed slightly then leapt forward. The driver of the Mercedes matched his move and closed the slight distance between the two cars with little effort. Just as the Mercedes began to weave in preparation for another hard slam, the driver heard the ear-piercing scream of the Corvette's tires as the little car vanished from his view. Ted had slammed on his brakes.

Ted's arms ached from fighting the wheel. The Corvette went into a wild skid but stayed on the road. It spun around in two complete circles and came to rest again facing the direction it had been going in. Ted jumped out, his legs weak, and pulled the Walther from his belt.

The Mercedes has stopped some 150 feet ahead. Ted heard the hard crunching sound as the driver shifted into reverse and began to come towards him rapidly in reverse. Ted leveled his gun at the fastly approaching car and let off three quick shots into the rear window and then several more at the tires.

The big car stopped for a split second and then shot forward, coughing black smoke as it raced away. Ted emptied his clip at the rapidly vanishing car, then regretted spending all his bullets in anger. He was tempted to persue the Mercedes and give the driver a taste of his own medicine but realized it was a foolish thought. The big car had proved more than a match for his and it certainly had more weight on its side. Furthermore he had to assume that the driver was probably armed.

Jil was pale when Ted got back into the car. "Please wait a minute, Ted." Her voice was trembling. Jil opened her door and ran into the bushes nearby. Ted could hear her retching.

The driver of the Mercedes looked at his sideview mirror several times during the next few minutes to see if Ted was chasing him. When he got as far as the main road he turned back in the direction of Washington. A few minutes later he pulled the black sedan into a service station and parked it behind a large truck, blocking view of it from the highway. Before going inside to use the telephone he gave the car a quick inspection.

The bullets that had entered the rear window had exited through the windshield. One had nicked the steering wheel, missing his hand by a fraction of an inch. There was no way he could drive this car back into Washington without causing attention. He decided he better call the Organization and get instructions.

Ted and Jil had turned their car around and were backtracking to the main road they had entered from. The trip to Reynolds house would take longer but there was more safety on the main road than on any more shortcuts.

At the same time the driver of the Mercedes was informing the Organization of his failed attempt, Ted was on a phone telling Dick Reynolds what had just happened.

"We're at a roadside restaurant right now. It will probably take another twenty minutes to get to your place, Dick."

"Just stay put, you two. I'll borrow a car and meet you there. We're going to have to find a place for you to stay. I don't think it would be wise to return to your apartment. Give me the name of the restaurant and expect me in a half hour."

Reynolds got off the phone with Ted and searched his brain for someone in the neighborhood he could borrow a car from. He was standing by the bay window overlooking his front lawn when he saw a local police car getting ready to leave from where it was parked several houses away. If he could get them to drop him off at police headquarters he could talk one of the local cops into lending him their personal car for a few hours. Several of them knew he was with the Bureau and it shouldn't be too hard to get a car in an emergency.

Across the street Mrs. Flynn sat rocking in her chair by the window, thinking. Too bad those two fine young men hadn't come to Mr. Reynolds house a few minutes earlier, before he left in the police car. They certainly were determined to see him, ringing the bell that many times and knocking on the door. Must be friends of his from the F.B.I., she thought, look at the way they are walking around the house peeking into windows!

Mrs. Flynn smiled. If her legs didn't bother her so she would go to the front door and call to them and let them wait in her house for Mr. Reynolds until he returned. Besides if they were G-men, she thought, they'd probably have all kinds of good stories! Better than some of that stuff she had to watch on television. It would be a nice way to spend a morning. Since Mrs. Reynolds died last summer she really had nobody to talk to much. If only she had the strength to climb down the stairs and call them from the front door.

Chapter 6

Ted and Jill were seated in the last booth of the long, diner-shaped restaurant. Across from them were the rest rooms and directly behind them was a rear fire exit door in case they had to leave in a hurry. Ted raised his arm and waved to Reynolds as the F.B.I. man paused near the front of the diner and looked around.

Reynolds joined them and the trio ordered more coffee. As soon as the waitress retreated Reynolds began.

"You two alright? From what you told me on the phone, Ted, that must have been some ride you had. Did you get the guy's plate number, and where is your car? I didn't see it out front and that threw a scare in me."

"I got in the back, near this door," Ted said, pointing to the exit behind him.

"Good thinking. Now let's get down to business. First off, I think this thing is getting out of hand so I called Mitchell at the Bureau and asked him if we could come in a little later and talk to him about some urgent business."

"Who's Mitchell?" Jil asked and Ted answered.

"The associate director of the Bureau," Ted let out a lung full of air and continued. "You've gone right up to the top, Dick, thanks."

"No thanks necessary. The people who want that package you got from Bauman play rough and since they may represent a threat to national security I figure Mitch will listen and put the Bureau on this officially."

There was a trace of satisfaction in Jil's voice as she spoke again. "Well, Dr. Bauman is getting his wish after all. Now these rotten Nazi killers will be dealing with the F.B.I."

"Hold on." Reynolds put his hand up much in the way a traffic cop would to halt vehicles. "I said we had a meeting with Mitch, but there isn't anything solid yet. He could very well dismiss the whole thing as being a matter for the local police." Reynolds paused and let a long moment of silence pass before continuing, with a slight smile.

"That's why I made another phone call before getting here. This one was to an old friend in the Israeli intelligence gang that operates here 'unofficially' if you know what I mean. The man I called is Uri Moertz, a very talented, highly skilled character who has a strong dislike for anything that even sounds Nazi."

"What do you mean he operates 'unofficially'?" Ted asked.

"Just that. No foreign government is supposed to have agents of his type assigned to duty in this country but almost all of them do. Uri isn't part of the Israeli Mission, holds no sort of diplomatic credentials, isn't even listed as an Israeli on the passport he carries. He is supposed to be a Canadian involved in some kind of electronic data processing work. His cover is that of a buyer, which gives him freedom of movement. But I'll tell you this, Uri is probably one of the top foreign agents operating here and one who knows every trick in the book when it comes to survival. The Israelis are very interested in several former Nazi bigwigs and a host of lower types who managed to escape the hangman when the war ended. If any of the old crowd are involved in this Bauman thing Uri will be delighted to remove them."

Jil gasped. "Remove them? Will he kill them?"

Reynolds looked at her with a long hard stare then shifted it to Ted. "Uri was part of the team that picked up Eichmann years ago and removed him from South America to Israel. He was tried and executed there, if you remember. Uri has also been involved in a few cases where the people played as nasty as the bunch that is giving you two trouble now. Sometimes this business gets hairy and, yes, he'll kill them if it comes to that—if his life, or yours, is in danger he will respond accordingly."

"You talk about him as if you know him very well," Ted remarked.

"I do. Let's just say there have been times when it was convenient for our government to look the other way while he was working." Reynolds paused again and took a long sip of the coffee the waitress had just brought. As soon as she was gone he added. "I trust him and like him. He will be your edge when it comes to dealing with these people in ways the Bureau can't. Now let's see this package I've been hearing about and tell me what you can about the information in it."

Ted reached down under the table and grabbed an airline overnight bag, placing it on the seat next to Reynolds.

"The stuff seems a bit disorganized and is probably out of order. It is all photo copies of original material Bauman must have kept somewhere. Quite a bit of what's here are pages from a journal, and Bauman made foot-notes for me that relate to other papers also included. I started reading the low numbers of the journal pages and here is what I put together.

"Bauman first got wind that he was on the right trail in his search for Adolf Hitler's children when he received a call last year from a French Nazi hunter he knew through correspondence and work they both did for a Jewish World Refugee Committee based in Paris.

"The man who wrote to him, Lucien Gertz, or Grotz, I forget which, but it's in there."

"It was Grotz, I remember," Jil offered.

Ted smiled at her and continued. "Anyway, Grotz asked Bauman if he could check on a residence in the U.S. for a Dr. Helmut Wolf. No state, no city, just check to see if there was a Dr. Helmut Wolf alive and practicing in the U.S."

"A tall order," Reynolds offered, raising his eyebrows.

"It would seem so but later in the pages, quite a bit later, Bauman notes that he is convinced that if Wolf is alive in the U.S. he has changed his name. Bauman mentions that his sources were unable to locate him."

"I'd like to know who his sources are," Reynolds mused.

"According to Grotz, Wolf was a doctor in the SS with the rank of Standartenfuhrer, or colonel. He wasn't one of Hitler's intimates in public but apparently he was part of a quiet circle that Hitler associated with out of the public eye. Wolf did some little favors for the Fuhrer. Things like making sure the women Hitler would want to spend time with were VD free."

"Hitler the Lover?" Reynolds seemed surprised. "I thought he had a long time involvement with Eva Braun?"

"Well, according to what Bauman has written elsewhere, the savior of Germany had quite an appetite for ladies. He had at least five different mistresses during the years he was in power, and we're not even counting Eva.

"Anyway, Grotz passed this information on to Bauman. It is based on an interrogation the French Secret Service had with an old man in the coastal city of St. Nazaire on May 29, 1945. The old man claimed to be out past curfew and hiding in a tool shed on the quay on the night of May 1 when an ambulance with an SS escort raced onto the quay and delivered someone on a stretcher aboard a U-boat. He claims to have heard one of the men clearly identified as Dr. Wolf and a short time later this man boarded the U-boat and ordered the sailors to gun down the SS escort on the quay. The U-boat men then attached a rope to the ambulance and, after dumping the SS men and their motorcyles into the back of it, towed it off the quay and into the drink when they departed."

"That's fantastic. Did the French conduct an underwater search for the ambulance?" Reynolds asked.

"If they did there is no record of it that Grotz found. But the old man then says a short time later he heard someone screaming for help and he pulled a Wehrmacht sergeant from the water. The sergeant told him he was the ambulance driver and had escaped being slaughtered because they must have forgotten he was sitting inside the vehicle's cab. He further avoided detection by huddling on the floor and only had a chance to escape when the ambulance was sinking to the bottom of the harbor."

"Who was the passenger that was delivered to the U-boat with Wolf?" Reynolds asked.

"The old man said the sergeant told him he thought it was Eva Braun. She was pregnant."

"That's impossible. Eva Braun died at the bunker with Hitler, according to the dental records."

"Right. And Grotz and Bauman both believed that the woman in the back of the ambulance was one of Hitler's other mistresses and she was carrying Hitler's child."

"It seems a bit far-fetched, if that's all there is. What else do you have," Reynolds queried.

"Oh, there's more, and it weaves a pretty convincing picture," Ted added.

"Through other sources Bauman uncovered a report on record with the French Ministry of Marine and Fisheries that documents the discovery of an ambulance filled with old motorcyles and some skeletons, all identified as World War II German vintage, that were removed from the mouth of the St. Nazaire harbor in 1949 when it was being restored for commercial use. Bauman uncovered this information early last year and when he brought it to the attention of French officials and also reminded them of the interrogation report their own secret service had on file with the old man, he ran into a stone wall. He returned from France and left Grotz to keep pestering them to locate a copy of the report. He had shown them the copy Grotz had given him but they claimed it was a bad joke and that no such report existed in their files. Bauman was home hardly two days when he received word that Grotz had died in his sleep.

"Furthermore, again working through people who were part of the Jewish relief group, Bauman went to Germany to search the records of the SS and trace the career of Helmut Wolf. Bauman and a man named Feltzer couldn't find anything in the files about Wolf after an entry that indicated he was assigned to a general's staff at Stalingrad. At the bottom of the file someone wrote 'Died there.' There is no date but the memo is accompanied by an official U.S. Army seal and an unreadable signature. Bauman notes that the battle for Stalingrad was in 1942 and by mid April 1943 the Russians had pushed the Germans back several hundred miles."

"Could be a fake, the signature and seal, I mean. Those things are easy enough to get if you want to get your hands on one," Reynolds volunteered.

"Exactly what Bauman and Feltzer believed. They copied Wolf's last-known address in Berlin and also his hometown near Munich then they began posing as a couple of old veterans and asking a lot of questions. They struck out in Berlin but got a good break in Munich. They actually found a family that knew Wolf's family before and during the war. According to what they learned Helmut Wolf did not die at Stalingrad but was alive and well right up to the end of the war. An old woman in the family remembers him being treated like some kind of hero when he came home for his final leave in late April, 1945. There was a party for him and the quiet talk was that he was returning to Berlin to spend his last days with the Fuhrer in the bunker."

"O.K.," Reynolds interrupted, "This all hints around that Wolf may have boarded a U-boat with a woman who was pregnant, possibly with Hitler's kid, and departed France in May, 1945. What else do we have and, specifically, what do we have to show that he actually got to America and raised her and that now she is here in Washington?"

Reynolds looked down at his watch and stopped Ted before he could continue. "Tell it to me in the car. We've got to meet Uri and then go over to the Bureau to see Mitch. We'll take the car I borrowed from a friend of mine at police headquarters. It's not as easy to pick out of a crowd as that red rocket you drive. Besides the car I have can seat three *comfortably*!"

The three of them were only a few minutes down the road heading for Washington when the two men who had visited Reynolds' house earlier pulled into the restaurant parking lot. They sat at the counter and had coffee while they discussed how they were going to explain that they had missed finding Reynolds at home. When they left they had no idea that Ted's car was parked around the other side of the diner and that they had missed by minutes finding the three people they wanted so much.

Chapter 7

Susan Benedict's breath was fogging the cosmetic mirror that she held close to her face. She was searching the area around her eyes for any signs of wrinkles and was so intent she didn't notice her husband come into the bedroom behind her.

"My, my, if you get any closer you may as well kiss it," he said with a trace of sarcasm as he passed her and went to his closet to retrieve his tuxedo jacket. As usual he was finished dressing but Susan, he knew, would need another half hour of self-examination before she was ready to be seen in public. She shifted her eyes in the mirror briefly and locked a cold gaze on him.

"I thought you found it beneath you to be thought of as the young and virile vice president who had an aging wife, so I've been doing something about it."

"Really? And what is that?"

"I'm taking extra care of my complexion. When we arrive at The White House in a little while I intend to have everyone remember that I'm the most attractive woman present . . . and that includes that broadcasting bitch, Sharon Franklin."

Elliott Benedict tensed up at his wife's hostile tone when she mentioned Sharon's name. He finished putting his jacket on and came up behind her. She had put the mirror down and was now checking items in her purse while seated before her dresser.

He slipped his hands onto her shoulders from behind and began a hard massage of the area around her neck.

"And what makes you think Sharon will be among those at tonight's function?"

"I overheard your phone call to the Secretary of State this morning. You're not very subtle, Elliott."

"Subtle? Who's trying to be subtle. We have a marriage of convenience, it's not a secret in this town, but I assure you I have no interest in Sharon Franklin. I wouldn't think of leaving you for her or any other woman." He dug his fingers deeper into her neck. "It wouldn't serve my purpose. And what's this about overhearing my phone call? I thought you had left the house early on some mysterious errand this morning, about eight o'clock, wasn't it?"

She spun herself loose fron his grip and ignored the last question. "You wouldn't leave me? It wouldn't serve your purpose?" She was on her feet and facing him. There was rage in her eyes.

"I'll tell you about 'purpose.' I have a purpose to remain Mrs. Elliott Benedict, at least until after the election. That is provided this time you have the guts to take on old man Chandler and his flunkies and get the party's nomination and then have what it takes to win the election. Then we'll see who has served whose purpose, you bastard!"

He turned away from her and began walking into the hall but paused and shook his finger while permitting a sly grin to cross his lips. His remarks were condensending.

"Now, now, Susan. Don't threaten me. Once I've won the Presidency I don't care if you stand on top of the Washington Monument and tell the world your husband is an unfaithful cad. We both know you won't say a thing before the election because you want to be the First Lady more than anything else in the world." He let out a hardy laugh and left the room.

She stood there frozen with her eyes directed at the doorway he had just gone through. The blood was pounding in her head. In an almost inaudible voice, she answered, "not more than *anything* else."

***

Congresswoman Leona Crawford Gordon tapped her fingers impatiently on her knee as she sat in the back of her private limousine waiting for her aide Jim Hanlon. She looked at her watch and to no one in particular asked, "What's keeping him? Where the hell does he think we are going, to a bowling dinner?" The chauffeur looked at her through the car's rear-view mirror.

"Shall I beep again, Miss Gordon?"

She ignored the question and simply let out a disgusted grunt. Almost on cue Jim Hanlon appeared exiting from the main door of the highrise apartment. He exaggerated a trot to the car and quickly slipped in the rear next to Leona.

"What the hell kept you? This is only my third invitation to The White House in ten years in this shitty town and you're making me late!" The chauffeur politely closed the privacy window between himself and his passengers and guided the long-wheel-based Lincoln into traffic.

"I'm sorry, Leona, I kind of fell behind with those phone calls you asked me to make and . . ."

She cut him off in mid-sentence. "Listen, buster. I don't tolerate mediocre performance from anyone in my organization. Is that clear? When I give an order to move, people move or they find themselves another job." Without missing a beat she asked another question, this time in softer tones. "How do I look?"

Hanlon blinked. He could hardly believe the change in her tone.

"What?"

Again, softly, she repeated it. "How do I look?" and added, "You're a man. Do I look attractive?"

Hanlon was almost speechless but he managed a fast nod and mumbled, "You look great, as always. You look terrific." He was slightly embarrassed after he said it but she had caught him off guard. In fact he had told her the truth but it was the first time in the more than three years he had worked for her that she had ever asked such a question. She was beautiful, he thought, but she was also one of the most ruthless politicians in the city.

***

Sharon Franklin moved through the television studio barking commands at the frail secretary trailing behind.

"I want a complete tape of my interview with the Vice President on Herb's desk by the time I get to his office tomorrow morning. We'll settle this bullshit once and for all. Nobody is holding my White Paper project on the shelf unless I hear it directly from the head of this network." She stopped in her tracks and turned on the secretary. "If Herb Cowan thinks he can screw around with me this time he's in for a real surprise. Mark my words. When I come out of his office tomorrow we will have a schedule for the White Paper and we'll be kicking it off with the Benedict interview. Now where are those goddamned phone messages?" She turned on her heel and retreated into her private office. The secretary again began to follow her and checked her watch.

"Miss Franklin, the Secretary of State's car will be calling for you any minute. Should I send a message downstairs that you'll be slightly delayed?"

"No! Let the prick wait. That's all he's good for anyway!"

In angry moods, then, three of the most attractive women, and three who all coveted power, prepared to attend the bipartisan reception President Chandler was hosting at The White House this evening for a trade delegation from Central America.

Meanwhile, Ted and Jil were on their way back to their apartment after having met with Uri Moertz and later with Lucien Mitchell, the associate director of the F.B.I. Dick Reynolds had driven them back to the restaurant where they had left the car earlier in the day.

Now, as the sky selfishly coveted the last tint of daylight before darkness cast its velvet cloak over the region, Ted and Jil silently made their way back to the capital city. Each was privately reviewing the two meetings they had just had.

***

Uri had insisted that Reynolds, Ted, and Jil join him having a cup of tea. His apartment was spartan, so much so in fact it made Ted think that if this man were to leave on a moment's notice anyone going through the apartment after his departure would find very little to indicate the characteristics of its occupant. The more Ted thought about it the more convinced he was that there was nothing to even hint at the man's personality.

Jil smiled and Ted simply nodded as Uri placed their teacups before them. Reynolds had successfully refused the offer by claiming the caffeine was no good for him. Ted and Jil were seated at the two kitchen chairs and Reynolds made do with a director's chair he brought in from the small living room. Uri had positioned himself across from them, leaning against the sink.

"From what Dick had a chance to tell me this morning you two seem to have opened up a hornet's nest of trouble." He was smiling as he spoke but his cold blue eyes belied any degree of casual interest. Without missing a beat he continued. "What makes you think the people you are dealing with are Nazis?"

The question really wasn't necessary, Ted thought, but it was as good a way as any to get into the story.

"Well, it began last Friday with a call from a man I had met several years ago, Dr. Aaron Bauman . . ."

Jil slowly sipped her tea as Ted brought Uri up to date the same way they had with Reynolds. As Ted spoke and Uri occasionally interjected a question, she studied the undercover Israeli agent. She had had reservations about him after Reynolds first spoke about involving him but the man she envisioned and the man who was now less than ten feet away from her in the apartment were quite different.

Uri Moertz appeared remarkably similar to Ted, she thought. A fraction of an inch under six feet tall, she estimated, with a lean body that hinted at constant conditioning. His arms, though not overly muscular, appeared strong. His movements were rapid but graceful. But there the similarity ended. Ted was a boyish twenty-eight years old. Jil guessed that Uri was in his early forties. His rugged good looks, however, made him appear younger at first. She found herself looking from Uri to Ted and thinking how pleased she would be if Ted were in as fine physical shape as Uri when he was the same age.

Uri ran a hand through his wavy light brown hair and shut his eyes for a moment. He was obviously in thought.

"Now you know as much as I do, Uri," Reynolds offered. Ted and Jil were going to fill me in on the rest on the drive over here but instead we got into a debate about where these two should stay for the next few days. I don't think they should go back to the apartment. Do you?"

"Yes and no. Naturally there is a chance for more

trouble if you return there and hiding out might not be a bad idea. However, at least this time you won't be caught by surprise and now they know you are armed. But most importantly," Uri was addressing Reynolds question but he was looking at Ted and Jil, "if you let Dick set you up in a 'safe' house you'll be out of contact with these people."

"You mean we won't be around so they can try to finish the job they've already tried?" Ted questioned.

"Yes, from their point of view, maybe. But maybe not. If you want to get this thing over with and out of your lives I think the best way is to continue living at your apartment and going on about your regular business or something else but at least be *reachable*. It is the only quick way to draw them out." Uri leaned across to the stove and turned on the tea water again.

"You want to use us as bait?" Jil's voice carried a hint of tension.

"Let's not use the word 'bait.' I'd prefer to say you will be our decoy and . . ."

Reynolds interrupted. "Now wait a minute. We're getting a bit ahead of ourselves." He rose from the chair and stuck his hands deep into his pants pockets, pacing back and forth in the tiny kitchen. There were a few moments of silence before he paused and spoke to Uri.

"These people are my friends and even if they weren't I wouldn't want to expose them to this kind of risk unless it could be controlled. If Mitch agrees after hearing the story that this is a Bureau job we can get twenty-four-hour protection for them. That way I'd agree with what you've just suggested, Uri, but not unless we know the Bureau is covering them night and day."

"That would be ideal. And you and I, Richard, could then check out the information Ted got from Bauman."

"Does anybody here care about how Jil and I feel?" Ted's question was light, without a trace of hostility.

Jil spoke first. "I don't like the idea of being a sitting target for these madmen but I think what you've both just said makes a lot of sense. Let's do whatever is necessary to flush them out from under their rock. Ted?"

"I agree. It is probably the only way. But whether or not the Bureau supplys bodyguards we are not going to move out to some 'safe' house and hide. If any son-of-a-bitch tries to get near me or Jil again I'll fill him full of holes."

Uri let an amused grin glide across his face. He moved over to the stove and took the teapot. When he lifted it he shook it.

"Empty. I lose more teapots this way. You drank all my water. And I thought you Americans all had coffee running through your blood streams!" The quip served to break the tension that had been building.

"Now let's get on with the other documents. What else do you have?"

Again, almost without a pause, Uri had switched mental gears and was again serious and businesslike. Jil concluded that she liked him.

Ted began shuffling through the pile of papers he had taken out of the flight bag.

"Here's the copy of the French interrogation of the guy who said he saw the massacre on the quay at St. Nazaire. He was found floating near the shoreline a few days after he told his story to the French."

"What about the ambulance driver he mentioned? The man who survived?" Uri asked.

"Bauman ran into a stone wall there. He tried to locate him when he was in Germany tracking down Wolf. There are several pages that note his progress in that effort but each time Bauman seemed to be on the right track he came up with nothing."

"Then it's possible the man is still alive, or did Bauman conclude that he is dead.?"

"He thought he was alive. It seems he heard three different versions of how the man died. His name is Heinrich Trautman."

"Hmmn," Uri again ran his hand through his wavy hair. "It is a possibility. Sounds like he is still covering his trail. Why didn't Bauman pursue it?"

"He had to get back to the States already. Grotz was also going to follow up on this, but his sudden death . . ."

"The bodies are starting to pile up," Reynolds added.

"Here is the report of the French Ministry of Marine and Fisheries that the bureaucrats claim also doesn't exist and here is a newspaper clipping photocopy Bauman located that confirms the story. The English translation is attached to it.

"Now this is something interesting. It is a copy of a sworn statement by a Captain Rolf Brunner of the SS Gross Deutschland Division describing the last days in Hitler's bunker."

"It is certainly thick. What was he doing, writing a book?" Uri asked.

"No, trying to save his neck it seems," Ted responded. "He was one of a small group that escaped before the Russians captured the bunker. He stayed right up to the end, leaving only after they had been told Hitler had killed himself. Brunner managed to make his way into the British area and then surrendered. He wrote this testament with very little urging while awaiting trial for war crimes.

"There is one section near the end in which he names the others in the bunker. The English provided a translation, but it did little good for Brunner. He was hung anyway. I'll read a paragraph to you:

'Around lunchtime on the day before Adolf Hitler finally admitted to himself that he had betrayed the German people and ended his own life I observed Standertenfuhrer Kleist and another officer of equal rank who I did not personally know but recognized as an SS doctor leaving Hitler's private quarters. Kleist came over to me and asked if any word had come from Tempelhof Airport concerning a medical plane having arrived yet. I answered no. Kleist and the other officer left the bunker and a short time later one of my men came running in to say he had seen the other officer shoot Kleist in the head before speeding away. I later discovered that the officer who shot Kleist was thought to be Standartenfuhrer Dr. Helmut Wolf.'

It was quiet in the small kitchen. Several moments passed before Ted spoke again.

"This seems to place Wolf in the bunker and knocks some holes in his earlier death report. And add this to Trautman's statement that Wolf borded a U-boat with a pregnant woman and it reinforces Bauman's theory about Hitler's daughter, right?" Ted was seeking a sign of agreement from Uri.

"It might. But all of this is history. Why did Bauman believe that Wolf and the woman succeeded in making a dangerous transatlantic trip in the U-boat to America? South America would have seemed a better choice. And why or how did Bauman determine the sex of the child the woman was carrying?" Uri's questions were fast and hard. He seemed to be playing the role of antagonist on purpose.

"Here." Ted located another sheet of paper. It was a copy of a newspaper story from *The Boston Globe*. He handed it to Uri while telling him what it contained. "It's about a fire in a rooming house in August, 1945.

Two women died. One, the woman who owned the house told authorities before she died that a male tenant, a German doctor, and a woman who had given birth to a baby girl lived in the top floor apartment. A neighbor told police that she had often heard the woman crying at night after she and the man had loud arguments and several times heard the woman scream his name 'Helmut.' The woman was found dead upstairs but no trace of the man or the baby were found.

"The fire was listed as suspicious but never solved or formally called arson."

Reynolds looked at his watch and got out of the chair. "Ted, why don't you leave a lot of this other stuff with Uri. We've got to be getting over to see Mitch. Just bring the material Uri has already seen. Besides, the Bureau will only be interested in the material and events related to the current problem and I think we have enough of that."

**

Ted slid the Corvette into a parking space some distance from the front of their apartment. He and Jil walked briskly toward the building, both scanning the area for unfamiliar vehicles or anything else out of the ordinary.

"I feel better about the Bureau being involved. How did Mitch strike you?" he asked.

"Very formal. Very businesslike. At first I thought he was annoyed with Dick for bringing us in, but it worked out the way you and Dick wanted it to and that's what counts."

"Yea, I guess so. I don't really like to know somebody is watching everything we do but it is for our own good. Mitch was really concerned, I thought. Actually it all went easier than I expected."

They climbed the steps to the building and reached

the front door but before opening it Ted turned and looked up and down the street.

"Do you see something?" Jil asked and she also searched the block.

"No. But they're out there. Mitch said we'd have surveillance by the time we got home." They paused for a moment before turning and entering the building.

They no sooner shut the door and began climbing the inside stairs when the black Mercedes that had been parked outside the building the previous night turned the corner and slowly passed the Corvette.

"Well, well. It seems our two lovebirds have returned to their nest," the driver said.

In the back seat, nervously dragging on a cigarette, Dr. Harold Lupo snapped, "Let them be for now. We must first locate and remove their protection. Call the van and tell them to get working."

Chapter 8

The phone was ringing as Ted pushed open the apartment door. Before moving into the room to get it he impulsively stopped and looked for any signs of visitors. Jil swept past him and darted for the phone.

"There is nobody here, Ted. Reynolds said the phone calls this morning were nothing more than a ruse to make sure we both left the apartment. They wanted us together for their dirty work." She picked up the receiver.

"Hello? Oh hi, David. Yes he is, we just got in. Thank you for the lovely flowers. Yes, I'm feeling a lot better. Here he is," she covered the mouthpiece on the phone before handing it to Ted.

"I thought it might be the airline," she said almost apologetically. "Sorry."

He took the phone from her and waved a pointed finger as if to scold. She headed for the kitchen.

"Hello David, what's up?"

"Ted, I've been trying to reach you all afternoon. I thought with Jil recovering from that nasty incident yesterday you two would be around the apartment all day . . ."

"We had some urgent business that had to be attended to. A piece of property we've been looking at in Virginia," he lied. "The real estate agent called and said

75

someone else was preparing to put a deposit on it and we had better make up our minds quickly. But it didn't work out. By the time we got there the other people had made a bid."

"Real estate? My, my, that sounds serious. Does this mean you two are thinking about tying the knot?"

"Could be, but we'll let you know for sure when there is something definite." From where he was in the living room Ted was watching Jil rummage through the refrigerator.

"Ted, I'm sorry I didn't get you earlier. I realize this is short notice but we could really use you tonight at the reception. Think you can freshen up and get into your tux and be at The White House in half an hour?"

Ted didn't respond quickly but finally said, "I thought you and DeMarco were covering this one. I'm supposed to be off for a few days, remember?"

"DeMarco won't be there. Something about an impounded wisdom tooth, or at least that's what the message I got said. Frankly, I think he is drunk again. It is really important for you to be there, I wouldn't ask otherwise." Now Holland paused, then added.

"I'll tell you what, bring Jil. I'll arrange it with security. That way you can be together. That is if she is up to coming out after the active day she has just had."

"Hang on, David, I'll ask her." Ted held the phone to his chest and called into the kitchen.

"If you put the leftovers back in the refrigerator I promise to get you your own tray of hors d' ouvres at The White House reception tonight. Want to go?"

Jil looked up startled. She had just taken a mouthful of cold meatloaf and frantically began shaking her head up and down while making sounds Ted could not understand.

"David, I think she just said yes. We'll see you in forty-five minutes."

***

The old Chevy stopped in front of the apartment but before getting out the driver adjusted his shoulder holster. He looked up and down the street and was satisfied he wasn't being observed. Nonetheless he picked up the large pizza pie box as he left the car and began whistling while he climbed the steps.

In the apartment foyer he found the mailbox belonging to Ted Scott and pushed the buzzer under it. A few seconds later came the buzz reply that released the lock on the foyer door.

"Who is it?" Jil asked from behind the apartment door as Ted quickly loaded the Walther.

"Pizza delivery," came the reply.

Jil looked across at Ted who had positioned himself behind the door. He shrugged and motioned to Jil to talk more.

"You have the wrong apartment. We didn't order any pizza," she said loudly.

"But this is special pizza. Israeli pizza!"

Ted and Jil both recognized Uri's voice at the same time. She opened the door and the agent quickly came in. Jil closed the door behind him as he opened the box to reveal it was empty.

"Just a precaution. Delivery people come and go without attracting much attention. I thought it was a good way to get over here." He raised his hand to prevent Ted and Jil from talking. He motioned them into the hall.

When the three of them were outside the apartment Uri explained his visit.

"I was going to call you but it is possible they bugged your apartment today while you were out, after the attempt to kill you failed. Don't say anything in there that you wouldn't want overheard. If you want to discuss what's been going on with each other write notes or come out here in the hall."

"Write notes?" Ted was annoyed. "That's dumb. Anyway what makes you think they'd bug the place. I was getting the idea they just wanted to kill us and retrieve the documents."

"They do want to kill you but if you carelessly mention Dick Reynolds' name, or Mitchell's or even mine as others who are aware of the Bauman material we'll be on their list too. And why do I think they'd bug your apartment? Simple. That's what I would do. Depending on the size of their operation you can expect they have a physical base nearby. An apartment across the street somewhere or a vehicle with a tape recorder in it."

Jil answered. "No chance of an apartment. Space is impossible to get in this neighborhood, isn't it Ted?"

"Yes hon, but if they have a car with a recording device . . ."

"Probably not a car," Uri interjected. "My bet would be a van, a station wagon. If I were doing it I wouldn't use the same one all the time either. Keep an eye out for an unusual number of new vehicles of that kind that show up. If you can get license plate numbers Reynolds can check them out at the Bureau.

"The other reason I came over here is Bauman's list of suspects. Did both of you read it?"

"I glanced at it but didn't actually read it. The names meant nothing to me," Jil offered.

"Ditto here," Ted replied. "There were over a dozen names."

"Well I not only read it I took special care to find out all I could about three names Bauman had made little marks next to."

"Already? We only left you a few hours ago," Jil said.

Uri smiled. "One of those names rang a bell. Leona

Williams was adopted and her name was changed to Crawford. When she was nineteen she had a brief marriage to a Navy pilot, Captain Edward Gordon. He became an MIA in Vietnam in 1964."

"Oh my God," Ted blurted. "Leona Crawford Gordon is a Member of Congress."

"That's right," Uri continued. "All of the women on Bauman's list now live in Washington and were born in Boston between May and August 1945. The time period that falls between the departure of the U-boat from France and the fatal fire in Boston. According to Bauman's theory Hitler's daughter was born there during that time."

"That's incredible," Jil said, "Bauman said she was close to power." Ted stood there dumbfounded.

"It gets better," Uri noted. "A baby christened Mary Lipscomb grew up and became a weather girl on a New England television station and decided for professional reasons to change her name to Sharon Franklin, now sometimes known as 'Miss Television America' and also the mistress of the Secretary of State, I'm told."

"Any more?" Ted had regained his composure.

"Yes, one more. The third one to have a mark on Bauman's list. Susan Gilson. Reynolds immediately recognized her. Gilson was the maiden name of none other than the wife of the Vice President of The United States, the present Susan Benedict."

"There they are. Three women close to the center of power. Maybe your Dr. Bauman had other hints as to which one it might be but all I found in what you gave me were the small marks he had put next to these three names on the list."

"That's some trio," Ted said. "Anything on anybody else on the list?"

"Not at first check but Reynolds has the boys at the Bureau giving them the once over."

"You did some job Uri," Jil offered.

"Don't thank me. If it wasn't for Dick and a priority search release that his boss Mitchell authorized this could have taken several days. Now comes the real undercover work: asking questions about their unpublished pasts without attracting attention."

"Maybe I can help a little in that department," Ted said. I'm fairly certain all three of them will be at the reception we are going to at The White House in a little while. I think I'll strike up some interesting conversations."

"Ted!" Jil was looking at her watch. "Look at the time! We've got to get going, we should be leaving here in ten minutes.

***

The van driver cursed as he came down the street for the second time. Still no place to park, he mumbled.

"Hey that car is still double parked in front of their building," the man in the back called. "Do you think they have a visitor?"

"Let's find out. I'll double park a bit ahead and make as if I'm changing a tire. Turn on the equipment."

Uri carried the empty pizza box as he came down the front stairs two at a time. He acted annoyed as he opened the back door of the car and placed the box on the back seat and slammed the door. He mouthed a few curses in the direction of Ted and Jil's apartment as he got behind the wheel of the car and screeched away. To any casual observer he appeared to be a delivery man who was the victim of a prank call. That's exactly what the occupants of the van thought as he swept by them. Uri noticed them and memorized their license plate number.

Chapter 9

"David," Susan Benedict called, "Isn't that Ted Scott from your staff that just came in? And who is that young woman with him?"

David Holland excused himself from the polite conversation he was having with the couple directly next to the Vice President and his wife and turned to answer Susan. He looked toward the entrance to the East Room and immediately saw Ted shaking hands with Jim Hanlon and introducing him to Jil.

"Yes it is, Susan," he glanced at his watch, looked up and smiled at her. "I asked him to be here tonight so he could help me with any press needs the President or Vice President may have." He gave Elliott Benedict a big wink and smiled broadly.

"Naturally you will be tending to the Vice President's needs," Susan queried sarcastically.

"Naturally," Holland answered. He either ignored or failed to detect her tone.

Elliott Benedict gave Susan a long cold stare. The United States Marine Corps Orchestra was playing a romantic two-step and he gripped her arm at the elbow firmly. With an artificial smile he asked, "Care to dance, darling? I see the President is on the floor dancing with Leona, shall we join them?"

As they moved toward the dance floor Holland looked around again and saw that Ted and Jil were still talking to Jim Hanlon. He decided to wait until their conversation broke up before approaching.

Leona Crawford Gordon held herself stiff as President William Chandler tried desperately to lead her while they were dancing.

"Relax, Leona. Enjoy the dance." He smiled at her and nodded to several people watching them from around the perimeter of the dance floor.

She returned his smile, adding, "I could have a genuine reason to smile and relax, Mr. President, if I knew you were endorsing my immigration bill. I can't understand why you haven't so far. We both know that in your heart you agree with what I've proposed."

"Dear Leona. Is that why you accepted the invitation to come here tonight, so you could button-hole me on your pet project?"

"Honestly?" she queried.

"Yes, honestly. Why did you come?"

"Well, for one thing my invitations to social functions at The White House haven't exactly been overwhelming. For another, yes, it's true I was hoping we would have an opportunity to talk about the immigration bill a bit. I at least want to get some kind of reading about how you feel."

"You've read my guarded comments about both your bill and the Vice President's opposition to it in the papers . . ."

"The hell with the papers. I don't for one minute believe the trash Dave Holland has been issuing as your 'position' on this. Everybody knows that Holland is working overtime helping Elliott Benedict carve his image so that he can get your party's nomination at the convention. I don't trust him. If you know what's good for you you shouldn't either."

Chandler stopped dancing in mid-step and brought his full six foot three-inch frame rigid. He looked down at Leona and there was an unusual firmness in his voice.

"Madam, I am still the President and will be until my second term ends on January 20.

Leona let her eyes scan the other guests around the dance floor and realized several people had noticed the two of them standing in place. Likewise Chandler was aware that people had seen but not heard the exchange. He immediately set his face into a broad smile and began dancing again. Leona remained silent.

***

Dick Reynolds pulled a five-dollar bill from his wallet and handed it to the young man standing on his front porch.

"Thanks a lot, Jerry. Now at least I'll be able to drive the car to the paint shop tomorrow. You did a great job removing the paint from the windows."

Reynolds said goodnight to his neighbor's son and for a moment toyed with the idea of putting the car into the garage. He decided against it. It was unlikely that vandals would come by again tonight.

***

The Secretary of State lifted two drinks from the tray proffered by the waiter and as he handed one to Sharon Franklin asked, "Would you care to dance? They are still playing slow ones."

"Not as long as Elliott is out there with his wife. I hate being in the same room with that woman, let alone on the same dance floor."

She looked at Chester Manning and added, "Besides, Mr. Secretary, I have more important things to do than dance." She walked past him, heading toward a small group that included a Supreme Court Justice and two Senators. Just as she reached the group she noticed David Holland joining Ted Scott and Jil.

"Ted! It was good of you to come," Holland was pumping Ted's hand as if they were old friends who had not seen each other in years. "And my dear Jil," he released Ted's hand and gripped her on both shoulders, gently kissing her on the cheek," You certainly look all recovered from your ordeal."

"What ordeal?" Sharon Franklin had joined them.

David Holland turned to face her, startled. "Sharon. I thought I just saw you and the Secretary halfway across the room! My, you move fast."

"In this town you have to, David." She turned to Ted. "I don't believe I've ever had the pleasure of being introduced to your ladyfriend."

"Sharon Franklin, meet Jil Baker," Ted said clumsily.

"Now, my dear." Sharon locked her eyes directly on Jil, "What's this talk about an ordeal?"

The orchestra finished its set and prepared to take a brief break as a pianist continued the music. Elliott and Susan Benedict, along with everyone else on the dance floor, waited until the President and Leona Gordon rejoined the crowd off the floor before following.

"I wonder if Chandler has something up his sleeve, inviting her here and then making a point of dancing with her." There was a trace of worry in the Vice President's voice.

"Why don't you find out? I see Holland over there with young Scott and whoever that girl is that came with him." She tightened when she realized that Sharon Franklin was also in the small group.

"If David was aware of anything other than what he told me that the President wanted as mixed a bag of official Washington here as possible—I'm sure he would have informed me. . . . but maybe Scott knows something David doesn't know. Susan, I have an idea but you'll have to help me."

***

The President refused a drink offered by the waiter but turned to Leona and asked her if she wanted one.

"No thank you." She quickly looked around the room at no one in particular and added. "I'd like to use a phone for a few minutes, Mr. President. Would that be possible?"

"Certainly, Congresswoman. We'll take care of that in a jiffy." He hardly raised his hand and a Secret Service agent was at his side.

"Bill, please escort Congresswoman Gordon to the phone in the library." Chandler darted his eyes to her and added, "Of course, Leona, if it is an extremely private call we can use . . ."

"No, that will be fine, Mr. President . . . as long as I may close the door."

Chandler again addressed the agent. "And Bill, as you pass David Holland over there please tell him I'd like a word with him."

The pianist changed the mood to a lively rumba in deference to the President's Latin American guests just as the Secret Service man passed Chandler's message on to Holland.

Sharon Franklin took the opportunity to excuse herself from Ted and Jil's company at the same time Holland departed to converse with the President.

"Ted, do you think we did the right thing telling her about the attack in the apartment?" Jil asked.

"Sure. What did we have to lose? I was trying to read her reaction but didn't pick up anything, did you?"

"No. She certainly is a cool customer."

"That she is. If she is Hitler's daughter she already knew it wasn't a burglary and assault. If she isn't then we did no harm anyway. It's not the kind of story she would use on the news."

"I hope not, especially after the pains David took to

keep it quiet from the press." Jil wanted to say something else but before she could Elliott and Susan Benedict materialized out of the crowd.

"Number two," Ted mumbled as he also saw them closing in.

"Good evening Ted," the Vice President said with a smile, extending his hand.

"Vice President, Mrs. Benedict. May I present my fiancee Jil Baker."

Jil was surprised to hear Ted use the term and Susan quickly picked up the change in her expression.

"Well, well. What a historic building to make such an announcement in," Susan said. "Miss Baker didn't seem to expect it. At least not here." Susan enjoyed watching Ted and Jil squirm.

Caught off guard, Ted tried to explain his impulsive remark away. "Well, actually you're right. In a way. We've been planning to make it official. I just thought I'd surprise her and do it tonight." He turned to Jil who found herself blushing and lost for words for some reason.

Elliott Benedict seized the opportunity he and Susan had discussed a short time ago. "Ted, let me be the first to congratulate you both . . . and the first to have the honor of dancing with the future Mrs. Scott." Benedict offered his arm to Jil and silently prayed the pianist would not play another rumba.

Jil was so startled she could only accept his offer and head toward the dance floor. As Susan took a step, closer to Ted, he tried to avoid noticing her firm breasts' heave with every breath she took.

"My husband tells me you are one of two people writing versions of the President's position on Congresswoman Gordon's disastrous immigration bill." She slowly sipped her drink and coyly looked at him over the rim of her glass.

***

Dick Reynolds couldn't imagine who would be ringing his front door bell at this hour of the evening. He rarely had evening visitors. He looked at the clock on his study wall. It was only 9:30 but he had been reading copies of the documents Uri had left with him earlier and somehow thought it was much later.

As a precaution he slid his revolver out of its holster and went to the door. He was relieved to see Jerry, the neighborhood boy who had cleaned his windows.

"Hi, Mr. Reynolds. I have a special favor to ask."

"Sure, Jerry, what can I do for you?" Reynolds kept his hand with the gun behind his back.

"Well, it's like this. I've got this important test in history tomorrow and for some dumb reason I didn't bring my book home. I wanted to run over to my friend Nick's house but then I remembered our car's window still had paint on them and I . . ."

"You want to borrow my car? Sure, kid, no problem. Just let me get the keys."

Reynolds watched Jerry go down the path and then closed the door. He had hardly gotten to the study again when he heard the roaring explosion.

He stood frozen for an instant, trying to convince himself it had been a trick of his imagination but he knew it wasn't. He ran from the house and down the path.

As he rounded the side toward the driveway his worst fears were realized. What was left of his car was a burning, twisted hulk of metal. A chunk of the steering wheel and a piece of Jerry's shirt were directly at his feet.

"Jerry! Oh my God! Jerry!" he screamed.

Across the street Mrs. Flynn was propped against the inside staircase that led to the second floor. Her legs were flat on the floor and her eyes were locked into a position that made them stare at her toes. Her neck was broken.

The two nice men who had been so intent on seeing Dick Reynolds earlier that day had come back again, just before he returned home earlier this afternoon. This time she made the fatal mistake of banging on her window and attracting their attention while they tinkered around with his car.

She was happy that they saw her and even though it took some time for her to make her way downstairs and open the door she was sure both they and Mr. Reynolds would appreciate her offer for them to wait for him here in her home.

She was wrong.

***

Though Susan Benedict had made an excuse about visiting the ladies room some time ago, her husband stayed on the dance floor with Jil. Apparently he's in a dancing mood, Ted thought.

The pianist had been replaced by the orchestra and now they were going into their second set. Ted attracted a waiter's attention and took a drink. At the same time he was joined by Jim Hanlon.

"Hi again, Ted. It looks like our *loving* Vice President enjoys the way Jil dances."

Ted grunted.

"Theodore, a little bird tells me you're the scribe that's doing the President's endorsement for Leona's immigration bill. How does it sound?"

"That seems to be a popular item for discussion around here tonight. But to answer your question it will sound good if he uses it. Did that little bird also tell you that DiMarco is doing the version the President will use if he comes out against it?"

"Sure, but DiMarco is a lightweight. He's never done anything stronger than the annual Christmas message and some college speeches for The Man. The feeling in our office is that if the Prez wanted a hatchet job on the immigration bill you'd be doing *that*!"

"I guess that is some sort of compliment, right, Jim?"

"Take it anyway you want but the truth is we feel it's

a cinch that Chandler is going to come out for stricter immigration quotas."

"Why all the mystery, Ted? Why doesn't he just come out and say it's a good bill and forget party politics. Isn't the opposition entitled to have some good ideas?"

Ted gave him a side glance, revealing a smirk. "C'mon, Jim, don't patronize me. If I have to give you an answer to that one you don't belong on the Hill."

Hanlon broke into a broad grin. He couldn't resist continuing the exchange.

"Alright, Shakespeare, what would you say if I told you some people have their own scenario about why Chandler is still on the fence?"

"Such as?" Ted inquired.

"Such as Chandler thinks Leona's bill is pretty good. Oh, he may find a few faults with it, but overall it is something he can live with. The old Conservative likes the fact that it finally puts a lid on some of the crud that's been creeping up on our shores for years.

"However, his liberal Vice President, the ambitious Mr. Benedict, is bent out of shape trying to keep Chandler from endorsing the bill.

"Benedict, they recall, almost wrested the nomination from Chandler after the old man's first term. But then, with all the aplomb of a shotgun wedding, the kingmakers came up with a peace treaty. It resulted in the most mismatched ticket in American political history: Chandler the Conservative and Benedict the Liberal. That made the Kennedy-Johnson and Reagan-Bush duets seem like they were made in heaven."

Hanlon was obviously enjoying himself. Ted let him continue.

"The deal, so the pundits say, cost first-term Vice President John J. Felker his spot on the ticket. The gullible Mr. Felker was assured he would receive an appointment to the Supreme Court. After all, everybody knew Mr. Justice Steinwitz was no more than a few breaths ahead of eternity.

"But the White House crowd read the actuary tables wrong and Justice Steinwitz continues to celebrate birthdays.

"That was the gamble. That was the long shot. Chandler wanted re-nomination without a war . . . and sacrificed his lifelong friend to get it. He may have honestly thought they'd all be attending Steinwitz' funeral, who knows? Benedict was told to hold his breath for four more years and then his hour would come.

"Felker stepped down for 'health reasons'. But he has become increasingly healthier this last year after having a heart-to-heart talk with the medical marvel Justice Steinwitz. It seems Steinwitz was properly outraged when he heard that Chandler had Felker waiting in the wings for his black robe.

"Steinwitz has been telling people he has no intention of dying to help consumate the Chandler-Benedict marriage. Now former Vice President Felker is making sounds, and lining up delegates, for a run at the convention. He no longer wants to be a Justice but thinks, instead, he should be President.

"The President never really felt comfortable with Benedict and has had pangs of regret for shit-canning Felker. Some 'informed sources' go so far as to say he wouldn't be at all unhappy if Felker did knock Benedict off, however remote the possibility. But Chandler has been thinking that if he breaks with Benedict early enough, and throws his support behind Felker it just might happen."

Ted wasn't surprised that Hanlon's information was one hundred percent correct. There were few secrets in either party. He decided, nonetheless, to dampen Hanlon's glee.

"OK, Jim, let's suppose some of what you say may be true, or reasonably close. Then the theory is that if the President does something like coming out for Leona's bill against the opposition of the Vice President he would then be playing hardball in Felker's court, right?"

"Right!"

"What does Leona have to gain?"

"Well, Teddy boy, for openers it weakens Benedict and strengthens Felker. And Felker, by the way believes as Chandler does that it is a good bill.

"The feeling is that if Chandler succeeds in helping Felker get the nomination there will be such a backlash from the Benedict wing of the party that many of them will stay home on election day or, worse for you, cross party lines."

"Suppose Benedict gets the nomination, Jim. Can't you expect a backlash from the Chandler-Felker wing?" Up until now both men had exchanged information they both knew. Ted now tried to feel Hanlon out for what might be an important reading of the other camp's strategy.

Hanlon didn't hesitate answering.

"Not really. Chandler is the key. If he remains behind Benedict, as per their deal four years ago, your party will remain solid. However, we think The Man will put the good of the country ahead of political loyalty. Chandler doesn't want to see Benedict in the White House. We think he'll bolt and support Felker. He has a chance to move in that direction by supporting Leona's bill based on his own conviction. He really couldn't ask for a better opportunity."

Ted thought for a moment and then answered.

"I still can't imagine Leona having that much to gain personally. Let's be honest, Jim, she has never really been one of your party's most loyal members. She does what is good for Leona and the party be damned. Why is she fighting so hard for this particular bill? It's certainly not out of some urge to champion her party. She doesn't need that, and her Congressional District is safe."

"You're wrong, Ted." Hanlon was equally candid. "The lady is as ambitious as anyone else on the Hill."

Hanlon paused and weighed the next words very carefully. "She's got Potomac Fever."

Ted was truly startled. "You can't be serious! Does she actually think she has a chance of being nominated? What about Rutledge?"

Ted's reference was to Senator Virgil Rutledge, the Majority Whip in the upper house and his party's strongest announced candidate for the Presidency.

Before Hanlon could answer they were joined by Congresswoman Leona Crawford Gordon.

"Good evening, Ted. Where is that lovely young lady I saw you with earlier?"

"On the dance floor with the Vice President," Ted replied, just as the orchestra paused between sets.

Leona bristled. "I would have thought you cared more for her than letting her become a victim of his lewd gyrations." She followed the cutting remark with a satisfied grin. "Come along, James, we have to talk for a few minutes."

Jil managed to deposit the Vice President with his wife and made her way back towards Ted. As she neared, she passed Leona and could feel the Congresswoman's eyes examine her from head to toe.

"I thought I'd never get away from that man!" She was annoyed and a little out of breath as she spoke to Ted.

"Did he make a pass at you?"

"Ted! What an awful thing to say."

"Just kidding. Even he wouldn't be so obvious here. But he does have quite a reputation with the ladies."

"Never mind that. What did you find out? After his wife left I saw you were talking to Congresswoman Gordon also. Did you learn anything from them?"

"No, not really. Except that for all their beauty they are three of the most undesirable women I've ever met."

A young man tapped Ted on his shoulder. "Excuse me, Mr. Scott," the White House page said. "There is an urgent call from a Mr. Richard Reynolds."

Chapter 10

The Phoenix watched Ted and Jil huddle briefly with David Holland and then make a hasty departure from the reception. Scott was obviously upset, she thought. He must have received the news that his dear friend—the FBI agent—encountered a bit of a problem starting his car.

She felt a sigh of relief that one of those meddling do-gooders had been eliminated. The two that just left would be next, she promised herself.

As David Holland made his way through the crowd she noticed a worried look on his face and decided to engage him in conversation. As he neared she attracted his attention with a slight wave.

"Is anything wrong, David? You have a troubled look, and I noticed Ted and his lady friend also seemed a bit perturbed as they left. What is it?"

"Oh, some sort of family matter. Ted's mother was rushed to the hospital a while ago and he and Jil are leaving town to be at her side." Holland frowned. "God, the timing is just awful! He just told me he would be away from the office until things get better. As if things weren't hectic enough around here already, now we've got to pick up the slack created by his absence!" Holland had worked himself into a disagreeable mood and simply nodded to her and moved on.

If you think it is hectic now you pompous ass how will you act when your fair-haired boy turns up dead within the next twenty-four hours? she wanted to reply.

For an instant Phoenix thought about alerting Lupo to the news that Scott and the girl would be attempting to drop out of sight but checked the impulse. They were under surveillance. It would be easy enough to follow them wherever they went once they returned to the apartment.

***

Ted spotted Uri waiting in the public parking garage as soon as the Corvette entered. He quickly completed the arrangements to have the car kept there for an extended period and then he and Jil immediately got in Uri's car and drove away.

"How did it happen?" Ted asked as soon as they were out of the garage and in traffic.

"A neighbor's kid came over and wanted to borrow Dick's car. He is real broken up about it but he called me at once when he couldn't reach you two at the apartment. Luckily I knew where you were. I thought it would be better to use his name when I called for you."

"Have you spoken to him since you reached us?" Jil asked.

"Yes, I called him back right away and told him what we were doing. He agrees you shouldn't go back to the apartment for a few days. I'll stop by tomorrow and pick up some things and bring them to the safe house."

"Suppose you're followed?" Ted questioned.

"I hope I am," Uri replied through clenched teeth. "There'll be one less Nazi around," he added.

Ted was silent for a few minutes. He looked at Jil sitting between himself and Uri in the front seat of the late model Buick.

"I can't get very excited about holing up somewhere doing nothing. How long do you think this could take?" he asked.

"There is no way to tell. We could get lucky and blow the whole thing in a couple of days," Uri replied, adding "Or it could take longer. Weeks, months, no way to predict it."

"Ted, I can't stay away from my job for an unspecified time, this will never work," Jil said. She turned to Uri and added, "Besides, I agree with Ted. We'll go stir-crazy sitting around not knowing what's going on and just waiting for them to discover us."

"Who said anything about sitting around? You two will be very busy. There is quite a bit of investigating to be done and it is all to our advantage if these killers don't know I'm involved. We now know they know Reynolds is in this with you but the boldness of their attempt to kill him makes me believe they think it is on a personal rather than an official level. I don't think they would have made such an obvious move if they thought you or he had discussed this with anyone else at the Bureau."

The three of them remained silent again for some time. The car moved through the outskirts of Washington and glided over the rolling hills of Virginia.

Finally, when they had been driving for some time, Ted asked, "Who operates this house? I mean is it yours or does it belong to the Bureau?"

Uri grinned. He kept his eyes on the dark road ahead which was lighted only by the shafts of illumination from the car's headlights. "It's ours. Compliments of a wealthy American who survived the horrors of the camps."

He prefered not to tell them anything more about it and changed the subject back to the investigations he had spoken of earlier.

"You'll probably only spend a day or two here, until we can move you somewhere else. A permanent base, somewhere that you can operate from with more freedom.

"Jil, you will probably return to work in the next couple of days or at least be flying again," he added.

"What do you mean 'flying again'?" she queried.

"Just that. Reynolds has someone working on locating Dr. Bauman's apartment. The phone number that he spoke to Ted from is not a regular listed number, its a floater."

Ted was puzzled. "A what?"

"A floater. A number tied into an existing exchange illegally. It prevents anyone from tracing a call and pinpointing the location of the caller."

"How is that done? Can't the phone company detect something like that quickly?" Ted asked.

"Most of the time, yes. But if the caller is clever enough and disconnects the float after each time he uses it the best they can do is get a general service area. In this case Reynolds believes we have a good chance of getting it down to a one or two block area."

"Why?" Both Ted and Jil asked the same question together.

"Because you have Bauman's phone number. People using a floater usually do not give out a number because anyone trying to locate them can activate the floater by calling the number."

"But suppose Bauman disconnected it, like you said, after using it?" It was Ted who was pursued the questioning.

"Then whatever number was used as the tie-in for the floater will record an unusually large surge of power. That's what Reynolds has people doing, calling that number over and over again while an agent in New York is checking power surges on a computer at the phone company."

"Doesn't the phone that the floater is connected to ring?"

"No. In most cases the party whose phone is used in this kind of operation is never aware of it."

The car suddenly turned off the main road and began a bumpy ride along a dusty dirt road leading to a dilapidated two-story frame house. The dwelling sat on a knoll, affording an excelent view of the surrounding countryside. Even in the darkness Ted and Jil could see how difficult it would be for anyone to arrive here by surprise. Despite a considerable number of trees and overgrowth which almost made the house invisible from the main road, once anyone was on the dirt road their presence could not be concealed.

"This place looks like something from an old Hitch-cock movie," Jil offered.

"It's not the Plaza, I'll grant you that," Uri answered. "But all the windows are bullet-proof. A little renova-tion some friends of mine did."

As Uri wheeled the Buick around the back and pulled it under a make shift carport Ted decided he and Jil would not be spending more than a night here.

***

A short time earlier the FBI agent assigned to watch Ted's apartment glanced at his watch.

Dolan had seen a man enter the building less than ten minutes ago. Enough time, he thought, for him to be fully involved in whatever it was he was up to. Dolan had earlier in the day visited the apartments of the other three people in the building in order to recognize any strangers who might appear. His cover for doing this was the pretense of soliciting for Jehovah's Witnesses. Now he decided it was time to find out who it was that had fumbled with several keys before entering the building.

Ronald Briggs stood in the center of Ted's living room. He took a final look around, satisfied that no gas could escape through the windows which he had carefully placed towels snugly against. The fumes from the four stove jets were beginning to permeate the air around him. In another fifteen minutes the apartment would be a sealed bomb.

He carefully set the spring mechanism of the crude device that would create a spark when the apartment door was opened. Other than the plastic spring the contraption was totally made of cardboard. After the explosion and fire there would be no trace of foul play. It would just be an unfortunate residential accident.

Briggs checked the self-setting mechanism again and backed out of the apartment, closing the door.

The cold steel muzzle of Dolan's gun pressed hard against his neck.

"Easy, buddy, a fast move and you're dead." Dolan kept the gun tightly against his captive and gently pushed him forward.

"Spread eagle," he said and used his left foot to kick Briggs feet apart. Briggs positioned his hands up against the door frame. Dolan ran his free hand along the man's torso and stopped when he felt the bulge he was looking for.

"I'm a cop. Detective Ronald Briggs of the Washington P.D. I don't know who the hell you are, Mac, but you're in for a heap of trouble unless you've got a good explanation," he said.

"Really?" There was sarcasm in Dolan's voice. "What reason does a cop have for breaking into an apartment?"

"Who the hell are you?"

"FBI."

"Show me some proof." Briggs was trying to buy time in the hope of catching Dolan off guard.

"Now, now. That's not fair. I asked you first. But

nobody ever said cops were smart, so I'll repeat my question. What were you doing in there? And why did you come out so carefully?"

"The people who live here were mugged and robbed yesterday. I'm following up on the case. I was just trying to figure out how somebody got in there without them knowing it." Briggs realized how weak his excuse sounded even before he finished. He hoped Dolan had not noticed the damage on the door jamb where he had to force the extra locks Ted had put on.

"I'm not buying that. I think the reason you went in was to rig a special welcome for these people when they return home. Suppose we find out how it works. Open the door."

A cold sweat began on Briggs forehead. He hoped there was enough time to open the door before the gas had become strong enough to cause the explosion. He had to take the gamble and try to overpower the FBI man.

"You want me to open the door?"

"That's what I said." Dolan eased the gun away from his neck and took two steps back toward the rear of the building and away from the stairs.

Briggs lowered his arms and got out his master keys. He quickly found the right one and inserted it in the lock. Before turning the key he filled his lungs with air trying to detect any odor of gas. There was none.

He turned the key and flung the door open.

Nothing happened.

He and Dolan stood there immobile for an instant then the slight trace of gas drifted towards them. The FBI man was concentrating on the smell and shifted his eyes into the apartment for a split second.

It was enough time for Briggs to let go with a high

kick, catching him in the groin. Dolan dropped to his knees and let out a painful moan but did not let go of his gun.

For an instant Briggs contemplated finishing him off but he was directly in front of Dolan's gun. Instead he turned and ran toward the stairs. He was going down them at breakneck speed and was surprised to hear the commotion behind him as the limping FBI man began to follow.

Briggs pulled the front door of the building open and started down the old stone stairs two at a time. Then he tripped.

He tumbled head over heels and struck his head several times. He was just getting up and trying to reorient himself when Dolan emerged from the building and began coming down the stairs at him.

Briggs dove out of his way and from a crouched position shot forward into a sprint. He was several feet away from Dolan when he heard the command to halt. He didn't.

It was the last sound he ever heard. A bullet from Dolan's gun crashed through the upper part of his skull and sliced off a chunk of his head, killing him instantly. His momentum carried him forward a few more steps before he began to weave and finally topple onto an ornate spiked wrought iron fence.

When Dolan reached him he immediately felt sick as he saw the protruding black spike bathed in crimson liquid sticking through Brigg's back.

Dolan never heard the van pull up in the street next to him. He turned toward it for no apparent reason and suddenly felt a heavy pressure in his chest. He looked directly at the man pointing the gun with the silencer on it at him. He felt a second and then a third thud hit him. He opened his mouth to say something but couldn't speak. Everything went black around him as he crumpled onto the pavement.

"Help me get him and Briggs into the back of the van," the gunman said. "Then get rid of them."

Chapter 11

The atmosphere in The Shingle Club was conducive to quiet luncheon conversations between the power-makers in this city. Once a reserve only for lawyers, its membership in recent years was opened to a select handful of Washington residents—both in government and the private sector—who wielded power in one form or another. Not a few high-ranking members of both political parties enjoyed the privacy of the richly tufted velour booths over the pedestrian decor of the nearby Republican and Democratic national clubs. More decisions affecting the American way of life were made around the tables of The Shingle Club than in any other forum in the capital, some believed.

Harold Lupo let his eyes follow the trail made by the celery stalk as he casually moved it around in the large glass of tomato juice. He was sitting across from Phoenix who was more distressed than he had ever seen her previously.

"I don't like what's been happening, doctor. There has been one major foul-up after another. What has happened to the 'finely tuned' organization you so often speak about? The comedy of errors we've been involved in these last several days befits a Mickey Mouse operation. TELL ME, NOW! WHEN WILL IT END?"

"My dear Phoenix, calm yourself. True, we've had a few setbacks but there is no reason to believe you are in jeopardy. The destruction of the FBI man Reynolds' car has been explained away as an act of revenge by underworld thugs. They are also blamed for killing the old woman across the street because she saw too much. The incident at Scott's apartment was a burglary-mugging. And as you know the White House kept that quiet, thanks to Mr. Holland.

"As for the missing FBI man Dolan, his body will never be found and Detective Ronald Briggs—whose car will be found in the long-term parking lot at Dulles International Airport—will be listed as a fugitive. There will be some incriminating evidence connecting him with a narcotics operation discovered shortly." He sat back and sipped the Virgin Mary.

"That's all fine," she snapped, "but we are still no closer to recovering the documents Bauman sent Scott or locating the old Jew's complete journal."

"Patience, have patience. The FBI is doing their best to trace the phone number Bauman gave Scott. I assure you that the instant Bauman's apartment is located by the Bureau's good efforts we will know it. In fact we may know it even before Reynolds." He reached into his breast pocket and removed a long Havana cigar from a hand-tooled case. He slowly lit it and looked at the Phoenix through the smoke as he puffed.

"Besides, this can all be considered a training exercise. A form of weeding out the bad from the good. Isn't it better to find out now where our individual strengths are than a year from now, when you are living in the White House?"

She didn't find his remarks comforting or amusing and her cold stare said it without her uttering another word.

***
Miles away, in the safe house tucked into the Virginia Hills, Ted and Jil prepared for lunch as Dick Reynolds was busy on the telephone. Uri had left earlier to follow up on other arrangements.

Reynolds had arrived at the house a little more than an hour ago and told them there had been another attempt on their lives at the apartment last night but that a neighbor who had heard noises in the hallway and then a gunshot outside discovered their apartment opened and the rooms filling with gas.

As he put the phone down and walked over to the table Reynolds had a worried look on his face.

"What now?" Ted asked.

"Nothing. That's the trouble. Dolan is missing. Gone. Vanished, and nobody in the neighborhood admits to seeing or hearing anything other than your neighbor next door who says she didn't look outside after she heard the gunshot."

"What about the blood you mentioned up the street and on the fence?"

"It's not Dolan's type. Whoever it was apparently came out of whatever kind of fight they had in pretty bad shape. The lab boys found a chunk of human skull nearby. But nobody saw anything!"

"Well I guess that settles it," Jil said in a dejected tone. "We aren't going back to the apartment."

"But we're not going to sit here and waste away either," Ted replied. "Dick, Uri said there would be some investigating we could do. When can we get started?"

Reynolds was surprised at the statement. "He told you that? Look kids, this is serious business. They've tried to kill you, me and maybe succeeded getting Dolan. I don't think. . . ."

"Don't think, Dick. Just let us do something. If they're intent on killing us at least let us have a chance to fight back. What about going to New York and looking for Bauman's journal and any other clues we can find when you locate his apartment?"

Reynolds turned a kitchen chair around and straddled it. He rested his chin on his hands which were folded across the high back.

"Christ, I wish Mitch had given me more men. With Dolan missing that leaves me and Berger alone on this."

"What about the guy in New York working on the computer at the phone company?" Jil asked.

"He's not mine, just on loan for a few days, courtesy of the senior agent in Manhattan."

"Then you *do* need us to do something," Ted responded.

"I hate to admit it, but you're right. Let's see what Uri comes up with first. Maybe by that time we'll have word from New York and at least have a few options open."

***

Congresswoman Leona Crawford Gordon studied the list of delegates who would be selecting her party's Presidential candidate when they convened in Miami Beach in less than a month's time.

Nearly a dozen close aids and staunch supporters were gathered in her quarters in the Cannon House Office Building. She finally put the list down and looked at the influential men around her.

"That's it. Rutledge has it sewed up. There is no way in hell he won't be nominated on the first ballot." She took off her reading glasses which she never wore in public and let herself drop into the oversized leather chair behind her desk.

"I told you we should have entered the primaries,"

the chairman of the board of a Fortune 500 company stated.

A member of the board of one of the seven sister oil companies replied: "No. It was correct that Leona didn't. Rutledge was just too strong out there. We all saw what he did to the other hopefuls. He gobbled them up. If Leona had been up against him in the primaries she would be a casualty now also. As it is now she can meet him one-on-one at the convention. He's not invincible."

"Didn't you hear what she just said? He's going to be nominated on the first ballot," a Wall Street financier butted in.

Several of them began to argue pro and con at once and Leona had to slam a book on the top of her desk to get their attention.

"Yes I said he had it in the bag. . . . but only providing we sit on our hands and do nothing. I still think he will get the nomination but we can make him fight for it. You can all go back to your state committees and put the pressure on. Without your financial help the party is going to lose quite a few congressional seats and more than a few state houses.

"We may not get the top of the ticket this time around but we can get the message to Virgil Rutledge that having Leona Crawford Gordon as his running mate makes good sense, politically and financially."

For the first time several men in the room realized that it had never been Leona's intention to secure the Presidential nomination. All along she had been planning and setting up the other candidates in a process of attrition so that she would attend the convention as the only leader in her party who had not been beaten badly by Rutledge.

Maybe she secretly believed what some of them privately thought: though women's rights had come a long way in the last decade the country was still more than a few years from coming out and electing a woman President. But a woman as Vice President, a heartbeat away, that was another story.

"Leona," another power-broker asked, "Even if we succeeded in turning the screws our ticket will be up against Benedict. He eliminated his competition in their party with almost as much ease as Rutledge did."

"Except for Felker," big oil corrected.

"Except Felker," Leona repeated. "Gentlemen, former Vice President Felker is preparing to drop a political bomb at the convention and bolt from the party if he doesn't get a solid guarantee that Mr. Justice Steinwitz is indeed retiring so that he can finally get the seat on the bench that President Chandler promised him four years ago."

There was a stunned silence in the room. Then, after the full implications of what Leona had said sunk in someone asked, "How do you know this Leona?" Her statement was almost beyond belief but they all knew she wouldn't have said it if it were not true.

She looked around the room at all of them and simply replied, "Trust me."

***

Sharon Franklin leaned over and lit the small table lamp on the rustic night table in the cottage at Camp David. She fumbled with a pack of cigarettes and slowly lit one.

Leaning back against the headboard of the bed she took in a lung full of smoke and glanced at the sleeping figure of the Vice President next to her. He was snoring.

Her eyes again adjusted to the relative darkness of the cabin and she considered getting out of bed and opening the blinds. She decided against it as she was sure Secret Service Agent Brock Davis was out there with an eye glued to the cabin. Instead she shook the prostrate figure next to her.

"Wake up, Elliott. It's time to get back to work."

He responded with a startled look and a few seconds passed before he realized where he was.

"Oh shit, Sharon. I've told you never to let me fall asleep that way. What time is it?"

"Ten after one in the afternoon."

"Damn it. That's a half hour we were out. Damn!"

"What's the big deal? You suggested the privacy of Camp David as an ideal place to work on the script for the follow-up on the Profile," she teased. "And to have privacy the Vice President and the television journalist selected a small cabin that they could draw the blinds on for total concentration. It's not as if we've been in here all night. We only arrived a little over an hour ago but your active libido demanded love-play over news play."

"Yeah, fine," he said as he rose from the bed and dragged a sheet with him for cover. He moved over to a window and peeked out of a corner of the blinds. "And there's eagle-eye Davis out there counting the minutes we've been holed up behind closed doors." He returned to the bed and began dressing.

"I thought you told me you trusted him with your life?"

"I do but he doesn't have to know about this, us. We've taken great care up til now to be discreet, using Manning as a cover and all. I wouldn't want to blow anything this close to the convention. All Susan needs is a single piece of evidence . . ."

"Oh, stop with that bullshit about Susan! We both know she could catch you bare-assed in bed with ten women and not do a thing about it. She wants to be the First Lady more than you want to be President."

Elliott Benedict stopped in the middle of pulling a sock on and half-turned to face Sharon.

"Is that what you think? You think we have nothing to worry about because my wife is ambitious?"

"Correct. And for you to continue patronizing me with that sad story just doesn't wash anymore."

"Sharon, I've told you once I'm elected, once all this is over I'll get a divorce and we can be married."

"Why wait for a divorce? A *widowed* Presidential candidate can pull a lot more votes than a henpecked one. And that way we'll both get what we want." She extended her arm around his neck and pulled him back down to her breasts."

"Please, Sharon. I've told you before. I don't want to hear that kind of talk."

She didn't answer him. Instead she took a long drag on her cigarette and reached over to crush the butt out in the ashtray. When she had finished she began to stroke his hair.

"Everything will work out fine. Just get the nomination and then win the election. Everything else will take care of itself," she said softly.

***

Susan Benedict stepped from the limousine and thought how ridiculous the young Marine saluting her looked. Maybe she expected Elliott to come out of the car behind her, she thought.

A White House Protocol Officer greeted her at the side entranceway.

"Good afternoon Mrs. Benedict, Mr. Holland is waiting in the Press Room."

"Thank you," she said. She wanted to add the man's name but hesitated when she wasn't sure if it was Selter or Selver.

Her high heels clicked along the polished floor and seemed to fill the chamber with a muffled echo. The aide opened the Press Room door and announced her arrival to David Holland.

"Hello Susan," he bubbled. "What a delight to see you like this during the middle of a business day!" His artificial smile said more than the tone of his voice.

"Please, David, spare me the dramatics," she said as she swept by him and headed for the lone high-backed chair in the room. "You have no more interest in seeing me here today than I have in telling *The Washington Post* that the Vice President of The United States is up at Camp David screwing the ass of that television bitch."

Holland choked at her frankness and made a feeble effort to explain that he was unaware of anything along the lines she suggested. But she cut his awkward plea short.

"Can we change the subject, David? I could care less if you know, or what you know. Just so long as that bastard of a husband of mine doesn't flaunt it in my face." She paused for a moment and then started up again, pointing a finger directly at Holland.

"You can tell him this, though. One more stupid stunt like this so-called interview session in a private hideaway and I'll make sure that silver-voiced tramp of his has her appearance changed so that a team of plastic surgeons won't be able to fix it. Do you understand?" She was almost out of breath from the degree of anger she had worked up. "Now let's get down to business." She took a deep breath and regained her composure.

"I understand young Scott has suddenly taken a leave of absense and will be out of town for an indefinite period. Is that true?"

"Yes, Susan. His mother is ill. Believe me I want him back . . ."

"I don't."

"What?"

"I said I don't. He was writing Chandler's endorsement of the Gordon immigration bill, wasn't he?"

"Yes, he was and DiMarco is doing the opposition statement the President will use if he comes out against the bill."

"Well, with Scott away you'll just have to get someone else to finish that job won't you? Why not let DiMarco do that also . . . by starting from the beginning."

"I can't make that kind of change. The President himself requested Ted to do the pro and DiMarco to do the con."

"Then that sounds to me like Chandler has already made his mind up to endorse the bill." Her eyes were fixed on a wall across the room but her mind was racing through other things. There was a long pause before she continued.

She looked directly at Holland and he could almost feel the heat from her burning eyes. "You must do whatever is necessary to persuade Chandler *not* to take a position on the bill before the election."

"But Susan, that's more than three months away. I truly believe Chandler will hold off on any announcement until after the convention . . . but to hope that he'd wait until after the election . . ."

"David, let me put it this way. You like your job and want to keep it in the Benedict Administration, don't you? If Chandler makes a foolish statement in support of the Gordon bill that will be all the Felker people need to either fight us at the convention or worse, sit on their hands on election day.

"What do you think your chances are of being White House Communications Director in a Rutledge Administration?"

She didn't wait for or expect an answer. Instead Susan Benedict lifted herself from the chair and again swept past Holland. As she reached the door she paused.

Without turning to face him she asked. "Do you know where it is that Scott went?"

"Wherever it is his mother lives. Why do you ask?"

"I may feel like sending flowers." She slammed the door behind her as she left.

Chapter 12

Ted and Jil both sipped coffee at the second floor snack shop in the north wing building of the Port Authority Bus Terminal in New York City.

They had flown into Newark Airport aboard the Eastern Airlines shuttle and caught the airport bus over to the huge Manhattan terminal. Since Dick had assured them that he expected to know the location of Bauman's apartment by the time they arrived in New York, the first thing they did was call him from a pay phone hardly five feet away from where they were now sitting. He took down the number and promised to call them back momentarily. That was nearly a half hour ago.

"Do you think he copied the number down wrong?"

"Reynolds? Wouldn't that be a pisser. We come here to await the great telephone search results the Bureau is conducting and an FBI man screws up on a simple pay telephone number. God! I hope not!"

Almost on cue the phone rang. Ted jumped up and got to it before the second ring.

Jil watched the animation in his face as he took down the information on the back of a paper napkin. He thanked Reynolds and said something about checking in every four hours up till midnight and starting again at 8 a.m.

"Where are we going?" Jil asked as he came back to the table and took her hand.

"Just across the street! Do you believe this? The power surge was traced to a restaurant off the corner of Eighth Avenue and 41st Street. That's hardly a half a block from here. Reynolds says it makes sense, especially if Bauman had to get to fast transportation. What luck!"

"Now all we have to do is break into a few apartments or buildings without getting arrested," Jil said laughingly as she and Ted practically skipped down the staircase to the first floor.

It was rush hour at the bus terminal. Thousands of commuters were making their way into the building to begin their rides to the New Jersey suburbs.

Ted and Jil made their way through the human stampede and walked the short distance southward to the northwest corner of Eighth Avenue and 41st Street. They paused and surveyed the facade of badly kept buildings lining the street across from them.

"It's got to be one of those on either side or above that restaurant. Feel like another coffee?" he asked.

Jil made a face. "Only if they promise to boil the cup and spoon before I use them. Why do you want to go in there?"

"I want to find out who, if anybody, lives in the adjoining lofts or behind the front floor stores."

As they crossed the avenue she replied, "I doubt it. Those places look almost abandoned except for the stores." She stopped in the middle of the avenue just as traffic began to move rapidly towards them. She pulled Ted's arm. "I hate rats and roaches, Ted, and this looks like a breeding ground."

They had to dodge a truck and two cars in order to make it safely to the other side of the avenue.

"Did you hear what that man yelled at us?" she asked.

"I'm sure it was nothing personal. Just a welcome to The Big Apple."

They were both in better spirits than they had been at any time in the last three days as Ted held the door open for Jil and they entered the restaurant.

***

Across town on fashionable Sutton Place a well-dressed man emerged from the hallway of an apartment building and entered the waiting car. Less than a half hour ago he had received a call from Dr. Harold Lupo advising him that something they were very interested in was in the neighborhood of Eighth Avenue and 41st Street near a dingy restaurant. He was pleased that Ruder was driving the car. Now Ruder would have a chance to recover the journal, which was something he bungled the first time by killing Bauman before they found out where he lived.

The car turned the corner heading west towards Eighth Avenue.

***

"You get much business in here this time of night?" Ted was pumping the toothless old man in the dirty white uniform which meant he was both counter man and short-order cook.

"Nah," he replied as he placed the two coffees before them.

"Not like the mornings, huh? I'll bet this place really hops when the commuters get off the buses."

"Nah. They don't stop much for coffee or breakfast. They rather have their secretaries make it for them in the office. Those guys all act like big shots, even the ones who got small jobs, know what I mean?"

"Sure, boy, some people." Ted shook his head in

sympathy. He was delighted the man was in a talkative mood.

"Say, I'm trying to locate an old friend who lives in the neighborhood, or at least he used to. Dr. Aaron Bauman. Do you know him?"

"Nope."

Ted tried to visualize what Bauman had looked like but realized the man could have changed considerably over the years. He decided to give it a try anyway.

"He's a short guy, maybe five-feet, five-inches. Gray hair but kind of balding on the top, wears thick eyeglasses . . ."

"Mister, that's a lotta guys. You know how many people look like that? Like I said, I don't know no Dr. Bowlding."

Ted started to correct the name but decided against it.

"Does anybody live above the restaurant or next door?"

The man stopped drying a dish and looked at him with narrow eyes.

"You a cop?"

"No I'm not. I'm just trying to find someone who might know my friend."

The man began drying the same dish again and remained silent for several seconds. He put the dish down and came over to a place at the counter directly in front of Ted and Jil.

"You two want anything else with them coffees?"

Jil started to say no but Ted touched her foot with his.

"Sure, how about a couple of burgers?"

"Cheeseburgers?"

"Yea, make them cheeseburgers, with everything, French fries, the works."

"Got no French fries, just lettuce, tomato and cole slaw."

"That'll be just fine."

The man retreated to the far end of the counter where the grill was and slowly located then dropped two meat patties on it.

"Hey," he called to Ted, "You might try the Dummy. He hangs around here sometimes. He's seems a little weird, suspicious of everything. I seen him a few times with an old guy. I bet the Dummy would know if your friend lived around here. He's the type that knows everything and says nothin!" The man made a toothless grin and laughed at his own joke.

"Why do you call him the Dummy?" Jil asked.

"Cause he don't talk. I once heard he was in one of those camps as a kid during the war. You know, those places where they cooked Jews in the ovens." He stopped abruptly. "You two ain't Jewish, are ya?"

***

Ruder pulled the car into the Park and Lock enclosed lot between Ninth and Tenth Avenues on 42nd Street. It was close as they could get except for the roof garage on the bus terminal building which neither of them cared to use.

While Ruder was busy fitting a silencer on his gun his passenger—import-export merchant Mel Peters—checked the gun he carried in an ankle holster. Peters didn't like silencers. He prefered to hear the ear-shattering blast whenever he used a weapon.

If they ran into any trouble Peters intended to let Ruder try to get them out of it first. If that didn't work out Peters was prepared to rectify the situation and eliminate Ruder. You weren't permitted to make two mistakes in the Organization.

They left the parking building and began to walk eastward on 42nd Street.

***

With the description the counter man had given them of the Dummy, Ted and Jil had little trouble locating him with his shoeshine box around the corner on Eighth Avenue. Jil stayed several feet away as Ted went up to the man and sat down on the folding chair used by customers.

The Dummy was a huge man who appeared to be in his late forties or early fifties. Ted watched him begin the process of dusting loose dirt from the shoe and then start applying a moistening liquid. Even squatted down with his head slightly bent working Ted could see he had sad eyes. His forearms were muscular and the upper portion of his torso hinted at the body of someone who exercised frequently. Despite his age Ted determined that the Dummy was in fine physical shape.

"I was told by the man at the counter in the restaurant around the corner that you might be able to help me locate someone I was looking for. Dr. Aaron Bauman," Ted said in a hushed voice.

The Dummy stiffened. He stopped working on Ted's shoe and brought his eyes up to look directly at Ted.

Ted had the uncomfortable feeling that he was no longer a customer but a captive. The Dummy seemed poised to lunge at him and Ted knew he better say something to gain the man's confidence quickly.

"Dr. Bauman called me last week. He wanted help with a search he was conducting for a Nazi. Then he sent me a package of some documents but I haven't heard from him since." Ted didn't want to mention that he knew Bauman was dead. He was worried that if the Dummy didn't know this the news might cause him to react violently.

The Dummy slowly rose from the squat position, never taking his eyes off Ted. He stood in front of Ted and his eyes began to fill with tears as he closed his hands into fists.

"Look, I'm Ted Scott. I work in The White House, I . . ."

With the mentioning of his name Ted noticed an immediate change in the man's facial expression. It showed more surprise now than anger. There was a hint of excitement as he extended his right hand and mouthed the word "proof."

Ted fumbled for his wallet and opened it to his driver's license and at the same time extracted a business card with the richly emblazoned gold seal of the President of The United States on it along with the legend: Thedore M. Scott, Special Assistant.

The Dummy inspected the license quickly but spent considerable time looking at the card. He smiled broadly and handed the wallet back to Ted.

Then, abruptly his mood changed again. His face became stone blank and emotionless as he dug into his own pocket and brought out a crumpled newspaper clipping. It was the wire service obituary on Bauman.

"Yes. I read it also. I didn't know if you knew about it, so I lied. Do you know where Dr. Bauman lived? There may be something there that could help us find out if he was murdered or actually died in an accident." Ted still felt better treading lightly with this huge man, who towered over his own six-foot frame and outweighed him by an easy forty pounds.

The Dummy made some fast hand gestures and twisted his face in disgust. He shook his head violently and grunted what Ted believes was "no accident, murder."

"I think so too. Can you help me find where he lived?"

The Dummy rapidly nodded, but indicated he wanted Ted to wait where he was. Turning away, the Dummy picked up his shoeshine box and folding chair and went into a liquor store a few doors away to deposit them inside for a while.

Ted gave Jil a hand sign that let her know they had found the right man.

Ruder and Peters walked by him and then past Jil as they saw the restaurant around the corner. They paused at the corner and looked over the buildings around the eatery the same way Ted and Jil had a short time earlier.

"Let's have some coffee," Peters said.

Chapter 13

The Dummy had taken Ted and Jil back around the corner to a hallway in an abandoned building next door to the restaurant. They exited through a broken window in the back that led to a dark alleyway and after climbing a fire escape ladder the Dummy pulled down for them, found themselves entering another window to a rear apartment above the restaurant.

As they climbed in Ted noticed a thin wire running out the window and attached to the telephone circuit box secured to the side of the building.

"Is that the telephone line?" Ted asked.

The Dummy proudly acknowledged that it was and patted his own chest.

"You did that? You made the illegal connection?"

Again the Dummy shook his head affirmatively. They were in a small alcove shut off from the rest of the apartment by a locked door. The Dummy dug a key out of his pocket and opened it and motioned for them to enter ahead of him.

"Do you live here also?" Jil asked.

He hesitated answering her but instead looked to Ted.

"It's alright. I told you she is working with me. She is my friend. They tried to kill her just like they did Dr. Bauman."

The Dummy looked directly into Jil's eyes then turned away and walked over to a small table lamp resting on the floor. He turned it on and pointed to a photo of Dr. Bauman in an old newspaper clipping hanging on the wall. He touched the photo and then his own chest answering her question with a sweeping motion around the room to indicate that the two men shared the apartment.

"A journal, a book or papers that Dr. Bauman kept. Anything that mentions his hunt for Nazis? Do you have them?" Ted asked.

The Dummy motioned for them to take a seat on a badly torn couch and he opened a clothes closet. He began to rummage through boxes and piles of rags on the floor.

The apartment was a railroad-room affair which didn't look as if it had been occupied for several years. Chunks of plaster were missing from the badly cracked ceiling and walls. Ted tried to look beyond the room they were in but it was too dark to see down the hallway. He wondered if the two men lived in this single room and if they had working plumbing facilities. The electricity, he thought, must also be an illegal hook-up since it would be unlikely to still be a regular service.

Jil was sitting at the edge of the couch. She couldn't bring herself to relaxing fully in the dingy, dirty apartment.

"God. I don't believe some people have to live like this," she whispered to Ted.

The Dummy brought a large scrapbook over to them and indicated that he was looking for something else.

The scrapbook was obviously also Bauman's. It was filled with newspaper and magazine stories about the capture and trials of Nazis in several countries. Ted studied an old photograph which showed the most famous and successful of the Nazi hunters, Simon Weisenthal, clutching hands with three other men. All had broad smiles on their faces. One of the men was a younger Dr. Bauman.

Their scrutiny was interrupted by the strained sound of the rusty fire escape ladder being pulled down, causing the three of them to freeze in mid-motion.

Ted and Jil remained immobile, holding a page of the scrapbook partially turned. The Dummy slowly and without a sound moved away from the rubble in the closet and moved to the side of the doorway that led back into the alcove.

Ted looked at the light but knew he couldn't get off the couch quietly enough to extinguish it without being heard. Fortunately the couch was not in a direct line with the doorway. Whoever it was that was coming would have to step into the room before seeing them. Ted brought his Walther out and aimed it in the direction of the door and at the same time put his left hand against Jil's back, whispering for her to get down on the floor. She did it swiftly and quietly.

Ruder and Peters had seen the glow from the light from the alley below. Since it was the only sign of life in the darkened area they were investigating it. There was no need to be overly quiet as they felt more than able to deal with anyone they came across.

"What do you think?" Ruder asked in low tones as he helped Peters onto the fire escape landing outside the open window.

"Derelicts, winos. Then again it could be the headquarters for the Jewish Defense League," he quipped. They both laughed louder than they realized. "Go ahead," he ordered Ruder and prepared to follow him through the window.

"Hello in there," Ruder called out when he was in the alcove. "Anybody home?" He cocked the hammer on his gun and stepped into the room where Ted, Jil and the Dummy waited.

***

Uri paced the living room of the safe house. His hands were on his hips and he was angry.

"Damn it, Dick. Why did you let them go? They spent one night and a half a day here and they're complaining about being cooped up. I could have sent someone else to New York to find the apartment. Shit!"

"Don't worry. They'll be calling in every four hours. Besides when you didn't come back last night and still weren't here this morning I thought it was a good way to keep them busy while getting them out of the Washington area," Reynolds replied.

"The Lufthansa flight leaves tomorrow. When they call in this evening we can tell them to get back here and I'll go up to New York and hunt for Bauman's apartment, if they haven't found it already," he added.

Uri plopped down in a living room chair. "Yea, I guess you're right. I just don't like surprises. I just wish I knew what they were up to. I could have met them in New York. It would make me feel a hell of a lot better.

"How good is your information from Germany?" Reynolds asked.

"Very good. One of our men there has known that Heinrich Trautman has been living in a village outside Stutgart under another name for several years. We checked him out thoroughly but could find nothing in his war record to connect him with any crimes. He was a simple Wehrmacht sergeant, a soldier, not a Nazi killer, so we left him alone."

"Didn't it seem strange that he wasn't using his real name unless he had something to hide?"

"No, not really. Thousands of ex-German servicemen dropped their real names after the war. Most were just scared of Allied justice. You must admit, toward the

end the International Tribunals were on pretty thin ice
with some of the convictions they got."

"That's an unusually benvolent statement from an
Israeli. Especially one who has been involved in more than
his share of capturing these killers."

"I'm a *sabra*, not an immigrant Jew from Europe. I
was born in Israel. I fought in two wars for my country
. . . the same way you would for yours or Trautman did
for Germany. Regular soldiers are just people. They
should be able to forget the past and live like everybody
else if they want to."

He got out of the chair and walked toward the
kitchen. "How about some tea?"

***

Ted could feel the blood pumping madly throughout
his system. He steadied his gun with both hands and
prayed that the figure that came through the door was a
policeman or someone from the restaurant downstairs.

It wasn't.

The direct glare from the floor light prevented Ruder
from immediately seeing Ted when he stepped into the
room. Before his eyes had a chance to adjust the meaty
forearm of the Dummy struck him a vicious blow across
the back of the neck and he was carried forward by the
impact. He squeezed off a shot from his gun but the
silencer muted it.

The Dummy spun around in time to deflect Peters
aim by smashing his arm against the door jamb and in so
doing forced him to drop his gun. Peters, however,
pushed the Dummy away with a hard kick in the stomach which sent him sprawling into the larger room
almost on top of Ruder.

Jil watched in horror as Ted sprang off the couch and
wrestled with Ruder for the gun with one hand while
still holding his own cocked gun in the other.

The Dummy recovered from his fall instantly and

dove for Peters, who was searching for his own gun on the near dark floor of the alcove.

Jil heard Ted's gun bounce on the floor but miraculously it did not fire. Ted and Ruder were rolling on the floor, fighting savagely. Near the doorway between the living room and the alcove she could see the Dummy lifting Peters bodily off the floor while they struggled. .

Jil crawled around on the floor and several times tried to get to Ted's gun but instead she was bumped and hit by the two tumbling bodies. Finally she managed get her hand around the gun but just as she did she heard the sickening thump of Ruder's silencer.

"Ted! No!" she screamed, but no sooner were the words out of her throat than she realized Ted and Ruder were still fighting for the gun. She thought the shot went wild until she noticed the Dummy coming across the room very fast. Peters was crumpled in a heap on the floor and a small pool of blood was forming near his left ear.

The Dummy grabbed Ruder from behind with one hand cupping his chin and the other palming the back of his head like a basketball. Ted was on the floor below them both with both hands locked on the gun, still struggling.

The sound of Ruder's neck cracking as the Dummy twisted his head ended with a popping sound. His body went limp and his full weight pressed against Ted who now had control of the gun.

Jil was speechless as she watched the Dummy help Ted push the dead man off him.

Ted got to his feet and looked over at the increasing red stain around Peters.

"Holy shit. They're both dead," was all he could say.

The Dummy rolled Ruder over and stared at his face.

"Nazi," he grunted. He said something else but Ted could only make out Bauman's name.

"Are you saying this is the man who killed **Dr. Bauman?**"

The Dummy nodded slowly and touched his chest with his index finger. He grunted a few more words that were easier to understand.

"Ted, I think he said he saw him do it," Jil said quietly.

"That's exactly what he said," Ted responded.

Chapter 14

Reynolds and Uri were waiting for them when they arrived on the shuttle.

Ted's phone call had filled them in on what had happened and a quick decision was made to bring the Dummy with them back to Washington.

"But for Chrisake, find out what his name is, will ya? We can't just call him 'Dummy,'" was Reynolds closing remark.

Now as the five of them left the airport packed tightly in Uri's car there was a uneasy silence that overpowered their individual thoughts.

Finally, after several miles of quiet driving, Reynolds spoke.

"These characters must have some network. They're all over the place. Did you remove all identification from the bodies like I told you?" he asked.

"Yes. It's all in here," Ted replied as he passed a brown paper bag up to the FBI man in the front seat.

"Now tell me about this flight we're taking to Germany," he added.

"We've got a solid lead on the Wehrmacht ambulance driver, Heinrich Trautman," Uri said. "We're going to pay him a visit and see if he knows anything besides what we've already heard.

"It seems like an awful great bother just to confirm information we already have. Besides he was just a driver, not a big-wig like Helmut Wolf," Jil offered.

"That's how it appears on the surface, you're right," Uri said. "But it is the only link we have with what actually happened in the French port almost four decades ago. We must talk to him," he added.

"While you three are off gallivanting in Germany I'll be working on the journal seeing what else we can come up with. Berger is looking over the lives of our three women suspects with a fine-toothed comb," Reynolds said.

"Who's Berger?" Jil asked.

"The only other FBI man working on this case with me since Dolan disappeared. I asked Mitch for more help earlier today but his whole attitude had changed. He played down the importance of what was happening . . . he seemed to think, or at least I got the feeling he was saying . . . the bombing of my car was some sort of vengeance from the underworld."

"That's crazy," Ted interrupted. "He was one hundred percent behind us when we spoke to him the other day. And what about what's been happening to us? What does he think about that now?" There was a strain of anger in Ted's voice.

"I don't know," Reynolds replied. "All I know is I never worked on a case that would have made anybody want to kill me and an old lady across the street." His tone was sullen.

The occupants of the car remained silent again for a long while.

Uri turned off the Interstate and onto one of the country roads which would lead them to the dirt road and the safe house.

***

A minute later a van speed by the cutoff they had taken and the two men inside cursed.

"The road ahead is empty as a dry well. They must have taken a cutoff back there somewhere. Lupo isn't going to like this."

"Too bad. He's gonna have to like it. It's too dark for us to be snooping around in these hills. I don't want to end up like Briggs. Turn it around. We'll call in and suggest an aerial search in daylight. That heap of a car shouldn't be hard to spot."

"Yea, but who was driving it? Who was that guy who picked up Reynolds and who was the other guy who got off the plane with Scott and the girl?"

"Just a few more victims, that's all."

***

"Of all the damn luck! I thought you said your people had been keeping an eye on Trautman?" Ted was pacing in the kitchen of the safe house. It was 2 a.m. and the phone call Uri had just received had woken him.

"They have been, or at least they knew where to locate him was my understanding. Somebody must have asked too many questions and scared him off," the Israeli answered. Both men were in their pajamas. The only light in the room was from a small night light near the phone on the wall.

"This means the trip to Germany is off til Trautman is located?"

"Naturally. I can't afford to go over there and conduct a search. I do have other responsibilities here, you know." The dissapointment and the hour had put an edge on Uri's voice.

"Well that's just fine. In the meantime I suppose Jil and I are supposed to hang around this place and count the blades of grass."

"I not only find your humor flat but your manners are sophomoric. If you don't want my help just say so. I have enough to keep me busy without . . ."

"I'm sorry, Uri. I really am." Ted realized how unfair he had been. "It's just . . ."

He pressed both hands against the sides of his head as if to contain an explosion.

"Alright my friend, I understand." Uri rose from the kitchen chair and rested a hand on Ted's shoulder. "Let's get to bed again and approach this with a fresh mind in the morning. Remember, we still have the journal to go through. Maybe there will be something in there that makes up for the delay in talking to Trautman."

**

Berger remained crouched on the outside back stoop for several minutes until he was sure both of them had returned to their beds.

He had been ordered to kill Reynolds, Ted and Jil once Reynolds brought him to wherever they were hiding out.

But the Israeli agent, and now the Dummy, complicated things. He never expected to discover anyone else involved. Lupo hadn't said anything about Uri. Reynolds hadn't mentioned him either.

He wondered if Lupo had known Ted and Jil had gone to New York. Probably not, otherwise the two who eventually died in the flat there would have expected trouble.

He ran his fingers over the binding of the journal. At least we've retrieved this for whatever it's worth, he thought. He looked longingly at Uri's car and Reynolds' car, both snugly in the car port and wished he knew how to hot-wire. It was going to be a long walk to the main road . . . and who knows where the nearest pay phone would be? Christ, he thought, I don't even know where the hell to tell them I am.

**

Berger thought he had been walking for at least two hours. He checked his digital watch and was disappointed to see that it had hardly been an hour and a half. It was 3:45. Only a few cars had passed him, but none would stop.

There was a bridge up ahead. He could see its outline in the moonlight. He remembered it from the ride up to the house earlier that evening. At least he was going the right way back.

Berger was almost halfway across the bridge when the policeman's voice startled him. The officer had silently driven up behind him.

"Hold it, buster. I realize it's a nice night for a walk but can you give me one good reason why you're doing it?"

"Holy cow! You scared the hell out of me. Where did you come from?" Berger held the journal low in one hand, hoping the officer wouldn't see it.

The officer didn't reply. He just kept his flashlight shining directly into Berger's face as he slowly got out of the police car.

"I . . . I had some car trouble, down the road . . . quite a ways back, and . . ."

"I've covered this road for the last twenty miles and didn't see any car on either side. You got identification?"

Berger almost identified himself as an F.B.I. man but hesitated. He decided instead to do something drastic.

He half turned and laid the journal on the thick cement guardrail while at the same time reaching for his gun.

"Sure, I'll just get out my driver's license and . . ."

He shot the policeman through his own coat. The first shot caught the officer in the throat but the officer fired back a fraction of a second later. Berger doubled up in agony as the bullet tore through his stomach. He put two more shots into the mortally wounded cop, both in the head.

The policeman was on the ground on the other side

of the car. He couldn't see him but he knew he had to be dead. Berger screamed from the pain he was experiencing himself and as he grabbed the guardrail for support he knocked the journal over the side. He reached after it, but the effort was in vain.

He didn't hear it hit the water below, but he felt it must have. He was bleeding badly and his legs felt very weak. Berger turned around and pushed himself away from the guardrail, lunging for the front fender of the car. He worked his way around to the driver's side and then to the back door.

He opened it and struggled with the dead officer's body, resting twice before getting it fully inside. He needed the car so he could get to a phone, any phone.

Berger lost all track of time as he drove the car erratically along the highway. Several times he cursed the dead police officer out loud.

Finally he saw an all-night gas station. It was on the opposite side of the road about two hundred yards ahead. There had to be a phone in there, he thought. He tried to gather his full concentration for the small journey but his mind kept blanking out.

Berger felt very contented. He was sitting on a beach at the waterline and he could feel the water running underneath him. It was much warmer than he remembered it. Then he was fully conscious again for a few seconds and realized it was his own blood which was soaking the seat of the car.

He was no closer to the gas station than he had been before. The car had rolled to a stop. Berger no longer had feeling in his legs and couldn't control them.

He cursed out loud and began to cry. He wanted to climb into the back seat and empty his gun into the cop. He blanked out again and when he came to he had an idea.

He used all his strength to press his right leg against

the accelerator pedal. The car shot forward very fast. He kept pressing down with his right hand and used his left to steer.

The station was getting closer. He was racing toward it in the wrong lane, the lane for oncoming traffic and something was distracting his attention but he no longer could rationalize what it was.

The police car was about thirty feet past the gas station when it was hit head-on by the eighteen-wheeler.

The impact drove it backwards, screeching and sparking against the asphalt as it spun wildly. It severed the pole carrying the high neon sign advertising the price of diesel fuel and knocked down the row of pumps with the ease of a bowling ball getting a strike.

The fire ball rose several hundred feet into the sky and debris started several small brush fires. The police car melted into a grotesque lump of metal within two minutes.

***

Uri, Ted, Jil and the Dummy were all in the small kitchen having breakfast and listening to the radio.

"And in local news, County Police this morning were still trying to identify the passenger or passengers of a car involved in a fiery crash with a tractor-trailer on Bellam Road. One police official was quoted as saying there was a strong possibility that the car was one of theirs which hadn't checked in or been seen since before the time of the accident at approximately 3:45 this morning. The driver of the truck, who was uninjured, told police . . ."

"Good morning everybody," Reynolds said as he entered the room. "Anybody seen Berger yet?"

Chapter 15

David Holland was very formal behind his desk. His hands rested on the immaculate blotter as he slowly rolled a new, freshly sharpened pencil between his fingers. His mood was distant and Ted realized it would be difficult to explain the absence of three weeks easily.

"You could have called, Ted. I think I deserved at least that much. You knew how busy things were here—and still are. If you wanted to quit your job wouldn't it have been the proper thing to just come out and say so rather than make up a story about your mother being ill and then vanishing for three weeks?"

"I'm sorry, David, at the time there was no other way to tell you or anybody else what was happening without it sounding crazy.

"That night at the White House reception I received a call that an innocent young man had been killed by an explosion meant for someone who was helping me and Jil, it was all very . . ."

"Ted, why don't you start from the beginning. I must admit your cryptic phone call confused me. If someone has been trying to kill you and Jil I can't understand why you haven't reported it to the authorities.

"But go ahead, I'm sorry, tell me what this is all about right from the start. Who is trying to kill you?"

David Holland let his body weight ease the high-back chair into a slightly reclining position. He tossed the pencil onto the blotter and folded his hands across his stomach.

Ted collected his thoughts for an instant and began. "Remember the night we were at Secretary of State Manning's for one of his frequent cocktail parties and you told me you had something to talk to me about and you had left a message in my call box at the EOB? Well, I went back to the office instead of going home—I had the feeling you knew I would—and there was a message for me to call a man I had met several years ago in Bayonne, N.J.. His name was Dr. Aaron Bauman."

Ted told David every detail of the story including the names of the three Washington women who were suspects. He didn't, however, mention Uri but instead credited Reynolds with specifics that related to Uri. As for the safe house, he told Holland it was something Reynolds had arranged.

As he spoke he continually tried to detect a reaction from Holland but was unable. Holland listened to the tale without the slightest trace of emotion or expression. Not until the story approached the present did Holland interrupt.

"And after Berger vanished with the journal we waited for word that Trautman had again been located in Germany. In the meantime we concentrated on the three women, using a sort of process of elimination to select the prime suspect."

"And who might that be?"

"Susan Benedict. She has the only shot at getting into power, real power, as the First Lady."

"Ted, do you realize what you have been saying to me? You have accused the wife of the Vice President of The United States as being the mastermind behind several tragedies you are calling murders and, if that wasn't bad enough, you are saying she is the illegitimate child of Adolf Hitler." Holland's voice was calm but his tone carried a trace of sarcasm.

"Well, David, you wanted to know why I have been playing hookey from the office and I told you. Ever since I got that call from Bauman people have been trying to kill Jil and me. There is a trail of bodies in New York, here, and in Virginia. How can you call them tragedies? They are murders, plain and simple."

"Ted, have you been under medical care?"

"What are you saying, David, I'm crazy? It's all in my mind?"

"Look at it this way. Sometimes things happen and when we expect a certain result, we read that result into the outcome. I don't doubt you received a call from this doctor who spent his life hunting Nazis but that could have upset you far greater than you realized. Then when that incident happened at your apartment and Jil was assaulted, your mind could have begun to add two and two and come up with five."

Ted rose from the chair he was in on the other side of the desk. "David after all that has happened I should be furious at you for your reaction but I'm not. I thought this out before I came here and realized how incredible it all sounded. I only half expected you to believe the whole story on face value.

"But think about what I've said, David, the names of the other people I've mentioned. Dick Reynolds is a solid type he . . ."

"I'm afraid I don't know Mr. Reynolds," Holland said coldly.

"But you know the associate director of the F.B.I., Mitchell, don't you?"

"By reputation only."

"Call him, David. Call the Bureau and talk to Mitchell.

Ask him to confirm what he knows about what I've said."

David Holland stared directly at Ted for a long several seconds then uprighted himself in the chair and lifted his phone to make the call. He paused midway through dialing and looked again at Ted.

"You realize that if the Bureau is involved in some sort of witch hunt that includes the wife of the Vice President there will be hell to pay if this craziness gets out." He resumed dialing.

Now Ted was angry. Holland's comment was offensive and revealed that David was not interested in checking the validity of Ted's story but more concerned to find out if the F.B.I. was actually connected with the affair.

Ted wanted to shout at Holland. He wanted to drag him from the office and take him to the safe house and let him meet Uri, talk to Reynolds and then maybe he would believe what had been happening.

"Good morning, this is White House Communications Director David Holland. I'd like to speak to Associate Director Mitchell please. It's urgent." There was a slight pause while Holland waited for him to come on the line. He avoided making eye contact with Ted.

"Director Mitchell? David Holland here. I need a little information concerning one of our staffers, a young man named Ted Scott."

Ted felt his face warm as it reddened. Holland was speaking about him as if he were the chairman of the board of a giant company who was being bothered with some small detail about a very low echelon office worker.

"I'm interested in finding out whether he has been over to see you within the past several weeks requesting an investigation into neo-Nazi activity here." There was a pause as Holland listened to Mitchell's reply.

"I see. Can you tell me if there is any sort of inquiry

going on *at all* concerning Nazis in or around Washington?" Holland pushed the swivel around so that he was facing the wall while he listened. His back faced Ted.

"I see. One final question, and I apologize for taking so much of your time with this sort of thing," Holland made a weak attempt at a laugh. "Do you have an agent named Dick Reynolds stationed in this area?"

From what he could gather Ted was aware that Mitchell had either refused to comment or denied the whole affair. The Associate Director's reply to the question about Reynolds was receiving the longest answer yet.

"Well, thank you very much, Director Mitchell. Again, I'm sorry to have bothered you with this but it came to me from a usually dependable source. Good-bye." Holland slowly spun the chair back to its correct position and replaced the phone.

"Ted, I don't want to believe the story you just told me but neither do I want to believe it was all some kind of preposterous lie, which leads me to the conclusion that *you* believe it." Holland got out of his chair and came around the front of the desk to where Ted had been standing for some time. He gently placed his arm around the younger man's shoulder. When he spoke he was patronizing.

"Look, Ted, we can work this thing out. Whatever it is, we can work it out. You need some rest. Why don't you let me make arrangements to have you quietly admitted to Bethesda for some tests and . . ."

Ted shot his arm up and knocked Holland's hand from around him.

"What did Mitchell say David? What did he say?"

Holland composed himself and stood squarely in front of Ted.

"He said he didn't know you, never heard of you and never met you. As for an investigation about Nazis the

Bureau was doing nothing out of the ordinary which includes keeping an eye on any subversives in the area. There was no new investigation."

"What about Reynolds? What did he say about him? I suppose Mitchell denied there was a Dick Reynolds so naturally he couldn't have been assigned to work on this case."

"On the contrary. the Associate Director said Reynolds was affiliated with the Bureau here in Washington. He has been on light duty ever since his wife died last year and was going to retire very shortly. He also mentioned that Reynolds had recently been the target of an underworld attempt on his life in which a neighbor's boy and a woman across the street were killed."

"He lied, David. As God is my witness he lied to you. Both Jil and Reynolds were with me in Mitchell's office when he agreed to put Dick in charge of this case."

"Yes, I know. And he gave Reynolds two agents, a Dolan and a Mr. Berger I think you said, who are now both missing, right?"

"Why didn't you ask him about them? He can't explain away two of his agents."

Holland again placed his arm on Ted's shoulder. "Ted, let's be reasonable. A few days in the hospital for some tests . . ."

"No, David. I'm not crazy and I'm not coming back to work yet either. I called you because there is a real and present danger that Hitler's daughter will be moving into the White House come January 20. That's the reason I called. I wasn't looking for sympathy. Susan Benedict is at the top of the list. We're sure she is the one."

Holland pulled away from Ted and his voice became harsh. "Ted you must get this wild idea out of your head! I've known Susan as long as I've known Elliott, that's more than six years. Don't you think somebody would have discovered this great, dark secret by now? Afterall the press digs deep into public officials backgrounds—including their relatives—you ought to know that."

"She has covered her trail very well, I'll admit. In fact we couldn't find anything in her background or the other two's that would give us a solid clue. But since Elliott stands to be nominated at the convention Susan is the one who has the most to gain."

"You keep saying 'we'. I presume you mean you and Jil?"

"Yes, and Reynolds," Ted caught himself before he included Uri.

"What about this mute fellow you mentioned?"

"The Dummy? I mean Ari . . . that's his name. He stays with us, sort of a bodyguard. He knows nothing of the suspects, per se. He is a lot brighter than we first thought, but the situation in Washington is over his head."

"So you and Jil, along with an F.B.I. man who has never recovered from his wife's death, and a mute who knows little about the people you have as suspects, have been sitting around in some old farm house in Virginia deciding that Susan Benedict is a danger to the national security? Really, Ted. Can't you hear how implausible it all sounds?"

"David, come with me to the house. There is someone else I want you to meet."

"Someone involved in all this with you? Someone you haven't mentioned up til now?"

"Yes. Furthermore, while you're there I'll have Reynolds call the Bureau and talk to Mitchell, you can listen in on an extension. I can prove he lied to you a few minutes ago."

"I'm sorry, Ted, I just can't take time off to go gallivanting around chasing phantoms."

"Funny, that's an expression I used when this all began, to describe to Jil what I thought of the wild charges Dr. Bauman was making."

"Yes, and don't you see? Events, coincidences have come together to throw this whole thing out of proportion. A few days rest in the hospital, peace, quiet, and you'll be able to look at what has happened objectively. You'll see how it has all somehow become distorted.

"Ted wait, where are you going . . . ?"

"Back to the safe house. I don't have time to convince you that I'm as sane as you are." Ted had reached the office door and opened it. As he began to step through it Holland called.

"Ted, please reconsider what I've said. A few days rest and you can be back here in your job with all of this behind you."

"No thanks, David. There is an organization out there that has tried to kill me more than once and succeeded killing God knows how many people. I believe that organization is under the control of Susan Benedict, and I aim to prove it." Ted let the door swing shut behind him as he left.

David Holland looked blankly at the closed door for several seconds before he reacted. He quickly returned to his desk and lifted the phone, paging his secretary.

"Get me Security," he demanded.

Ted reached the elevator bank in the EOB and hesitated. He turned quickly and made his way toward the back of the building and the fire stairs. He was afraid Holland would try to stop him from leaving after the discussion they just had. Luckily the meeting was in Holland's EOB office and not his chamber in the White House next door. There would be no chance to get out of there if someone were trying to keep him, he thought.

Ted was nearing the first floor landing when he heard

footsteps rapidly approaching the fire door on the other side. He pressed himself against the wall just as the door swung open and two security men came rushing through and heading up the stairs. The heavy metal door halted an inch from his nose and began to slowly close again.

The security men kept their concentration forward as they took the stairs two at a time, never expecting that Ted was safely behind them.

Once they had rounded the turn atop the midway landing and began going to the next level Ted quickly opened the door and stepped into the hallway. He boldly walked across the marble floor and turned the corner that led to the parking lot door. All the activity was going on some distance away and out of his view near the ground floor elevators. The two security guards who passed him in the stairway hadn't expected to actually find him, just prevent him from escaping that way in case he got away from the agents going up to intercept him on the elevator.

They'll probably begin searching the various offices next, Ted thought, once they realize he wasn't on the elevator or stairs.

Ted slipped behind the wheel of Uri's car and quickly left the lot. Security hadn't yet alerted the guard at the gate and he swept by giving the man a broad grin and a wave.

Ted obeyed the speed laws but drove away from metropolitan Washington as fast as he could. Fortunately, he had deliberately misled David when the older man asked *where* in Virginia the safe house was. They'd be looking in the wrong county if they pursued the idea of apprehending him.

It was good to be out and away from the house. The sun was bright and there was a slight breeze making it an altogether lovely summer day. As the scenery changed from the fast-pace of Washington to the full, rich green landscape of Virginia, Ted was able to actually relax during the drive.

The first of the two national political conventions would begin in three days, on Monday. But this was a glorious Friday and he felt that for at least as long as it took to get back to the house he had escaped from the danger and pressures of recent weeks.

True, David Holland hadn't cooperated or believed him and chances were very good that Ted had just forfeited his job but for some capricious reason it didn't bother him.

Ted reached for the dial and turned on the radio. A familiar tune came on and he caught himself humming along with it.

Chapter 16

Secret Service agent Brock Davis could smell the aroma of bacon as it filtered through the exhaust of the palatial cottage Elliott and Susan Benedict were using on a private island southeast of Key Biscayne. He flashed the message to the other agents guarding the compound over his walkie-talkie so they all would be aware the Vice President and his wife were up and about.

The convention had begun two days ago and Benedict had somewhat broken with custom and arrived in the State of Florida before the formalities of nominating him had been completed. Tonight would be the nomination.

As expected, former Vice President Felker's name would be placed in nomination first, followed by a small list of favorite sons. Benedict would be the last one nominated but there was hardly a delegate in Miami now who expected any last minute surprises. He would be the overwhelming choice on the first ballot.

President Chandler had not, as some expected, publicly endorsed the immigration bill that Benedict opposed so strongly, the bill written and introduced by Congresswoman Leona Crawford Gordon. In fact the President declined to take a position on the bill one way or the other. The move was considered a deadly blow to the chances the Felker supporters clung to up until the very last minute.

Yesterday afternoon the President made it final.

"Inasmuch as the Revised Alien Quota Act legislation remains in Committee it would be inappropriate at this time for me to comment on its merits or lack thereof. Furthermore, for anyone to interpret my actions, whether they would be in support of or against the bill, as an indication of a preference of candidates at the convention, would be foolhardy," President Chandler told newsmen who spoke with him as he left the hospital bedside of ailing Supreme Court Justice Steinwitz.

"Mr. President, if Mr. Justice Steinwitz fails to recover as rapidly as everyone hopes he will, what are the chances that he will retire from the Court and you will appoint former Vice President Felker in his place?"

The President turned to face the newsman who asked the question. He had a disgusted look on his face. "Jack, you always were a crepe-hanging son-of-a-bitch!"

The remark brought a howl of laughter from the press corps and none of them, not even the man it was directed at, used the comment in their stories.

Now, in the warm Florida sun, Elliott Benedict was busy in the kitchen preparing breakfast, confident that the threat by the Felker faction was nothing more than an annoying exercise the delegates would have to sit through tonight.

Susan entered the kitchen wearing a form-fitting tank bathing suit. Elliott looked up at her and stopped in the middle of cracking an egg.

"Well, good morning, that certainly is a very complimentary bathing suit. You look simply great!" He was totally sincere but somehow he failed to convey it in his voice.

"Go to hell."

Elliott let his shoulders slouch and a sad look came over him.

"For a moment I thought you might actually be in a civil mood. Can't we avoid any friction today? Today of all days? Can't we spend the time together and . . . maybe try to work out what's gone wrong between us, at least take a first step? Our lives will be different after tonight. Being Vice President is one thing but being an incumbent Vice President who has received the nomination for President makes all the difference in the world."

"Not for me. You're still a cheating, sneaky bastard. Why should we try to hide that fact? My skin crawls whenever you're near me, so keep your hands, and your eyes off me." She walked briskly by him and toward the rear door of the cottage.

As he had so many times before Elliott Benedict ignored her acid remarks and instead again tried to make peace.

"I've made breakfast, Susan. Would you like some bacon and eggs?"

She spun around quickly as she reached the door. "Why don't you call Miss Television America over for breakfast? She can't be very far away, can she?"

Elliott watched her cross the flagstone patio and go to the dock where she untied the speed boat.

He was pouring himself a cup of coffee when Brock Davis knocked and entered the cottage. The roaring engine of the boat grew faint.

"What is it Brock?"

"Mr. Vice President, your wife has gone off in the boat without waiting for a detail to join her in a chase craft. I sure would appreciate it if you would talk to her about doing that again."

"Thank you, Brock. Care for some eggs?"

***

The network's emblem had been reproduced in full color and hung across the far side of the auditorium in a position that permitted it to be picked up on camera as Sharon Franklin and her co-anchor John Philips kept millions of viewers up to date on the convention proceedings.

Sharon was trying her best to make the report of the final meeting of the Platform Committee seem interesting. They had gone on the air for a fifteen minute *News Brief—Election '84 Report* at 11 a.m. and would do another one at 3 p.m. Both of the network spots were supposed to hype viewer interest for a larger audience share this evening when the nominating began.

"Sharon, our floor man Doug Stevens with the Ohio delegation reported in while you were bringing us all up to date on the Platform Committee and he has what may be a blockbuster of an item." The plastic smile Philips gave her was matched by her own back to him.

"Really, John? What did he have to say?" She hated to play second banana and help set him up for anything of value. But what could possibly be happening in Ohio that could matter at this late hour?

She listened as Philips reported that the chairman and several Ohio delegates had sent a telegram to President Chandler asking the chief executive to openly support either Benedict or Felker before the nominating tonight.

It was one of those impulsive, last minute moves that frequently happened at conventions and she knew it had as much chance of getting results as the governor of Ohio had in being nominated as the state's favorite son. Philips finished the report with proper amount of suspense, making it sound as if he almost believed that there would be an answer from the President.

"We'll naturally keep abreast of this and other late developments and break into regularly scheduled programming at any time today if there is a response from The White House. Until later this afternoon, then, this is John Philips . . ."

"And Sharon Franklin,"

". . . Saying good bye."

Sharon stormed out of the studio as soon as the red "on-air" light went off. Philips called after her but she ignored him. He caught up with her on the main floor of the convention hall.

"Hey! What's going on? Why the 'mood' all of a sudden?"

She stopped in her tracks and turned to face him. Her eyes flared with anger.

"Don't you *ever* set me up like that again. I am supposed to sign the network's coverage off at the conclusion of each broadcast, not you. Don't come along with some crap about trouble in Ohio or anything else. That's a cheap trick that's so old it stinks. You pull another stunt like that and I'll be working the Chicago convention in two weeks without you, understand?"

"Whoa! I don't have to take that kind of crap from you or anybody else. This was not only the first time we worked together, madam, it was the last." He turned and began to walk away but Sharon grabbed him by the arm.

"Nobody walks out on me, Philips, do you understand that? You're through because *I* say you're through, not because you think so. I decide who works with me, nobody else does!"

Philips looked at her rigid posture and aloof facial expression and couldn't resist shooting his free arm up in the air and shouting "Heil Hitler!"

Sharon swung her arm around in a mighty arc and stunned him with the force of her blow. She brought her other hand up with almost as much force and clobbered him on the other side of the head.

"Don't you ever, ever say that to me, you swine, you filthy pig," she was still shouting at him and preparing to hit him again while he tried to block the fast volley of blows. A security man and several Platform Committee delegates started rushing over to the part of the nearly empty hall where they were.

Philips managed to back step away and both of them realized they had attracted considerable attention. Almost in unison Sharon and Philips turned away from each other and walked in different directions.

John Philips found himself alone in the broadcast booth for the 3 p.m. *News Brief—Election '84 Report*. Sharon Franklin had made up her mind not to appear on camera with him again. Within a half hour after the news reached network executives in New York, another co-anchor was winging his way to Miami to join Sharon for the nominating session proceedings that evening. Philips had been replaced.

***

That evening, after the players on the convention floor had performed their obligations and Elliott Benedict was nominated much quicker than anyone had anticipated with half of the favorite sons dropping out. Ted and Jil sat in the darkened living room of the house in Virginia and watched as the television network introduced interview after interview and made small talk among reporters in order to fill the remaining time they had allotted for the proceedings.

Phoenix was asked if she thought the fact that President Chandler had not come out for or against the immigration bill was a factor in the swiftness of the Benedict nomination.

"That's hard to say. There has been much speculation in recent weeks as to whether the President would or would not come out for the bill. A position by

President Chandler would have been interpreted either as support for Elliott Benedict or former Vice President Felker. By announcing yesterday that he understood that and therefore would not comment on the bill, the President let the nominating process take its natural course."

"Political double-talk," Jil said as she watched the striking image on the screen.

"That's no way to talk about a lady," Ted chided.

"Who said she was a lady?"

"Our convention coverage resumes tomorrow evening when these same delegates welcome Vice President Elliott Benedict to this arena for his acceptance speech and to endorse his selection for a vice presidential candidate.

"Until 8 p.m. tomorrow evening this is Sharon Franklin . . ."

"And Dudley Knowles . . ."

". . . saying good night."

Ted got out of the chair and was about to turn the television off when Reynolds came into the room.

"Leave it on, Ted. I'll catch the news in a little while."

Ted smiled at him, "You got it. Nighty-night, we're going up to bed." He extended his hand to Jil and helped her out of the low sofa.

Instead of leaving at once, however, Ted paused at the door and turned to Reynolds. "Anything new from Mitchell?"

"No, not really. He said again that he thinks there is a leak high up in the Bureau . . . but nothing more. They still haven't found Dolan or Berger."

Jil had avoided commenting on the discussions Ted and Dick had concerning Mitchell ever since the argument the two men had the day Ted returned from his meeting with David Holland. But tonight she didn't hold back.

"I still think he could have helped us out when David called him by admitting he had met us and was conducting an investigation," she said.

"An investigation? Young lady I am the investigating team, as you know by now. The Bureau seems to have taken a 'hands-off' policy on this one. Mitch lied to Holland because he felt it was none of Holland's business to poke around. If Holland wanted information on an investigation he should have gone through channels, Mitch said."

"We know, you told us," she replied. "And it doesn't make any more sense now than it did the first time you said it."

"You people sound like a broken record," Uri called from the kitchen. "If you all still have that much energy left come in here and join me looking at the microfilm files. My eyes are getting tired anyway."

"Good night Uri," Ted called. He and Jil headed for their room.

"I don't feel like watching the news now after all," Reynolds said and switched off the television. "Good night, everybody."

Uri sat hunched over the kitchen table staring blankly at the wall as he listened to Reynolds heavy footfalls going up the stairs.

Finally he gave his attention back to the brightly lit box covering most of the table. He again began to slowly crank the pages of *The Boston Globe* onto the screen. The file he was going through was 1945. In the previous weeks he and the others had performed a similar search of *The New York Times* for that same year.

Several times they uncovered items of interest that proved to amount to nothing.

"But what exactly are we looking for?" Jil had asked.

"Something, anything at all about the three women

we suspect. I don't exactly know what myself but I will when we find it."

For the first few weeks Uri had managed to keep Ted, Jil, and Reynolds busy checking German Kriegsmarine records of U-boat combat patrols during the last month of the war. It wasn't difficult to get copies of this information through his connections overseas. The fact that it all came in the original German gave Ari, the mute, a part to play translating.

Uri was happy that Ari was a slow translator. It kept them all around the house during the day while he wasn't there.

But these projects to keep them all busy were wearing out. Uri needed something to happen. Otherwise the whole thing would fall apart and they would let their guard down.

He was sure that as soon as they did that they would be dead. The Organization was out there somewhere waiting for them to reveal themselves, he was certain of that.

Uri got out of the kitchen chair and turned on a pot of water for tea. He was expecting a call from Germany and was spending the night at the house.

***

Phoenix was also expecting a phone call. But hers was due at a respectable hour the following morning.

As she laid on her back in bed staring blankly at the ceiling her thoughts this night, as they had for several nights during the last few weeks, turned to Ted and Jil and Aaron Bauman's journal.

As each day passed she was believing more and more what Dr. Lupo had said:

"They no longer have the journal, believe me. Our man Berger is missing and it is very possible he is dead but then too Scott and the girl may also be dead. They haven't been seen for almost a month now. If they were alive and had the journal they would be visible and we would know it. The FBI man Reynolds has also dropped out of sight. It is possible Berger intended to eliminate them with a bomb and he didn't get away in time."

It sounded so convincing. She wanted to believe it but her instincts told her they were not dead.

Chapter 17

There was good news and bad news over breakfast the following morning.

Uri had received the call from Germany. Trautman had been located and was being held by Israeli agents as per Uri's request.

Mr. Justice Steinwitz had died in his sleep the previous evening and news commentators were having a field day speculating on how soon it would be before President Chandler nominated former Vice President Felker to replace him on the Court.

"Naming Felker to the bench will dry up any opposition to the Benedict nomination. The party will join hands and elect Elliott Benedict. He's a shoe-in," Ted said. "Now we just have to wait two weeks until Virgil Rutledge gets the nod from the opposition and the campaign will be in full swing," he added.

"Is Benedict really much stronger than Rutledge?" Uri asked.

"I think so," Ted answered. "There would have to be a major development, and I mean major, to swing the election to Rutledge."

"So Susan Benedict seems to be on her way to The White House," Jil said sullenly.

"Enough of American politics. Doesn't anybody want

to hear about the trip to Germany?" Uri asked. He looked around the table and all eyes were on him.

"Here's what I suggest. Ted, you and I will make the trip. I took the liberty of having new passports made for you and Jil last week. We don't know if the authorities are looking for you at points of entry and exit but it doesn't hurt to be too careful."

"What about me, am I a friggin' orphan? I'd like to get out of this place too, ya know," Reynolds blurted.

"Dick, I saved a special assignment for you. It is something Jil mentioned when we were going through the U-boat patrol files and I got confirmation of it in the phone call about Trautman. You will be going to a Caribbean island called St. Kitts to talk with a man who was aboard the last U-boat to surrender after the war."

"I don't understand. What did I mention? I never even heard of St. Kitts," Jil said.

Uri looked around at them and couldn't help preventing the grin from forming on his face.

"O.K., I can see everybody wants to hear about the U-boat before the Germany trip.

"Jil, you came across a story in the *Times* microfilm about a German submarine, U-977, which was the last holdout and didn't surrender until August 17, 1945, in Argentina. That was more than three months after the war ended . . ."

"Yes, now I remember. The U-boat had left Oslo, Norway in early May, the *Times* story said. There were other reports that it had carried Hitler and that's why it didn't or couldn't surrender when all the others did. But I don't remember anything about an island called St. Kitts."

"St. Kitts wasn't mentioned in anything you read. My associates overseas came up with it as the place where one of the crew members of U-977 is living. It is a tiny island in the Eastern Caribbean, about 160 miles southeast of St. Croix in the U.S. Virgin Islands. The former assistant radioman on U-977, like most of the rest of the crew, prefered to remain in neutral Argentina rather than go home after the war. The radioman we're talking about, a fellow named Fritz Frank, stayed there for a few years and then began moving from island to island in the Caribbean until he settled in St. Kitts. He owns and operates a small guest hotel high up in the mountains."

"You said there were reports that this sub carried Hitler," Ted asked, "What became of those charges?"

"Nothing. The U-boat commander, Heinz Schaeffer, and his crew denied it. Schaeffer remained in Argentina and eventually wrote a book about his adventures. A few years ago Schaeffer and all other surviving members of his crew began dropping out of sight. However, one of our people visited another island, Bonaire, with a group of Scuba buffs last Summer and heard about a very exclusive little hotel on St. Kitts that is run by a German. Fritz Frank apparently gets sentimental when he has had a few and brags about how the U-boats controlled the seas during the war. I had our people check him out and sure enough he is from the U-977."

"And I'll be visiting his hotel to talk to him?" Reynolds asked.

"Right. Jil will be with you if you'd like or she can stay here with Ari," Uri offered.

"Pardon me," Jil said in a huffy voice. "But I don't like being discussed as if I were a piece of baggage one could take or leave behind." She looked at each of the men around the table, adding, "I'm not staying behind to mind the store and I don't think it is fair to expect me to. I should be going with Ted to Germany."

"No."

"No."

Ted and Uri were agreed on that point.

"Then it's off to the Caribbean with Dick. Ari can play nursemaid to the house."

"Frankly, if you are going with Dick maybe Ari should be with you two also," Ted suggested. "He's additional protection."

"My God, I feel as if I'm planning a world tour!" Uri threw his hands up. He rose from the table and turned on the pot of water for more tea.

"As long as everyone can afford to pay for their own tickets they can go," he said, adding as he looked at Jil "I realize paying for an airline ticket will be a strange sensation for you."

"Strange but necessary. I can't very well take advantage of my free flying privileges while I'm supposed to be recuperating from a mini-bike accident, can I?"

"No you can't. And that's another reason you'll have to use the false passport Uri had made. By the way you're supposed to call somebody today and check on what's been going on since you've been away," Ted reminded her.

"What's that all about?" Reynolds asked.

"The girls I fly with, my regular crew. I call a few of them every few days to let them know I'm still on the mend."

"I just thought of something," Reynolds interrupted. "If Ari is going to the Caribbean who's paying for his ticket? He doesn't have that kind of money to spare."

"I'll pick it up," Ted volunteered. "We can stop by my bank on the way to pick up the airline tickets."

"Alright then," Uri cut in. "Let's finish breakfast and get this show on the road!"

***

Leona Crawford Gordon impatiently tapped her fingernails against the base of the phone which was on her lap.

The news of Steinwitz' death was the first thing she

heard as the clock-radio went off. Now sitting up in bed, she was waiting for The White House switchboard operator to give her David Holland's hotel room telephone number in Miami.

She closed her eyes and memorized the number as it was given and uttered a quick thank you as she hung up.

The phone in Holland's room rang several times before the tired voice of David Holland came on.

"Holland"

"David? This is Leona Gordon. I just heard on the news that Steinwitz died last night."

"Yes, I know. We got the news before retiring," he looked at the night table next to his bed and tried to focus his eyes on the small brass alarm clock. "What time is it?"

"It's 7:20"

"What did I ever do to you to deserve a call at this hour, Leona?"

"David, I want to know if Chandler intends to name Felker to the Court before the election."

"I don't know that and if I did I wouldn't be in a position to answer it. You're a loyal member of the opposition party, remember?"

"And a loyal American first, David. Felker is not the kind of man this country should have sitting on the highest court in the land."

"Leona, I'm surprised to hear you say that. I should think you would feel right at home with Felker's thinking, much in the way you and Chandler see eye to eye so often. The three of you are a bit to the right. Why the sudden anti-Felker talk?"

She bristled at Holland's glib remark. "I don't think you should start sounding so high and mighty yet, David. After all, your man only got the nomination last night. I believe you are still on The White House staff working for Chandler, and he is still President. Besides, my party meets in Chicago soon to offer our own candidate to the American people."

"And that's why you are sour on the possible Felker appointment, isn't it Leona? You know as well as I do that your strongest candidate would be Rutledge and the only way Virgil has a snowball's chance in hell of beating Elliott is if Felker bolts from our party and his faction follows him."

"That's not why I'm calling. I'll admit what you say has merit but it isn't the main issue here. The issue is Felker's integrity and ability to serve this nation as a member of the Supreme Court."

"And how's that?" Holland was getting bored with the call.

"He's a communist," she lied. "I know the President is flying to Miami tonight to be at the convention when Elliott picks his number two man. You've got to set up a private meeting for me with Chandler before he meets with Felker tonight and promises him the Court appointment."

"Suppose he has already done that, or is doing it today before he leaves for Florida? Anyway, how can you prove Felker is a communist?" Holland knew Elliott Benedict would be very happy to prevent Felker from getting the appointment. But at the same time Benedict wanted to be sure Felker was somehow removed from a position where he could create problems in the election. The Court nomination would do that, certainly. But if Holland could arrange to have Felker discredited publicly for a reason such as what Leona was suggesting then they would be rid of him fully.

"I can prove it, and will prove it. I'm flying down to Florida as soon as I can catch a plane. Tell me where we can meet."

Holland thought for a moment. "Chester Manning

has a place near Key Biscayne; Elliott and Susan are using it as a hideaway. Get down there early enough in the day and keep out of sight. I'll call the President and then Elliott and let them know you are coming."

"I don't look forward to spending several hours in the same house with Elliott."

"You won't have to. It's a complex, three or four cottages on a private island.

***

"There goes that news helicopter again," Ted said as he looked out of the window of Uri's car. "They've been by here quite a bit in the last few days."

"Really," Uri asked. "What are the letters on the side?"

Ted strained to read the inscription but was unable.

"I caught part of it yesterday, WD something. It isn't call letters I recognize. Look they're swinging back this way, now we'll be able to get a look."

Uri glanced in his rear view mirror and could see Reynolds' car getting ready to follow them down the dirt road. Dick, Jil and Ari were in it and on their way to do some clothes shopping while Ted and Uri went to the bank and picked up the airline tickets.

"Here it comes, wow is he coming in low," Ted said. "I can see the letters now, its WDJM-FM . . ."

Uri through the shift into reverse and gunned the engine. He was racing backwards up the dirt road and frantically blowing his horn.

"What the hell are you doing?"

"Suppose that's not a news copter? They already know what Dick's car looks like. We've got to alert Dick to pull his car back behind the house until that thing leaves."

Dick Reynolds sat behind the wheel of his car and watched Uri's Buick rapidly approaching in reverse.

"What's he doing that for?" Jil asked.

"I don't know but if we don't get out of his way he'll plow into us." Instead of backing up Reynolds pulled his car off the road and into the grass just as the clappity sound of the helicopter blades and engine passed between the two cars.

"They've seen us, both cars," Uri said. "We'll soon find out if it is a news copter. He pulled the Buick abreast of Reynolds car.

"What's going on?" Jil asked through the open window.

"Get back in the house, quickly!" Uri shouted, "That copter may be *them*."

Even before Uri finished the warning Reynolds had begun twisting the steering wheel and stepping on the gas, taking his car through some underbrush and tall grass and back onto the dirt road. He began making a rapid three-point turn in order to head back to the house, going forward.

Uri, meanwhile, pushed his accelerator to the floor and raced backwards up the road.

The helicopter made a tight turn and hung almost motionless for an instant before beginning another run at the vehicles below. When it moved out it moved fast.

"Here he comes again, Uri." Ted rolled down the window and reached into his belt for the Walther. The chopper swung wide to their left and Ted could see two men clearly inside. One had a rifle.

Ted decided he would shoot first but before he could take aim and squeeze off a shot the car jolted to a halt then bucked slowly. The impact knocked the gun out of Ted's hand.

"A friggin' tree stump, sorry," Uri explained. "I got too close to the side of the road."

"Stop the car. I have to get my gun."

Reynolds car went off the road and into the underbrush to pass them. Ted pushed his door open and snatched a look skyward before exiting to retrieve the gun. The chopper had positioned itself at the end of the dirt road up near the house, some fifty yards away.

It was starting to move forward toward them in a slow, deliberate run. Uri gunned the engine on the Buick but it wouldn't move forward. The stump was caught on the undercarriage. He slammed the shift into reverse, then into forward again creating a rocking motion but the car would not come loose.

"Give it up," Ted yelled to him, "C'mon over here." Ted motioned to a tree he was heading for. Uri pulled his own gun from his holster and slid across the seat, exiting through Ted's open door.

"Get out everybody. Get out and scatter into the tall grass," Reynolds ordered. He flung his door open while simultaneously hitting the brake and shifting into park. The helicopter was hardly ten feet off the ground and moving straight toward them. The backwash from its blades flattened the tall grass in a twenty foot area.

Reynolds dove out of the car and rolled into the brush along the side of the road. He managed to unholster his gun in the process. Jil had just gotten clear of the car when the high-pitched twangy sound of bullets ripping into metal followed. Instead of dropping to the ground she ran into the underbrush and headed for a large tree.

Uri reached the tree where Ted was and they both watched the helicopter riddle Reynolds' car and then swing in the direction Jil had run.

"Thank God they got away in time," Uri said.

"I didn't see Ari leave the car," Ted shouted. "They're going after Jil!"

Ted and Uri left the sanctuary of the tree and began running toward Reynolds car and the area Jil had gone. While they were running they heard more shots and realized Reynolds was also heading after the chopper and firing at it. There was too much tree cover where they were so Ted and Uri started running diagonally toward the road. Once they were in the clear and could see the helicopter they joined in the firing.

The chopper again hung almost motionless and slowly began to swing around to face its attackers.

Reynolds reached his car first and found a frightened Ari sitting paralyzed in the back. Bullets had ripped three large holes into the seat less than six inches away from him. They had entered through the roof.

"Ari! Ari! C'mon out. Follow me, back to the house," Reynolds ordered while still firing at the chopper.

"Take him in, Dick," Uri called. "We'll get Jil."

The second man in the chopper was firing at them even as they spoke. Bullets splintered the trunks of trees, cutting down saplings and sending wood chips flying in wild, jerky cascades. Ted and Uri could see that Jil was using the diversion to make her way clear of the firing and back in the direction of the house.

The chopper pilot began moving the craft in upward, downward and sideways movements. It succeeded in throwing off Ted and Uri's aim but it had the same effect on its own gunman.

"We're getting nowhere fast," Uri said. "We'll be out of ammunition before he is, then we're sitting ducks. This standoff is coming to a close very quickly."

"O.K. then let's start falling back toward the house. Jil is in the clear. She'll be inside in a minute."

They alternated firing at the helicopter as they back-peddled up the dirt road. The gunman pulled the rifle inside and exchanged it for a sub-machine gun. His first burst ripped a stitched path between Ted and Uri missing both of them by less than a foot. They could see the gunman and the pilot arguing and then the chopper lurched forward rapidly and came to a halt without the swaying motion it had employed before.

Uri immediately leveled at the glass dome, now less than sixty feet away and slightly more than ten feet off the ground. He squeezed off three fast rounds that shattered the dome. The pilot put the chopper into a steep climb as he swung the dome around and away from them.

"Great! You got them," Ted shouted and slapped Uri on the back.

"Just their protective windshield, I'm afraid. Not the occupants. Let's get into the house now. They're coming back."

Ted and Uri sprinted toward the house and made it inside as the helicopter did indeed swing around and chase them. The gunman fired the sub-machine indiscriminately. From inside the house the sound of the bullets hitting the door had a metalic plink sound and Ted realized that along with bulletproof windows the doors were steel core.

"It sounds like hail hitting the windows, doesn't it?" Jil asked. Nobody answered. Uri had immediately gone to a closet in the living room and extracted a high-powered rifle with a scope. Ted and Reynolds were busy reloading their handguns. Ari stood motionless in the kitchen with his hands pressed tightly over his ears.

"Ted, Dick. Upstairs. We can get a shot at it better from above." Uri led the way and the other two followed.

The helicopter had made several passes at the house and spent a considerable amount of ammunition.

"They must realize their bullets are doing little harm. Why are they keeping it up?" Ted was puzzled by the continued passes the chopper made.

"They've probably phoned our position in to some colleagues and now they are simply holding us until reinforcements arrive," Uri said as he opened the window in the center gable. He was getting into position and lining up the rifle for a shot when the helicopter lunged forward, almost on a crash course at him.

"Get down, they spotted us."

A fusillade of bullets tore into the small room ripping up chunks of floorboard and destroying the window frame. It ended abruptly as the chopper passed over the roof of the house.

"Christ, that was close. What happened to your bullet proof glass?" Reynolds asked.

"It doesn't work when the window is open. The guarantee becomes void."

"I'm glad you guys have time for wisecracks. Give me that rifle. I was best in my platoon in the army," Ted lied. Uri handed him the gun and he and Reynolds watched Ted stick it out the window and take aim.

The helicopter was making a tight circle around to the front of the house again and as soon as it was in range Ted waited for it to begin its run again. It was lining it up in the cross-hairs when Uri offered a bit of advice.

"The pilot. Right between the eyes would be just fine but if you can't do that hit the fuel tank. We want that plane to go down like a rock, not crash into the house and kill us."

Ted hesitated. The chopper began its run, sub-machine gun blazine away. He felt himself falling backwards and realized Uri had pulled him out of the window. Ted hit the floor and watched Uri grab the gun and quickly shove it through the open window, aim and fire.

The house shuddered from the explosion. Uri threw himself on the floor next to Ted and both men felt the blast of heat as it funneled through the open windows. Chunks of the helicopter bounced off the house and clanged as they hit the ground below.

"Holy hell, Uri, how close was it when you hit it?" Reynolds asked.

"Too close, my friend, too close." Uri lifted himself off the floor and extended a hand to Ted, pulling him up also.

"It's now time to leave here and fast. Gather up everything of value you have and leave nothing behind that could be traced to any of us. But first let's get my car off that tree stump."

Less than fifteen minutes later Uri, Ted, Jil, Reynolds and Ari were safely traveling away from the house on the main road as the black Mercedes and the van sped past them going in the direction of the safe house.

They could see the smoke and an occasional flame rising above the trees as the pulled onto the dirt road. The house was burning beyond control. "Do you think they were in that car?" the Mercedes driver asked.

"Of course not," came the reply from the back seat.

Chapter 18

Elliott Benedict stared unbelievingly at the procession of vehicles attempting to get clearance to enter the compound.

"What the hell is going on? Is the entire convention reconvening here?" He let the curtain fall back into place and turned to David Holland. "That bitch must have done it," he pointed in the general direction of the cottage where Leona Crawford Gordon had been put up hardly an hour earlier.

"This is her idea of a joke. I'm sorry I let you talk me into using this place for the meeting." He stormed away and picked up his tennis racquet as he headed for the rear door. "I don't want to see any of them now, do you hear? Tell them I'm working on my acceptance speech. Tell them anything." He paused halfway through the door. "Have you reached Chandler yet?"

"I left a message at his suite."

"Then he doesn't know about the meeting yet?"

"He knows we want to see him. He doesn't know Leona is here."

"He doesn't? Then he is the only person in the State of Florida who doesn't." Benedict continued his trip to the tennis court. Whacking a basket of balls was just what he needed now.

David Holland walked over to the window and looked out across the relatively narrow waterway separating the island from the mainland. Elliott was right, he thought, it seems as if half the State was trying to get clearance from the Secret Service in order to cross the single-lane bridge. What alarmed Holland was that nobody was being turned away.

He walked over to the Plektron unit sitting on the antique serving table and turned it on. Agent Brock Davis immediately responded.

"Sir?"

"Brock, do you know why they are letting that mob over the bridge?"

"Yes sir. They are on the invite list for the memorial service."

"What are you talking about? What memorial service?"

"The service for Justice Steinwitz. Mrs. Benedict and Congresswoman Gordon said the Vice President had asked them . . ."

"Raise your men at the bridge and tell them to stall or do something but not to let another vehicle cross over. This island will sink. I don't know what this is all about but I assure you the Vice President knows nothing about any memorial service." Holland replaced the Plektron and went back over to the window while also picking up the phone in an effort to reach the cottage Leona was at.

Midway through dialing he froze in stunned disbelief. The network television van followed by a limousine carrying Sharon Franklin had just crossed the bridge and was now on the island. He completed dialing in a hurry.

Leona picked up the phone before the second ring. She answered with a cheerful hello.

"Leona, the Secret Service just told me you and

Susan Benedict were responsible for this stampede. What's the meaning of this?"

"Isn't it a marvelous idea, David?" She was obviously enjoying herself. "Everybody was delighted to come. Look, there's another car with members of the loyal opposition." She was positioned by a window also.

"Leona, how did you do this? You only got here a little over an hour ago yourself. Some of these people couldn't have been here in Florida, they're not even members of our party."

"*Your* party, David, not mine. More than a few are from my party. Actually it was quite simple. I made a few phone calls after I spoke to you and *presto!* I had a corporate jet ready to deliver a bipartisan delegation, plus some sympathetic business leaders, to the memorial service for Justice Steinwitz."

"Why did you do that? I thought you wanted a private meeting with the President?"

"I do. But what better cover than a gathering for a solemn tribute to our dearly departed octogenarian Justice. I must admit Jim Hanlon of my staff helped considerably with mobilizing the telephone staff. We were very fair, you know. We invited as many delegates from your convention as we could reach."

"Plus the media. I just saw Sharon Franklin and her team pass by. I'm sure Susan didn't agree to that. And just how did you get her involved in this?"

"I left a message for her and explained the situation when she called me back. She agrees fully that we had to stop the communist Felker and the only way to have a meeting with the President was to create a cover.

"David, I'm sorry to say this but I just don't trust everybody in your camp. Wouldn't it have been very convenient for your party if someone leaked to the press that I had flown to Florida personally to discuss the Felker nomination with the President. That would have created a cloud over Felker while at the same time dealt me a serious blow politically. This way I'm just one of many who have journeyed to the Sunshine State for the spontaneous tribute the Vice President suggested."

"Leona this isn't going to work. It will backfire. I still can't believe Susan agreed to let Sharon on the island."

"She didn't. That was a little something extra I put in. It might provide an interesting diversion." She was laughing heartily as Holland replaced the phone.

Holland left the cottage and began walking toward the tennis courts to tell Elliott what he had just learned. Instead he noticed Susan Benedict on the dock preparing to take the speed boat out again. He called to her and she waited for him to come over.

"Susan, I just spoke to Leona and she told me what you two have been up to. How could you let her use you that way?"

"Use me? On the contrary, David. I thought having an abundance of people here while she and the President settled this Felker thing was a marvelous idea." She stared directly into his eyes and became quite serious.

"Despite the friction that exists between Elliott and me I want very much for him to win the election. Anything that can guarantee that will have my unconditional support."

"But it all seems so unnecessary. We could have arranged a private meeting for Leona with the President without creating this kind of circus. Anyway there is time, Steinwitz only died last night."

"And Felker's people were on the phone with The White House before breakfast this morning."

"How do you know that?"

"I have my sources, David. I am also aware that the President refused to discuss his thoughts on an appointment with them and they were outraged. David, Chandler *promised* Felker that seat four years ago when Elliott became the vice presidential candidate. If Felker doesn't have the President's word that he will get it before the session begins tonight I'm afraid Felker will create an embarrassing problem on the floor. I don't want to risk having millions of voters who love that old fart bolt and cost Elliott the election."

"Then you and Leona want this meeting for crossed-purposes. She thinks you want to help her convince Chandler that Felker is a communist and therefore discredit him. But you want her to meet with the President so you can convince the President that he *must* nominate Felker."

"One hundred percent correct, David."

Holland felt somewhat inadequate in view of the scheming Susan and Leona were capable of. He still had an edge, one little tidbit of information that would let Susan know her plans would not be as smooth as she thought. "I think I'll go tell Elliott . . ."

"No need. We've already discussed it. He agrees with me totally. But if you must talk to him, he's over there banging his balls against a wall . . . tennis balls that is." She permitted a sly grin to form on her lips.

"What I was going to say was tell Elliott that the media is here also. Sharon Franklin and her entourage arrived a short while ago." He turned and walked away briskly.

Susan Benedict got into the speed boat, her hands trembling, and gunned the engine to life. She pulled away from the dock with such force the mooring line whipped violently and slapped against the fiberglass body of the boat with a hard, cracking sound.

She put the boat into a tight turn and opened the throttle all the way. Several of the recent arrivals on the island watched her race very close to the shore, creating a huge splash wave that cascaded onto the shore. She ran the distance of the island down past the last cottage and again tightly turned the boat for a run in the opposite direction.

A Secret Service detail vainly tried to catch her but had little luck. The crowd on the shore was growing quickly as Susan provided a dangerous but thrilling exhibition.

She turned the boat away from the coast and headed into deeper water, aiming for a permanently moored waterski ramp.

Elliott and David had made their way to the shoreline too.

"What the hell does she think she is doing?" her husband asked.

Holland did not reply.

Leona watched the show from the second floor window. Several people who had been in her party had left the cottage and were among those watching from the shore.

Sharon Franklin ran over to the network van excitedly.

"Charlie get a camera on this. I think that's Susan Benedict out there trying to break her neck. Hurry!"

The speed boat met the ramp at a perfect angle and was thrust into the air. Loud gasps of approval and shouts of encouragement roared from the audience on the shore.

The boat seemed to glide through the air and return to the water as if it had been gently placed down by some giant hand. Susan let it run forward for several yards before cutting another sharp turn for a second run. She could clearly see the crowd watching from the shore. She pulled the boat into a wide turn to build up even greater speed than on the first jump.

Leona left the window and made her way downstairs and outside. She reached a place on the shore just as the boat again hit the ramp.

But this time Susan's approach was off. Instead of

rising gracefully and lifting into the air as it had before the boat fishtailed slightly and it wobbled as it bumped up and over the ramp.

There was a collective scream from the shore as the crowd watched the boat tumble in the air and arc sharply toward the water.

Susan Benedict was thrown clear of it a fraction of a second before it crashed into the water and exploded.

The Secret Service chase boat frantically closed in to reach her.

"My God, Elliott," was all that David Holland could say. Elliott stood motionless, unable to speak. The crowd on the shore became very animated and moved around rapidly as if they could somehow help the woman floating face down in the water.

The Secret Service boat pulled her out of the water and headed back to the small dock.

Holland grabbed Elliott by the arm and they both began to run toward where the boat would put in. As they got there they had to push their way through the forming crowd.

The boat was a few feet away as Elliott and David managed to get in front of the others, all except an old man using an ornate gold-topped cane for support.

He turned to Holland and raised his cane across the Press Secretary's chest.

"I'm a doctor," Harold Lupo said.

***

Jil, Reynolds and Ari handed their snack trays to the flight attendant aboard the BWIA flight from Miami to St. Kitts. There was no direct service between the small Caribbean island other than via New York or Miami. There choice had been to connect through either of those cities and Miami was selected.

As it was, however, they had lost a day since it was too late to make the island flight by the time they reached Miami. Now as the jet began its descent from the clouds and an occasional island appeared through the aircraft windows they prepared for their arrival at Golden Rock International Airport.

"I still can't get over how lucky we were to locate a decent room in Miami, what with the convention being there," Jil said.

"Yea, but it cost a bit more than I wanted it to. We'll have to watch our spending. I didn't count on shelling out money for a hotel in Miami," Reynolds replied.

Ari had a window seat and he hardly took his eyes away from the changing vistas below. This was his first plane ride, they had learned. He had come to the United States from Germany after the war via a ship. Jil was happy to see him enjoying himself but more than that she was glad he would be with them in case of an emergency. She could still clearly see him snapping the man's neck in the New York apartment. While the thought repulsed her it also provided a kind of comfort. Ari was a powerful friend to have.

It took less than twenty minutes for the jet to land and taxi to the modern two-story terminal building. Once they had cleared immigration and customs the three of them found themselves outside the building and confronted by a number of taxi drivers, all wanting to transport the new arrivals to any hotel they wished.

They selected a driver who offered to include a sight-seeing tour on the way to their hotel. Unfortunately the hotel run by the German, Mountainside Plantation, was booked solid, they were told, but the driver assured them he could get them rooms at a nearby property.

As they were entering the cab Reynolds spotted the headline in the *Miami News* being carried by one of the other passengers:

VICE PRESIDENT'S WIFE ESCAPES DEATH
IN FLORIDA BOATING ACCIDENT

"Hey mister, excuse me. Are you finished with that paper?" Reynolds called.

The man looked at the paper as if seeing it for the first time and wondered why he had bothered to carry it off the plane. "Sure, it's yours," he said, offering it to Reynolds.

"I could just kick myself for not listening to the news this morning," Jil said, but Reynolds didn't answer her.

"It says she will be O.K., just some bruises and a slight concussion. She was apparently horsing around and showing off to a large group of people who gathered for a memorial service the Vice President arranged for the late Justice Steinwitz. Quite an impressive list of who's who was there," he added.

Reynolds handed the paper to Jil and focused his attention on the scenery passing by.

The tall, blond man who had come off the same plane they had was seated comfortably in the back seat of his taxi. He alternately watched the island sights and kept an eye on the taxi some distance ahead of his own.

"You're sure you know which hotel they're going to," he asked his driver.

"Oh yes sir. They be going to Hillside Inn. That driver he work outa there. He always takes people there no matter what."

"Good. Then we're going to Hillside Inn also."

***

Several thousand miles away in a hotel near the airport in Munich Ted and Uri prepared for breakfast. They had arrived in the early hours of the morning and were now getting ready to set out on their trip to meet Heinrich Trautman.

Chapter 19

Jil turned over onto her back. She had taken enough sun there and now wanted to let the warmth of the celestial body embrace her other side.

"Are you aiming to be well-done or medium-rare?"

She lifted her sunglasses and smiled at Reynolds who was wiping his neck with his handkerchef.

"Hi. When did you get back?"

"Just a few minutes ago. Still no sign of our U-boat man."

"Well it's Monday. The manager at Mountainside Plantation said he was expected back on island today, but not what time. He'll know we want to see him. We've left enough messages."

"And we're running up some bill. Four days on this island cost a few bucks even if the prices are a bargain."

"Stop complaining and get into your suit. Join me here by the pool."

"No, thanks. I don't want to be a lobster look-alike."

"Where's Ari?"

"He got real brave and wanted to join that group that's climbing up to the volcano. I figured it was a good idea. He's been moping around doing nothing since we got here except eating like a horse. He'll be

O.K. He and the other guests are being taken up by a local guide."

Jil lowered her glasses and put her head back on the chaise lounge. "I still think you should change and get some sun."

"Negative, lady. I'm going to see if I can get through to the States and check my phone service for messages."

"Ted said they probably wouldn't call unless they had something extraordinary to report," she noted. "Besides, you left this number with your service for them in case they wanted to reach us."

"I know. But I still feel better checking in. I've got to do something to keep busy."

The tall blond man was sipping a drink at poolside bar as Reynolds passed. For an instant Reynolds had the feeling he had seen him before. Probably on the plane or here at the hotel during the last four days. He tried to push the feeling from his mind but it persisted.

He thought about it all the way back to his room. Then, sitting on the edge of his bed and waiting for the operator to connect him to an overseas line he was convinced that he had seen the man before.

And he had seen him in Washington.

***

Across the Atlantic Ocean, Ted and Uri had better luck in locating their man.

For the last three and a half days they had been having regular conversations with Heinrich Trautman. At first he refused to admit anything about the incident on the quay in St. Nazaire in 1945. He even denied his name, claiming to be a Swiss farmer living in Germany only a few years.

Before leaving New York Uri had called the agents who were holding Trautman and told them to fabricate a story about mistaken identity and let him go, with profuse appologies. They were also told not to let him go too far.

Upon arriving at the village where Trautman was, Uri introduced himself as a member of the West German intelligence organization. His credentials were convincing.

"I'm sorry for the inconvenience and alarm my men may have caused, Herr Trautman, but I assure you we meant you no harm," was the way Uri began the relationship. He then proceeded to ask Trautman several mundane and irrelevant questions about his memories of the war.

"The authorities are having a difficult time locating some men who served in your unit. Two of them turned in a large treasure to the Allies when the war ended. It has never been claimed and if they can be located now there is a good chance they will be entitled to a large reward."

"What kind of treasure?" Trautman had asked.

Uri made up the lie as he told the story. It sounded so good Ted almost believed it himself. Uri had introduced Ted as a representative of the U.S. Government. Ted's White House credentials were perfect to fool Trautman. Fortunately he did not read English.

The approach was totally soft-sell. Uri was extremely curteous and left Trautman with a hint that there could also be something in it for him if he helped them locate the men.

However, Trautman persisted in denying that he was ever in the German Army throughout the initial meeting.

It was the repeated visits by Uri and Ted and Uri's warm friendly talk about the "good old days" that made Trautman begin to open up. It was slow at first.

He admitted on the second visit that he had served in the Wehrmacht, but still insisted he wasn't Heinrich Trautman.

When they visited him the third day he opened up a little more.

"I'm seventy-eight years old," he admitted. "I was even too old to be in the army during the war but you know how it was then. Everybody served. Children defended Berlin from the Russians. Children twelve and thirteen years old fought next to men who were then the age I am now." He spat on the ground and cursed the Russians.

"You were lucky then, to get transferred to France and drive an ambulance," Uri offered.

Trautman looked deep into his eyes and smiled slowly. "Why do you try to trick me, young man? I've decided you are not who you say you are. But I am also convinced you are not one of the *Kameradine*. Why is it so important for you to know if I drove an ambulance in the war, eh?"

"What's the *Kameradine*?" Ted asked.

"The name used to describe former members of the SS," Uri answered. He was going to ask Trautman another question but the old man spoke first.

"Yes, I am Heinrich Trautman. What does it matter now? I have outfoxed them and lived a long life. They tried to kill me many times but always I was too smart for those swine." He touched an index finger to the side of his head and gave Uri an exaggerated wink.

Now Ted and Uri were meeting Trautman for the fourth time. The old man seemed to be happy to see them. They sat on stools on the porch of the farmhouse and Trautman excitedly told them humorous incidents that had happened during the war.

The conversation had been going on for almost two hours during which time Trautman only paused to offer them a drink.

"Tell me about the last days of the war, Herr Trautman, when you were in France driving the ambulance."

The old man stared at the dirt in front of the porch stoop. There was a long pause. Finally he began to talk again, without looking up.

"Only one time did I drive the ambulance. Only once, but you must know that, eh? You must know how I was almost killed when they pulled it into the water, right? That's what you want me to tell you about. That's why your men held me and then you came." He paused and seemed in deep thought for a long time. Then he began again.

"I'll never forget it, you know. Never for as long as I live. The war had turned some men into animals. I know, I saw how they acted.

"I was in command of a patrol that guarded the air strip several miles outside the city. It was a quiet duty and I thanked God for being assigned to this sector. The Allies had bypassed our region after the Normandy landings and pushed through France and into Germany. We followed the progress of the war on the radios many of the French had.

"By this time we were convinced the war was lost. Our duty at the air strip was just a formality, something to do to earn our pay. Nothing had happened in the region since early in the war when the Allies bombed the submarine pens at St. Nazaire, but that was before I was there.

"Then on May 1, I remember the day well, a motorcade of SS troops arrived at the air strip in late afternoon. They pushed people around and threatened to shoot anybody who didn't swear allegiance to Adolf Hitler. They were having sport with a French farmer who came by to see what the commotion was all about.

They made him dance as they shot into the ground around his feet. Finally they tired of the game and told him to run back toward his farm. When he was only a few feet away one of them shot him in the back of the head. It was sickening. They were animals, crazy animals.

"Since I was in command of the Wehrmacht men the SS Standartenfuhrer ordered me to take him and some of his men to the local hospital. I did and he selected an ambulance. I had no idea why he wanted it but he told me I would be its driver when the plane came in that evening.

"After dark that night a plane arrived. A woman on a stretcher was placed in the back of the ambulance and another Standartenfuhrer, who had come on the plane with her and still more SS men, joined me in the front of the vehicle. Before getting in he selected four motorcycles to serve as escorts.

"The SS colonel who was in command of the troops that had come to the air strip earlier in the day protested. He offered to have all his men escort the ambulance.

"The other colonel . . . he was called 'doctor' by his own men who took over the motorcycles, denied the request. He told the other colonel the patient was in his personal charge and his Gross Deutschland men would be the escort. Without further conversation he dismissed the other SS troops and ordered them into the plane for the trip back to Germany.

"Again the other colonel protested. The doctor listened to his words and shot him right on the spot. The Gross Deutschland Division SS men held the other SS and my men at gunpoint. Then they marched them over to the plane, took away their guns and made them board the aircraft. While the plane was taking off and heading back to Germany the doctor ordered his men to burn the remaining vehicles.

"When he got into the cab and saw me and my Wehrmacht uniform he was startled. In fact, he almost dropped his cane."

"What cane?" Uri asked.

"A gold-topped one. The doctor had a very bad limp. One of his men had to help him get into the front seat of the vehicle."

"You said he had a limp, a bad limp? Was his leg bandaged?"

"I don't believe it was a recent injury. I just think he was a cripple. There was no bandage. Besides, the cane was not something a person would have if they only needed it for a short while. It was very attractive, carved. A beautiful piece."

"What happened next?" Uri prodded.

Trautman recounted the story through to the slaughter on the quay.

"You clearly heard him addressed as Standartenfuhrer Dr. Helmut Wolf." Ted stated.

"Yes. That's how he identified himself when the U-boat captain asked his name and then, after the shooting, one of the sailors who was putting the dead bodies into the back of the ambulance called up to the captain and asked if anything should be done to wash away the blood.

"The captain was standing only a few feet away from where I was hiding on the floor of the ambulance. He called up to the deck of the boat: 'Dr. Wolf, should anything be done about these stains.' Wolf answered back that all Europe was covered in blood, a little more wouldn't mean anything.

"Shortly after that the sailors secured a rope or a chain, I don't know which, to the front of the ambulance and when the U-boat pulled away from the quay the vehicle was dragged into the water.

"I screamed and shouted as the ambulance was pulled into the water but they either didn't hear me or didn't want to. It seemed as if the ambulance was dragged in the water for a long while. When the water was already past the door line only then did it break free of the U-boat."

"Did you see anyone on the boat deck release it or did it snap away?"

"I didn't see anyone. It just slowed down and began to sink fast. The windows in the cab were closed but water had managed to get in anyway. It was up to my chin when I cranked down the window next to me. There was a great rush of water. It filled the cab in seconds and pushed me across the seat to the passenger side but I was able to get back to the open window and get out."

"Did you hear anything else on the quay or did Wolf say anything to you during the ride from the airport?"

"Only what I've just told you."

"Could you have forgotten something, try to remember it all again. Another name, a destination, anything?"

Trautman fixed his eyes on Uri and in a deliberate, slow tone replied. "I remember it exactly the way I have said it. You don't forget something that horrible. Every detail, every word spoken that night are as fresh in my memory as if they happened today.

***

The steel band had finished playing nearly a half hour ago and all but a few guests at the Mountainside Plantation on St. Kitts had retired to their rooms for the night. The hotel's staff were busy cleaning up empty tables and removing the leftover food that had been served during the West Indian buffet. Jil, Ari and Reynolds were together at a corner table on the fieldstone balcony overlooking the tiny lights of the capital city of Basseterre.

The selection of the table was not an accident. Earlier in the evening they had been seated elsewhere but as this table became free they took their drinks and moved to it, supposedly for the fantastic view it afforded. Actually it was the table next to the one the property's owner, Fritz Frank, had joined when he arrived that evening.

Frank had joined two couples who were middle-aged and repeat guests at the Plantation. It was a noisy group with much laughter and back slapping. Reynolds had stopped counting the rounds of drinks but noticed that Frank was being the gracious host and signing for them. More than once the conversation broke into a short German phrase at a point just preceding laughter. Though the English of the two women was perfect Reynolds noticed a slight accent on both of the men. Fritz Frank's English had a definite West Indian lilt to it from his years in the islands.

Reynolds waited to make his move as the two couples thanked Frank and made their exit. He was alone at the table finishing a drink as Reynolds went over and introduced himself.

"Mr. Frank. My name is Dick Reynolds, I'm a writer, and I was wondering if you would like to join my friends and me for a drink. You have a lovely property here."

Frank immediately gave Reynolds a wide smile and accepted the offer. "I am honored, Mr. Reynolds, but I insist on buying the drinks."

Reynolds introduced Jil as his niece and assistant and Ari as a researcher. Once they were seated and a round of drinks had been ordered Reynolds was sure Frank was on his way to getting very drunk. That was just fine, he thought.

But it was Frank who took the lead and began the conversation. Jil and Ari listened as Reynolds responded.

"Well, when did you three arrive on St. Kitts?"

"Four days ago. We're staying at the Hillside Inn. We had hoped to be here but you are full."

"Yes indeed. A very good season. I'm sorry you were unable to be accommodated but perhaps next time. We get a very high percentage of repeat visitors."

"I've noticed that here tonight. We heard a few of the guests talking and I got the impression that those people you were with at the next table were among those who have been here before."

"Ah, yes." Frank nodded his head. "One of the men has been coming here for years . . . always with a different woman," he said the last part in a conspiratorial tone with exaggerated wide eyes and followed by a hearty laugh.

Reynolds looked at Jil and smiled. She raised her eyes in mock horror while Ari beamed approval.

Reynolds had heard the word "reunion" mentioned a few times during the loud conversation from the other table earlier and decided to mention it.

"I couldn't help but overhear your friends talking about some sort of reunion and that interested me. My squadron is planning a reunion in a few months and I've been on the organizing committee."

"Squadron? Perhaps your reunion is a veterans group?"

"Yes indeed. Submarines. I was in the Pacific during the war. This will be the first get-together since the war ended," Reynolds lied. In fact he had done a little reading about submarines and U-boats in the last week. Enough to bluff his way through just this kind of conversation.

"Really!" Frank slapped his knee. "I too was in U-boats." He paused and added in a humorous tone,

"But on the *other* side!" He laughed loudly again and Reynolds joined him, feigning wonder at the coincidence.

"Was that other fellow in the U-boats too?"

"Yes, yes. But not mine. We weren't shipmates. In fact I didn't know him during the war. We met afterward, many years later, through a mutual accquaintance. These islands are popular now with German tourists. Many of them like Scuba and the water is perfectly clear with many coral reefs. I have friends who recommend my plantation to particular guests in Germany and they come."

"What do you mean 'particular'?"

"No riff-raff. I only want people of a certain calibre. People who can afford fine food and drink and people who are not ashamed to say they fought for their country in the war."

"Did your boat work in these waters?"

"A few times before I was on her. I didn't get into boats until near the war's end and by then they were no longer free to roam the high seas at will. Your Allied navies and stupidity in the high command saw to that."

"Don't tell me about stupidity, the German Navy didn't have a corner on that market. I can tell you stories about the American Navy you wouldn't believe."

"Ah, but all you had to worry about in the Pacific were the Japanese. In the Atlantic we had the Americans, the British, the Canadians and others out there."

Reynolds was happy that Frank spoke easily and openly about the war.

"There's no question you fellows in the U-boats had it rougher than we did in submarines. In fact I'm working on a book about the contrasts between our two navies, especially the lot of the submariners. A friend of mine back in the States mentioned you and the Mountainside Plantation. He said he thought you were an ex-submariner so I thought I'd look you up when we came down here."

Frank tightened his eyes as if it would help him remember. "I'm sorry, you said your name was . . .?"

"Reynolds, Dick Reynolds."

"Of course. The man who left all those messages for me which I received when I arrived back on island today." Frank emptied his drink and signaled the waiter for another round.

"So you want to know something about what it was like in a U-boat as opposed to an American submarine, eh?"

"Well, not exactly. I have quite a bit of comparative information already. What I'm interested in is an episode concerning a specific U-boat." Reynolds hoped he wouldn't blow it with his next statement. "I want to know about the last voyage of U-977, your boat." He held his breath after completing the sentence.

"Ah, and I suppose you want to know if I brought Hitler to Argentina, eh?" Frank seemed to find the question humorous.

"Certainly. We brought Hitler, Goering, Himmler, Von Ribbentrop, all of them. We left doubles behind in Germany!" He erupted into a loud laugh and pounded his fist on the table.

Reynolds wanted to get him to be serious but it might be difficult if Frank continued to treat the conversation as a mock.

"We carried no one other than a regular complement you would expect to find on a U-boat." He was still smiling but had stopped laughing. Beneath the smile Reynolds could detect a serious tone. "Those foolish charges were laid to rest years ago." Frank shook his head and a slightly disgusted look crept across his face, "But still the newspapers raise the question. Every so many years someone takes the tired old story and looks at it again trying to find something that will substantiate such a preposterous theory. I suppose when the editors have nothing better to do . . ."

"Mr. Frank, I read the book by your U-boat commander and I've done considerable research on the final days of the war. I'm not here to re-hash that part of the story. I'm interested in things, facts, that haven't been previously published.

"The U-977 was under the sea for over two months. It didn't give up until after the war was over for three months. A lot must have happened, things you may have considered routine, that were never mentioned. That's the kind of information I'm looking for," Reynolds lied.

"You're not a novelist hunting Hitler?"

"I give you my word I am not hunting Hitler or any of the others you mentioned."

"Aha!" Frank's eyes sparkled. "You want me to say we had Martin Bormann aboard." Frank was quite satisfied with the way he thought he had led Reynolds into a trap.

"Bormann may or may not have escaped from Germany. It's true that many writers have speculated on his disappearance over the years . . ."

"Decades."

"Decades, then. But I'm not one of them. I told you what my purpose was and is. I will not mention anything more about Nazi leaders being transported on the U-977 unless you decide to change your original story after all these years and say your boat did carry any of them."

"We did not. My story today will be exactly the same to you as it has been to others who have pestered me about such things. I moved out of South America some years ago to get away from exactly that kind of annoyance." Frank's mood had changed. He was holding hostility just below the surface.

"I'm sorry if I've upset you, Mr. Frank. But I thought you might be interested in relating the side of life in a U-boat that very few people are familiar with. I'm sorry you are unable to separate what I'm trying to do from the kinds of stories that thrive on sensationalism." Reynolds made a feeble effort to leave.

"Hold on. Wait a minute. If you really want a picture of the existence in a U-boat we can talk. I wouldn't mind that at all. However, I'm a bit tired now. Could we resume this talk sometime tomorrow?"

Reynolds hated to postpone the discussion but he had no choice. They set a convenient time for the next evening and Frank excused himself and left.

As Reynolds followed his departure across the room his eyes halted at the bar. There were a handful of people together drinking and talking softly. Several seats away from them, in the corner, was the same man Dick had seen earlier at his hotel. The man he was now sure he had seen in Washington.

Chapter 20

During the taxi ride back to their own hotel Reynolds told Jil and Ari about the man from Washington he had repeatedly seen on the island.

"Are you saying he is following us?" Jill asked

"I think so. It would be just too much of a coincidence otherwise."

Jil shuddered. "Will this nightmare ever end?"

Reynolds didn't have to reply to the question but instead noted something else. "This guy has had plenty of chances to get us but he hasn't. Do you realize this is the first time they've just watched and not tried to kill us?"

"If that's supposed to be comforting, Dick, it falls short by a country mile. I'm not impressed," Jil sulked.

"I've got an idea. We're going to turn the tables and hunt the hunter."

Ari and Jil gave Reynolds their undivided attention as he unfolded a plan. Meanwhile, several car lengths behind them, the man from Washington relaxed comfortably in the back seat of his taxi and looked out at the moon as it ducked behind rapidly passing low clouds. There was a slight breeze crossing the island and he was thankful that St. Kitts had very low humidity.

This wasn't a half-bad assignment after all, he thought.

He crossed his legs and lit a cigarette, all the while humming a tune the steel band had played earlier that evening.

***

Ted watched in amazement as Trautman cleared his plate and eagerly nodded in agreement when Uri asked if he would like another order.

They were at a corner table in a boisterous village restaurant having what Uri told Trautman was a "Farewell meal, a thank you for your help."

"Well Uri, I've finally met someone who puts you to shame in the eating department. Our friend is a bottomless pit," Ted said, motioning to Trautman who was sliding a large chunk of bread through the plate to pick up the last morsel.

"Tell me, Heinrich, just one more time. You're sure you haven't remembered anything else that was said by Dr. Wolf, the SS men or the U-boat sailors that night on the quay?"

Trautman's eyes widened as the waitress replaced the empty plate with a full one and another basket of black bread. His concentration was nearly totally on the food but he managed to answer through smiling lips that revealed teeth caked with food.

"No Uri, nothing. Just what I've told you." They had become familiar enough to use first names, something Uri had initiated in an effort to lower Trautman's subconscious resistance.

"I thought about it all again, like you asked, and there was nothing important that any of them said. I told you Wolf made a speech to the SS men and mentioned how honored they were to have served the Fuehrer. Ha, some honor! The next minute he orders the sailor on the U-boat to cut them down like paper dolls." Trautman lowered his head and rapidly shoveled the food into his mouth only breaking stride occasionally to wash the bulk down with a few mouthfuls of beer.

"They said nothing else about Hitler, none of them, and nothing about the *Golden Pheasants*," he offered.

"Golden Pheasants?" Ted was not familiar with the term.

Uri explained it. "That was a term used to describe those who were close to Hitler, the one's who were permitted to wear gilded swastikas, people like Goering, Himmler, Bormann, Speer, that crowd." Uri crossed his arms on the tabletop and leaned forward, his face only inches away from Trautman.

"Try hard to remember this. Did you see a gilded swastika on Wolf's uniform. Was he a Golden Pheasant?"

"Of course," Trautman replied without missing a mouthful. "That's what I said it for."

"You hadn't mentioned them before," Uri reminded him.

"I didn't?" Trautman seemed surprised. "Well, I should have. Wolf himself spoke about them in the ambulance during the ride to the quay. Didn't I tell you that?"

"NO!" The reply from Uri and Ted was in unison and loud enough to make Trautman cringe. He actually paused from eating and gave both men a scared look. "I'm sorry, I thought I did. I thought I did the night we drank all the wine."

"Maybe that was the problem," Uri offered. "You drank too much wine and *thought* you mentioned the Golden Pheasants but you didn't. I wonder what else you thought you told us but didn't?" There was a trace of anger in Uri's voice. Both he and Ted had locked their eyes on Trautman and the old man could see they were unhappy.

"Did I say anything about the Phoenix?" Trautman asked. "When Wolf looked back at the woman on the stretcher he said something, not to me, it was more like he was thinking out loud. He said something that sounded like 'Rest well, O mother of the Phoenix, rest well.' Some kind of poem, isn't it? But I don't think it's important."

***

The man from Washington paused outside Reynolds' cottage. He could hear Dick and Jil talking about Frank and neo-Nazis. He quietly moved himself into position against the wall next to the front window. Pressed flat so as to avoid detection, he strained to hear the conversation. A look of horror and surprise came across his face as the tremendous figure of Ari crashed down on him from out of nowhere.

Jil and Reynolds immediately responded to the noise outside. Reynolds came through the front door with his gun drawn and was satisfied to see Ari lifting the groggy man to his feet.

"Well, well. Didn't anyone ever tell you that snooping around can be dangerous to your health?" Reynolds was delighted that they had finally captured one of their antagonists alive.

"Bring him inside, Ari. This gentleman will be our guest, our talkative guest."

Reynolds removed the man's wallet and also discovered a snubnose .38 in an ankle holster. Just as he was about to sit down and go through the wallet the phone rang. Jil was closing the cottage door and Ari was lashing the man's arms to the arms of a wooden chair with his and Reynolds' belts.

"Dick Reynolds here"

"Dick? It's Ted. We're leaving Germany. We may have hit on something here. How is it going where you are?

"It was quiet until tonight. We finally got to talk to Frank and will be getting together with him again tomorrow. But the important thing is we got ourselves one, real, live Nazi prisoner."

"What? You mean they're down there too?"

"This one followed us here from Washington. We set a trap and caught him only minutes before you called."

"Dick when you question him ask if he knows anything about the Golden Pheasants or the Phoenix."

"What's that all about?"

"I can't go into it now, Uri is yelling that we have to get to the airport to catch the plane for Paris. Just be subtle. See what kind of reaction you get from him when you mention those names."

"Why are you going to Paris?"

"Can't talk. I'll call you tomorrow. It's another lead. Tell Jil I love her. Bye."

Reynolds replaced the phone on its cradle and looked across at the now fully awake man secured to the chair. They locked eyes for a long second but neither spoke. Reynolds opened the wallet in his hand and was surprised to see an identification card and gold shield.

"I'm with the Bureau also, Mr. Reynolds," the man said. "I'm Bob Taylor. Associate Director Mitchell personally asked me to keep an eye on you."

***

Susan Benedict clutched her husband's arm and smiled broadly for reporters who met her as she left the hospital.

"Mrs. Benedict, how do you feel now?" one reporter asked.

"Just fine. I was a bit shaken by the tumble. I'm feeling perfect now."

"Do you plan to do any more speedboat racing in the near future?" another asked.

"Certainly. I just had an unfortunate spill. I enjoy the water, boats and everything about them. I'll be back in the swim of things, so to speak, very soon."

"Not too soon," Elliott added, patting her wrist. "We're

going to take a brief vacation and get right into campaigning." He smiled affectionately at his wife as they made their way toward the waiting limousine.

"Mrs. Benedict, wouldn't you say you were lucky that there was a doctor nearby when you had the accident. Some reports said that Dr. Lupo actually saved your life."

"I think that is a bit of an exaggeration," Elliott replied as he helped his wife into the back seat. "We are grateful for Dr. Lupo's expert medical care but I don't think it is accurate to say that Susan's life was ever in real danger."

"Have you spoken to Dr. Lupo since the accident?" another asked.

Susan Benedict gave the reporter a cold stare. "No, I don't even know the man. We spoke briefly after he attended to me in the ambulance. I haven't seen him since."

"Mr. Vice President," another asked as Elliott entered the car, do you have any comment on the opposition party's selection of Virgil Rutledge as the man who will be running against you?"

"Any comment? Don't you think his nomination was a foregone conclusion? He clearly demonstrated to the American people that none of the other contenders in his party were qualified to run for president." Elliott offered. He was hoping this question would come up. "He seems to be the best of the lot in their camp. And if we are to believe what those members of his own party said about him during the primaries that isn't good enough for America! I think the big surprise at their convention was the fact that Virgil Rutledge was unable to mend his fences with his party bosses and had to select Leona Crawford Gordon as his running mate. She obviously wasn't his first choice. Rutledge had to go to the third or fourth string to find someone who would run on his ticket. America can't entrust its government to a party that is unable to offer the people the very best they have."

That evening and the next morning newspapers across the country carried page one photos of Susan Benedict being attended at the time of the accident by Dr. Harold Lupo. The caption under the photo began with the lead-in: Vice President's Wife Plays Down Role of Good Samaritan Doctor.

Elliott Benedict's remarks about the Rutledge-Gordon ticket were included in the last paragraph of the accompanying story.

***

Jil answered the phone and was happy to hear Ted's voice.

"Hi love, I finally got to Paris."

"Hello, darling. I wish I was with you. Is everything alright?"

"Yea, just fine. I told Dick last night I'd call him and fill him in on what we learned from Trautman. But first tell me what's going on with your prisoner."

"Oh he's not a prisoner anymore. We let him go. He's an FBI man that Mitchell assigned to protect us."

"What? Last night Reynolds was sure the guy was a Nazi."

"Yes, but he wasn't. Dick called Mitchell from here and got him out of bed to confirm the man's story. Mitchell said he was worried that we were getting in over our heads and with the other two agents still missing he asked agent Bob Taylor to take this on as a special assignment. Nobody at the Bureau knows he is working on this.

"That sure is some change from the attitude Mitchell displayed the last time Reynolds talked to him. Where is Dick now?"

"He and Ari went over to talk to Frank again. Taylor

went too but he is keeping out of sight. I'm here getting my things together. Dick says we will be leaving the island today. He is sure he can finish up with Frank in an hour. Actually, Ted, he doesn't hold out much hope of getting anything. Frank seems to be just an ex-navy man who has told everything there is to tell to anybody who would listen over the years."

"We thought we had heard everything Trautman had to say also until the last meeting with him. Then he remembered Dr. Wolf refer to the unborn baby the woman in the ambulance was carrying as the 'Phoenix'."

"What is the significance of that?"

"Uri isn't sure. But at least it gives us a possible code name to drop around. If it means anything our Nazi friends should get very uptight knowing that we've discovered it. Then again it could mean nothing."

"What's the lead you are following in Paris?"

"Uri had some of his people do some digging into the French National Archives. The German Kriegsmarine had a big headquarters in Paris during the war and the classified records of all U-boats operating from French ports are kept there. Uri's people think they found a copy of a secret message ordering a U-boat to pick up an important passenger at St. Nazaire on May 1, 1945."

***

Ari sat in the shade at a table at the Mountainside Plantation. He was breaking small pieces of bread and dropping them nearby for the birds to swoop down and get. FBI agent Bob Taylor was somewhere on the grounds also but not visible to Ari or Reynolds who was enjoying a tall drink at the patio bar with Fritz Frank.

Jil had interrupted their discussion briefly with a phone call to fill Reynolds in on her conversation with Ted.

"During the time the U-977 was crossing the Atlantic

did you receive any messages from other U-boats or have any contact with the Kriegsmarine?"

Frank narrowed his eyes and he studied Reynolds. "Mr. Reynolds I thought this conversation was to be about life in a U-boat, not the journey of U-977."

"I know, I'm sorry that's what I told you last night but I've just learned something that is very odd. That phone call I received? The person on the other end informed me that the Kriegsmarine records in Paris contain a secret message about a U-boat picking up a special passenger at St. Nazaire, France on May 1, 1945."

Fritz Frank visibly stiffened. "Go on, Mr. Reynolds."

"I also have heard that a U-boat did in fact depart from that port and it had a pregnant woman aboard. Some stories even say the child she was carrying was Hitler's daughter. Does the term Golden Pheasants mean anything to you? How about Phoenix? Did the U-977 receive any transmissions using either of these expressions?"

Frank tried desperately to remain calm. When he spoke it was hardly obvious that Reynolds' words had disturbed him.

"I'm forced to say that neither of those expressions were ever heard on or transmitted to the U-977. As for a secret message ordering a U-boat to pick up a passenger in France what kind of secret would it have been if a lowly radio operator such as myself were aware of it?" He laughed convincingly.

"I think you would be better off not chasing such phantoms, Mr. Reynolds. The war has been over for nearly forty years. All the talk about Nazis who escaped, conspiracies and the like, fail to take an important factor into consideration."

"What's that Mr. Frank?"

"Adolf Hitler would now be over one hundred years

old if he were alive. Martin Bormann would be in his eighties. All the others would be old men too. What can the world fear from such people even if they had escaped? The veterans on both sides who fought in the war are now old men passing away their final days in retirement."

"Not all of them Mr. Frank."

"No?"

"No. You are fifty-nine years old and quite actively operating this very busy plantation." Reynolds looked deep into Frank's eyes and thought for a moment he saw a spark of rage.

***

Ted and Uri were excited as they left the meeting with the Israeli agents who were colleagues of Uri's. The information given to them confirmed that a U-boat had been ordered to pick up a passenger at St. Nazaire along with SS Standartenfuehrer Dr. Helmut Wolf. Both men were pleased at the confirmation they now positively had.

As they left a sidewalk cafe on the Champs Elysees and strolled in the warm August sun, Ted stopped to purchase a copy of the *International Herald Tribune*. He carefully folded the English language newspaper and tucked it into his blazer pocket. The sights and sounds of Paris were far too great to be preempted by reading a newspaper now. He would save it for a quiet period in his hotel room later.

"Now I know why Jil loves this city so much. It's beautiful."

"Then you should plan to revisit it with her after this is over," Uri suggested.

"I intend to." Ted paused again and took in the full scope of the beautiful avenue. His eyes traveled from the high end where the Arc de Triomphe majestically rose above the treetops down to the terminus of the famous boulevard to the Place de La Concorde with its ancient Egyptian obelisk jutting skyward.

"It is almost unthinkable that Hitler ordered his generals to destroy Paris as they were retreating from the advancing Allies."

"Yes, that would have been a loss to all mankind, not just the French. However, the French have this foolish conviction that Paris belongs exclusively to them!"

Both of them laughed easily.

Across the avenue a rough looking man watched them continue their stroll as he spoke on the pay phone.

"I don't know what they got. I told you yesterday the Israeli agents were spending a lot of time with Kriegsmarine records. Whatever they found has satisfied them." He listened for several seconds and then continued.

"Sure it's easy for you to tell me you received a call from America and I should kill them. But who are they and what were they looking for? If you want me to finish them off you better at least let me know who it is and why they have to be eliminated. You can reach me at the hotel. Yes, yes, I checked into the same one they are at. The Plaza-Athenee.

"Remember. I want a call before I'll do anything. I don't run a sloppy business in Paris; we only eliminate people who we feel are a threat to the Organization."

***

Several thousand miles away Jil, Reynolds and Ari were checking out of their rooms at the Hillside Inn. Bob Taylor was waiting for them when they came into the lobby.

"All checked out?" Reynolds asked him.

"Yea. I was packed this morning before we left to see Frank. How did it go?"

"We came up with zero. For a while I thought for sure he was going to be a break for us. I thought maybe he would remember something that would at least establish if the U-boat from France ever made it across the Atlantic." Reynolds placed his room key on the counter and Jil asked him for money to settle the bill.

"You already know that the boat made it across, don't you?" Taylor asked. "I mean that's what Bauman told Ted Scott and all these close calls you people have been having seem to confirm that somebody is trying to protect that secret."

"Taylor, let me tell you something. You should have been in this business now long enough to know that what we have is a fistful of non-conclusive evidence. True, somebody has been trying to kill Ted and Jil, and me too for that matter. But we don't have one hard piece of physical evidence to connect these things with any of the three women suspects or a U-boat that we believe brought Hitler's daughter here almost forty years ago."

"I hate to interrupt this conversation gentlemen but if we don't continue it in the taxi we'll miss our connecting flight to St. Croix."

The desk clerk cut in. "That will be your only connection today. If you miss it you'll be spending another night here, unless you want to wait until Thursday for the direct flight to New York."

"Listen, we're lucky we're able to pay the bill up to today. We'll be on that flight when it leaves," Reynolds replied. Just as the four of them headed for the taxi the phone rang.

Jil was already in the cab. So was Ari, Reynolds and Taylor were just getting in when the desk clerk called to Dick.

"Mr. Reynolds, you have a long distance call from Paris. A Mr. Scott."

"Dick, that call could cost us our plane ride," Taylor offered.

"Yeah, but if Ted is calling again from overseas it must be important. Look, you three go ahead and try to hold the plane. I'll make it fast." He hurried back into the lobby and Jil got out of the taxi.

"Bob, you and Ari go ahead. I'll wait here with Dick," she said as she slammed the taxi door and watched it speed away toward Golden Rock International Airport.

"Hello Ted, what's up? It better be good. I may be missing a plane for this call."

"Dick? I think we've got her. Hitler's daughter, I think we know who she is."

"Well who is it and how did you uncover her?"

"There is a picture on the front page of the *International Herald Tribune* with a story about Susan Benedict's boat accident last week. The doctor who saved her life is named Harold Lupo.

"Lupo, Dick. Don't you get it? Lupo is Italian for Wolf! Even the first initial is the same: Helmut Wolf became Harold Lupo."

"It sounds very convincing but it's not proof positive that both men are one in the same Ted. Still it is something to look into."

"Dick there is more. There is a walking stick or ornate cane in the foreground of the picture. We already know Wolf used a gold-topped cane. Uri agrees that this is too much of a coincidence. They are both doctors, the same initials, the wordplay on the name, and he is at Susan Benedict's side when she needed him. Further, she says in the story that she doesn't know him. That denial rings pretty loud. The story makes it sound as if she went out of her way to separate herself from connection with him."

"Okay, Ted, okay. You've convinced me. Maybe there is more to this than just a coincidence. We're going now to catch a plane and should be back in the new safe house early this evening. What's your schedule?"

"Uri is checking on plane connections now. We will be leaving here tonight or first thing tomorrow."

"See you in Virginia, pal. Jil sends her love, bye."

Reynolds replaced the phone and turned to Jil.

"Sorry, honey. There was no time for you to talk to him if we're going to catch that plane."

Jil tried to supress her dejection. "I understand. Tell me what he said."

"Sure, but in the taxi on the way. Let's get going."

Chapter 21

The tall, dark cloud of smoke was drifting slowly toward the terminal building at Golden Rock International Airport as the taxi with Jil and Reynolds made its way through the increasing rush of people who were heading for the airport.

Bright yellow emergency fire vehicles with flashing red lights were visible at the southerly end of the airstrip and the din of approaching ambulances caused Jil to place her hands over her ears as she and Dick got out of the taxi.

"What happened?" Dick called to one of several men running in the direction of the activity.

"The St. Croix plane . . . it exploded just after takeoff."

Reynolds looked at Jil. Both of them stood there frozen for an instant. "If we had left a minute or two earlier, if Ted hadn't called. . . . my God, Dick, we would have been on that plane!"

It took Dick and Jil several minutes to locate Ari and Bob Taylor, who had both rushed out to the crash site to assist in the futile rescue operation.

"Everybody aboard was killed instantly," Taylor told them as they gathered around a table in the second floor restaurant and absent-mindedly sipped coffees.

"Did you see it happen, Bob?" Jil asked.

"Yes. Ari wanted to watch the takeoff. We were up here as a matter of fact, by that window. We watched the last piece of luggage go aboard, the slow taxi to the end of the strip and the liftoff. It hardly got more than a hundred feet above the runway when it exploded . . ."

"Excuse me, Mr. Reynolds! Miss Baker! You're all right! You didn't get aboard the plane, how fortunate." Fritz Frank's lower lip trembled as he spoke. He stood over them, accompanied by two men whom Reynolds recognized from the Mountainside Plantation. He was sure they were not tourists but they didn't seem to be hotel employees either. Their function became obvious without much delay.

"I really am surprised to see you, you know. I had been assured that you and your three friends were aboard the aircraft."

"Thank you for your concern, but as you see we are still here. I guess our numbers just weren't up yet," Dick offered, along with a weak smile.

"But not for long," Frank replied. His eyes were cold and his lips were tight as he continued.

"The four of you are leaving this island now, as my guests, aboard a boat. Once we are out to sea we shall resume the conversation you initiated concerning the Phoenix. Shall we go?" Frank moved his hand slightly and the two men with him slid their lightweight jackets back enough to reveal their weapons.

Reynolds looked briefly at Jil, whose frightened eyes indicated she understood their predicament. He glanced at Bob Taylor and both men felt their frustration at having packed their own weapons in their luggage. Only Ari seemed undisturbed by the change of events.

During the ride to the boat from the airport there was total silence in the van. Frank's men kept their weapons trained on the four prisoners throughout the ride and only attempted to conceal them when they boarded the boat at the old quay behind the French Colonial Treasury Building in the capital city of Basseterre.

Once on board, Reynolds and Taylor were thoroughly searched and then locked in a forward cabin below decks on the forty-foot cabin cruiser. Jil and Ari were kept above decks and searched quickly once the boat had moved sufficiently far enough away from the dock.

"Get the other two up here and lock these two below," Frank ordered. "We'll deal with the FBI men first and then we can have some sport with the girl and the Jew later." Their laughter sent a cold chill through Jil. She glanced at Ari but again the big man showed no signs of distress or anger.

The boat was now some distance from Basseterre. One of Frank's men handled her with experience as the sleek hull sliced through the rocky seas between St. Kitts and its sister island of Nevis.

"Over here, Kurt," Frank said to the man who brought Reynolds and Taylor up from below. He motioned to a place on the deck where he wanted them placed. Now Frank was also brandishing a gun. He waisted no time getting to the point. Reynolds and Taylor sat on the deck.

"Mr. Reynolds you seem to have made a fatal mistake. There is no one outside the Organization who knows the significance of the Phoenix and since you and your three companions are not part of our very select group it will be my honor to see that you take your knowledge with you to your graves."

"It's not only us, Frank, there are others who know. Killing us won't protect your secret."

"If you mean Scott and the Israeli I assure you they will be meeting the same fate as you within the next few hours, if they haven't already."

"But it's not only them." Reynolds was trying to buy

time. "The reason we missed the plane is because we contacted others in the States. The FBI . . ."

"Please don't fabricate stories at this late hour Mr. Reynolds. Face it, you're through, all of you. The call that delayed you was from Paris, not Washington. There is no one who knows anything of consequence. Even you and the girl have no idea what you almost stumbled onto."

"Then why don't you tell us. That is, if you really intend to eliminate us, what harm will it do. Besides it would be nice to know what we are dying for," Taylor said.

"Such a dramatic cliche. It almost sounds like the lines from one of your American B movies. I'm sorry, gentlemen, I shall not indulge your curiosity. The only talking to be done here will be by you, not me. Now let's start by telling me what made you come to find me on St. Kitts."

Reynolds and Taylor exchanged glances but neither spoke. They both returned their attention to Frank.

"Well, I see I'm going to have to prove we are playing hard ball."

Frank leveled his gun at Taylor's leg and squeezed off a round. The bullet was perfectly placed to shatter the knee. Taylor screamed in pain and rolled back and forth on the deck.

For an instant Reynolds considered jumping up at Frank but he knew he would be cut down either by Frank or Kurt. Taylor was in extreme pain and Reynolds knew Frank wouldn't hesitate to shoot him again if he didn't get some answers, and pretty fast.

"Well Mr. Reynolds do you have anything to say or should I blast away his other knee?"

Dick was about to tell Frank anything, even if he had to make up a story as he went along. Just as he nodded and began to talk there was a loud crashing sound from below decks.

"The big one and the girl, they are breaking out . . . get them," Frank ordered Kurt. Frank backed away from Reynolds and Taylor and turned his attention to the steps below deck that Kurt was just reaching.

Reynolds took the instant to grab hold of the ship's anchor and from a squat position prepared to lunge at Frank with it.

The sound was almost deafening and the flash that engulfed Kurt as the meteor flare exploded in his chest momentarily distracted Reynolds. Ari had apparently located the distress flare gun below decks and had now used it.

Kurt stumbled backward away from the steps. His body was aglow as he turned and faced Frank. His chin hung open and his eyes registered the horror of a man who knew he would be dead in seconds. Kurt's gun dropping to the deck was the only sound to break the sizzling crackle of flare burning through Kurt. He fell face-forward at Frank's feet.

Ari was now at the head of the stairs with the re-loaded flare gun but before he could fire Frank got off three rapid shots, all hitting the big man in the face and propelling him back down the stairs.

Reynolds lunged at Frank using the anchor as a bat and caught him in the arm, dislodging the gun. The third man had cut the boat's engines and was now coming down from the fly bridge.

Frank and Reynolds were wrestling and Reynolds was getting the advantage just as the third man smashed the butt of his gun across Dick's skull.

Frank pushed Reynolds' limp body off and picked up the anchor. He swung it back and was ready to dig it into Dick's chest when he heard Jil scream. He and the third man turned to see her standing at the top of the stairs aiming the flare gun at them.

"I suggest you put that gun down young lady. If you fire it at us you will kill your two friends also." Frank motioned to the unconscious figure of Reynolds and Taylor, who was barely conscious. He caught a side glance of the third man who was still holding his gun. Frank wanted to continue talking to Jil to distract her so the other man could get a shot off. But the man's move was too pronounced and Jil turned the gun on him and fired.

Again the blinding flash temporarily stunned those on the ship. The man had taken the shot in his right shoulder. As he screamed and spun backward toward the stern rail his gun dropped on the deck alongside Taylor. His body hit the rail and he jerked himself over it and into the cool water.

Jil stood frozen in the position she had fired the gun from. Frank began to move toward her with the anchor.

"You're a dangerous little bitch, Miss Baker," he said from twisted lips. Blood was now soaking his shirt sleeve from the wound he received when Reynolds had used the anchor to strike him.

"This anchor makes a nasty gash, take a look. A final look. I'm going to use it to remove your pretty eyes one at a time." He continued to move closer, slowly. Jil began to step backward down the stairs. Her mind raced wildly but she couldn't think where Ari had put the remining flares. In his pocket? There would be no time to get them and load the gun, Frank was too close.

"Frank! Another move and you're a dead man." It was Reynolds. He was up on one knee and aiming the gun that had fallen near Taylor. The blood from his head injury had created red rivulets from his forehead down to his chin and he looked grotesque. He aimed with one hand while using the other to steady himself against the rail. The boat was rocking heavily now at the mercy of the strong channel waves between St. Kitts and Nevis. Reynolds got to his feet and pulled back the hammer on the revolver.

"Now, Mr. Frank, you will do the talking or so help me God I'll use this gun on you one limb at a time."

The boat rocked violently as it caught a swell. Frank lurched forward, Reynolds reacted instantly and fired four shots at point-blank range. Frank was dead before he hit the deck.

***

"You go ahead, Ted. I want to make a last minute stop to the men's room before we board," Uri told him as they moved away from the newsstand at the airport. They had checked out of the Plaza-Athenee and arrived at the airline counter in plenty of time for their flight back to Washington from Paris.

Uri moved away from Ted and cut directly toward the toilet. Once inside he positioned himself behind the door and only had to wait an instant for the stocky man in the badly fitting suit to enter.

He immediately jumped the man and threw him to the ground. Using a neck lock and with his knee pressed firmly against the man's spine he introduced himself.

"I'm one of the good guys, so you must be one of the bad guys, right? Who are you and why have you been following us since we left the hotel?"

The man grunted, exaggerating his inability to speak while in the uncomfortable position. Uri bent his head a little harder, causing severe pain. The man yelled.

"Alright, alright. Stop, you're breaking my neck. Please stop!"

Before letting him up Uri frisked him and removed a knife and a gun fitted with a silencer. Once he was on his feet Uri pushed him into a toilet stall and closed the door behind them.

"Now why have you been following us?"

"There must be some mistake. I wasn't following you, there was someone else who left the hotel that I was trailing."

"Really?" Uri didn't conceal his disbelief.

"Yes, you see I'm a private investigator and my client is a woman who's husband is fooling around and . . ."

"You've got five seconds before I cut your tongue out." Uri flashed the man's knife close to his face and at that moment the man thrust his knee into Uri's groin doubling him up. He quickly smashed him behind the neck with a hard blow and used his other knee to deliver a fierce blow to Uri's face. Somehow Uri managed to clutch the knife and he used all his strength to punch it into the man's stomach.

The man continued to strike out at Uri but the power of his blows had decreased considerably. Uri turned the knife hard in his stomach and pulled it out with a downward rip. He pushed the dying man off him and was sure the man would be dead before his body hit the white tile floor.

Ted looked around the gate area and checked his watch. He noticed Uri limped slightly as he approached but failed to see the splashes of blood on his suit.

"Everything okay? Kidneys empty?"

"Empty and hurting. Let's get onboard. We were followed. I've just eliminated one but there could be another. I'll tell you about it when we're on the plane."

***

Jil and Reynolds didn't arrive at the safe house until two days after Ted and Uri returned.

They exchanged the details of their experiences and Jil explained how they remained behind on St. Kitts to bury Ari and Bob Taylor after he died. Now there were just the four of them again. Associate FBI Director Mitchell had not returned any of Reynolds' calls.

The four of them were undecided on how to use the information they had gathered. Ted wanted to simply send Susan Benedict letters with one word: Phoenix. The others felt this was trite and of no value.

Reynolds insisted they remain out of sight and follow her movements. Uri agreed but went a step farther. He wanted to have a hit-team eliminate her. No one supported that suggestion.

Jil insisted that Ted take the information he had to David Holland despite the risk that he would be arrested.

***

Days turned into weeks and the weeks slowly became months while this small group of people who believed they had information which would affect the course of world history found themselves unable to agree on an effective way to utilize it.

Finally the Presidential Election was a little more than a week away when Uri told the others what he had been doing.

"These several weeks we've been successful in avoiding detection," he told them as they gathered around the table for a meal on Sunday, October 28. "The election is nine days away. If something isn't done in this short time there is no way in the world to stop Susan Benedict from becoming the First Lady. Once that happens all our fears will be realized."

"Uri," Jil interrupted, "You sound as if you've rehearsed this little speech before a mirror a hundred times. What are you trying to tell us?"

He looked at her and his face quickly flushed. As he looked next at Ted and finally Reynolds he could see they shared her opinion.

"Yes, I've rehearsed it, and for good reason. I don't want what I'm about to tell you to come out wrong. But first let me tell you this. I've had some people checking on Fritz Frank and the man who we eliminated at the airport in Paris.

"Frank was never a member of the crew of U-977. He was a hardline Nazi attached to the Kriegsmarine. He was ordered out of Europe three days before the capitulation and told to set up residence in South America first and eventually the Caribbean, preferably an island with little tourist or commercial traffic."

"How did you find this out?" Ted asked.

"My colleagues in Israel. He wasn't thought to be a big fish and we had nothing really on him. The information you supplied, Dick and Jil, led us to fit in some pieces. Frank was one of several links in the worldwide transportation network that helps war criminals move from country to country."

"But Uri, he lost control when we mentioned the Phoenix to him. That's when he blew his cover. Surely he had to be more than a low-echelon member to be aware of what that meant," Reynolds offered.

"And just what does it mean?" Uri asked. "Ted and I stumbled upon it in our last conversation with Trautman. We still don't know if it is a code name for Hitler's daughter."

"C'mon, Uri, you know more than you are telling us. Phoenix means something, Frank's actions prove that. You're playing games."

Uri again looked around the table at them. This time he permitted a slight grin to cross his lips.

"Yes, it means something. And yes, it is not something that anyone but a favored few in the Organization would know about. Fritz Frank is the cousin of Dr. Harry Lupo, formerly Standartenfuehrer Helmut Wolf. From his quiet plantation on St. Kitts he headed up the Organization's efforts throughout the Caribbean and South America. His cover was so good even the American CIA believed he was a former radio operator from the U-977."

"What about the man at the airport in Paris?" Ted asked.

"He was a wanted war criminal. A former French member of the SS who returned to his country after the war and functioned as a roughneck, thug and killer."

"Did you say a *French* member of the SS? I thought the SS was made up of German supermen," Reynolds said.

"That's a myth," Uri answered. "In the early days of the war it was true but as things got rough for the Nazis they permitted foreigners to become SS. By 1945 the Waffen SS had approximately a half-million non-Germans in 27 of its 40 divisions. They were mostly Europeans—Dutch, Flemish, French, Norwegian, Danes, Swiss, Swedes—but there were some Asians and Americans as well."

"How did you find out about him?" Jil asked.

"Our people read in the newspaper about the body being found. Besides, I called them, once Ted and I landed in Washington, and told them to find out who he was."

"Okay. Now what is it you were going to tell us?" Ted asked.

"Just that I've arranged for some reinforcements. I have three men flying in this weekend to help us prevent Susan Benedict from ever creating a Fourth Reich in America or anywhere else."

"No, Uri. That's the hit-squad you've been talking about!" Jil was shocked.

"We won't be any part of that, despite what they've done," Ted followed. "We don't want to kill her or anybody else. There has been enough killing. We just want to expose her and let her face justice."

"Justice? You can't be serious! Can you count how

many people have died just since you've been involved in this? Multiply it a million times. This is the same bloodline that soaked the world in blood from 1933 to 1945 and they are still doing it only on a smaller scale. Justice! Did Aaron Bauman get justice? Or Ari? Or the people on that plane you, Jil, and Dick were nearly on? And Dick, what about your neighbor's son? Or the three FBI agents who are dead . . . and the old lady who lived across the street from you?"

"I didn't say anything about justice, Uri," Reynolds added quietly. "But I won't be a party to murder when we aren't even sure Susan Benedict is the woman we want."

The room fell silent. Reynolds got up from the table and walked to the large bow window. "All we know is that she was hurt in a boating accident and the doctor who first attended her was Helmut Wolf." He continued looking out the window at nothing in particular then finally added. "Before we pull the trigger we've got to be sure it's her."

***

Elliott Benedict sat hunched on a sofa clicking the remote control for the TV set. The final interview in the profile series that he had done with Sharon Franklin was about to come on.

He and Susan had shocked the campaign staff by taking this next to last weekend of the election off and were spending it at a lakeside retreat in Maine. He was holding the largest pre-election lead in U.S. history and was the odds-on choice by all the pollsters to win the Presidency by the largest landslide ever.

Susan passed in front of him and adjusted the band on her bathing suit top where it tied at the neck.

"I guess I can't persuade you to sit and watch this with me," he asked.

"No, thank you." Her mood was light. "I have no

interest in seeing Chapter Three of *A Man And His Mistress*." She looked back at him and forced a sarcastic smile as she opened the door to leave the cottage. "Try not to stain your pants when you ejaculate."

Elliott tried to ignore the remark and concentrate on the show as it began. The network's election logo zoomed into view and a deep-voiced announcer told millions of viewers that regular programming was being pre-empted for this special broadcast.

Susan Benedict walked along the slate path to the boat dock. She looked around and gave the Secret Service agents a wave as they hurried to get into a chase boat.

Elliott Benedict placed the remote control device on the end table next to the couch and sat back to relax and watch his interview.

Susan turned the key and started the fast little boat. With experienced hands she maneuvered it away from the dock and immediately opened up full throttle. The Secret Service boat was already a good distance behind her.

***

Sharon Franklin's lovely face filled the screen as she made opening remarks about the election and the interview which was to follow. She concluded with a bright smile and the camera cut to a commercial.

Elliott thought this was the right time to fetch a beer from the refrigerator. He lifted himself from the couch and quickly made his way into the kitchen.

As he pulled the refrigerator door open an explosion rattled the windows. He stood frozen for a moment before realizing that whatever it was had happened outside the cottage, not in it.

Another few seconds passed before he moved. "Susan!" he screamed. "Susan!"

***

Sharon Franklin sat in a comfortable chair of the network control room watching her interview with Elliott Benedict draw to a close. Though she had seen it several times previously she demanded, and got absolute silence. She had made it a point of being in the control room and viewing the broadcasting of each tape in the series as it aired. There was less than two minutes to go in the hour show when a member of the news staff burst into the room. All heads turned at the intrusion.

"Hey, we got a big one! Susan Benedict was just in another boating accident and she is dying at a hospital in Maine."

There was mild panic in the control room as various people made instant decisions about breaking the story.

"Sharon, get into Studio B right now and we'll cut to you making the announcement," a director said. "Phil, give her that wiry copy just as it is, we can expand on it later. Don, call our affiliate in . . . whatever the name of that Maine town is and get a remote plugged in as quick as you can to the hospital. Dave . . ."

"Larry," It was Sharon in a quiet, almost trembling voice. "I don't think I can do it . . . I, I'm too close to them as a family. Get Lowell to do it. He was here just a minute ago."

The director looked at her briefly then turned away. "Somebody get Lowell over to Studio B. Hurry!

***

Ted Scott took a deep breath and stepped out from the high bushes that graced the landscape of David Holland's palatial estate. It was just past dusk but vision was more than adequate.

"Good evening, David."

"Wha . . .?" Holland, who had been standing alone on the patio, was startled but quickly regained his composure when he recognized Scott. "My God, Ted, what are you doing hiding in bushes?"

Ted took a step forward, extending his hands before him in a calming gesture. "David, I had to talk to you, but please! Let's not go through another scene like the last time. Please hear me out."

Holland brushed the remark off with a wave. "It's all too late for that now, I have no stomach for hysteria. What is it you want?"

"When we last spoke, David, you didn't believe the possibility that Hitler's daughter actually existed and was here in Washington ready to orchestrate the rise of the Fourth Reich. I'll admit I didn't present my case very well at that time but since then things have happened which should make even you question what's going on."

"Ted," Holland interrupted, "I'm not at my best right now . . . I have to sort things out in my mind. So much has happened, so much I never would have dreamed possible. Please, can we continue this conversation at another time?"

Ted was surprised at Holland's obvious distraction. He wondered what caused his former mentor to be so distraught.

"David, are you alright? I've never seen you like this before. What is it?"

Holland looked at him for a long few seconds and then slowly contorted his face in pain. He brought his hands up to cover his eyes and conceal the tears but they were betrayed in his choking, gasping voice.

"I've been used. I was a decoy, an instrument to protect Elliott in his affair with Sharon Franklin." Holland was talking very fast, pouring out secrets he had kept for some time. He took his hands down and looked into the night, still talking but seemingly to himself rather than Ted.

"I arranged for her to be seen regularly with the Secretary of State. I created the rumors that she and

Manning were romantically involved and even got him to go along with it with a promise of a Cabinet position in the new administration. I provided them with the opportunity." Holland paused but continued to look into the night. Finally he turned to Ted and there was a firmness in his voice for the first time.

"Elliott told me only recently that Sharon had suggested they do away with Susan. He was frightened and asked me if I thought her remarks were serious." Holland paused again. Ted was confused by what David had been saying but did not interrupt.

"I told him it was Sharon's idea of a macabre joke and not to worry." Holland turned away and walked to the porch stoop and sat down, his hands braced against his knees. Ted followed but remained standing before him.

"On Friday, when Elliott and Susan announced that they were taking a respite from the campaign and spending the weekend in Maine, Sharon called me and asked if I could arrange for her to secretly get onto the compound for a few minutes Saturday. She said there was something she had to talk to Elliott about and it could only be done in person, and had to be done this weekend. She insisted I not tell him beforehand of her visit.

"Reluctantly, I arranged for it. She was to arrive with a man from the boat shop in town but slip away from him while he faked some repairs on the speedboat.

"The man came on schedule but Sharon was not with him. He puttered around with the boat and left. I thought Sharon had a change of plans for some reason. When I returned to Washington last evening I tried to call her but she was unavailable.

"She used me, Ted, and as much as I hate to admit it I now fear Elliott may be involved also . . . either before or after the fact, but surely involved."

"David, what are you talking about? What importance does this have to anything."

Holland's eyes softened and he looked at Ted the way a parent would explaining something to a child. "Have you listened to the radio or TV in the last two hours?"

"No. I've been very discreetly trying to get here without being followed. Why?"

"Susan Benedict died of injuries she received in another speedboat accident earlier this evening. She was dead on arrival at the hospital."

There was a long silence that was only broken by a slight breeze that rustled the leaves on the tall oaks that lined the pathway to the estate.

"Ever since I heard the news I have had this horrible feeling that Sharon Franklin's 'macabre joke' was serious and that I played the fool by arranging for the boat man to make the boat an instrument of death.

"Elliott will be elected, of course. He would have been without this but now the sympathy vote erases any chance of a last minute fluke.

"A year from now, maybe a little longer, depending on what public reaction is, he and Sharon will be married, I'm sure." Holland was voicing a projection he had obviously played over in his mind several times in the last two hours.

"It will be a fairytale romance. Sharon Franklin, the beautiful goddess of television filling the void in the life of the handsome, young President. Replacing his equally attractive wife." Holland lowered his head and added softly, "America will have another Camelot."

Ted's mind was racing these last few seconds since David told him of Susan's death. Now he couldn't contain himself any longer. He grabbed Holland by the shoulders and raised him to his feet.

"David, this is important, try to remember. When Susan had the first boat accident in Florida the first medical aid she received was from Dr. Harold Lupo. Was Lupo there because of Susan or somebody else?"

Holland couldn't understand the meaning of Ted's question but didn't hesitate to reply. "He wasn't with us, none of us on the White House staff knew him, and I'm sure Susan didn't either. In fact she made that quite clear when she was leaving the hospital."

"Yes, I know, I saw the picture in the paper. But Dr. Lupo is a link to Hitler's daughter. That's part of what I came here to tell you tonight. It's no crazy idea, David, it's a real fact. Was Sharon Franklin present at the boat accident, the first one? Could he have been with her?"

"Yes, Sharon was there, but Ted, this business about Hitler's daughter again, it really seems too much to believe."

"David you said it yourself only a minute ago. Susan is dead, Elliott and Sharon will marry. Sharon arranged for Susan to be murdered! Don't you see? Susan and Sharon were two of the three women who surfaced as the prime suspects in this nightmare.

"All along the clues were leading us to believe it was Susan but now it all fits. David, if you believe Sharon is capable of murder is it much harder to believe she is behind a string of murders that began since I became aware of Dr. Bauman's journal?"

"Ted, I must have time to think this out. It is just all too much at one time."

"David, take me to the President. You tell him what you know and I'll explain what's been going on and we'll at least have someone who can look at it all rationally."

"The President? He would have us both locked up in a looney bin . . ."

"No, he wouldn't David. He'd listen and look at the evidence. Even if he didn't believe my story he'd have to look into your charges. He'd be able to have an investigation conducted and if you are right, if Sharon had Susan killed, he would be able to stop her from ever marrying Elliott."

"And you'd be satisfied that you stopped Hitler's daughter?"

"Yes." Ted's eyes were pleading with David. He hoped Holland would want to get his own guilt off his chest by going to President Chandler. Even if the President discounted Ted's story it made little difference as long as action was taken to stop Sharon Franklin from ever becoming the wife of the President.

"This whole thing is so bizarre . . . I don't know what to think."

"Just say yes, David. Yes that we can meet with Chandler and tell him our fears. It is the *only* thing we can do."

David Holland turned away and began to climb the steps to the large double-doors. He paused and turned to Ted.

"Perhaps you're right. Meet me at my office tomorrow morning at nine o'clock and we'll approach the President." He looked once more deep into Ted's eyes and added, "God, I hope he doesn't think we're both mad."

Chapter 22

"Where's Uri?" Ted asked Reynolds as he and Jil entered the kitchen."

"And good morning to you too," Reynolds replied.

"Good morning. Where's Uri?"

"He left for the airport to meet his Israeli friends."

Ted poured a cup of coffee for himself and handed a tea bag to Jil. He sat at the table across from Reynolds as Jil prepared her tea on the counter near the stove.

"Did you talk to him before he left?"

"Yes. Susan Benedict's death throws a monkey wrench into his plans. He was sure she was the one."

Ted added milk to the overcooked dark brew. "I suppose now he and his gunmen will stalk Sharon Franklin?"

"You're full of questions for a guy who just crawled out of bed. But to answer you: no. He went to meet them and frankly he really doesn't know what he is going to say. He went out on quite a limb convincing them they had a chance to get the daughter of Adolf Hitler. He's very upset about what happened."

"Why? Because he didn't have a chance to put a bullet in her head himself?"

Reynolds slammed his fist on the table. "No, damn it! Because this means we may now never know if she was the Phoenix or not. If she was she may have taken the secret with her to the grave. If she wasn't then we are no closer to unmasking her than we were weeks ago."

Ted permitted a smile to cross his face. "Tell Uri when he gets back that before the day is over the Phoenix will be living on borrowed time. I have a meeting with the President this morning and we may finally be getting the kind of help we need to stop her."

"Keeping secrets, Ted?" Reynolds asked surprised.

"No, not secrets, just playing some trump cards close to the vest. The way we've been stumbling around these last several weeks has led us nowhere. Last night I met with David Holland and he agreed to arrange a meeting. I didn't wake you or Uri when I got in last night because I wanted to sort things out in my head first. I did, however, tell Jil."

"Oh Dick, this could be an eleventh hour shot in the dark but I believe when Ted and David tell the President what has been going on this veil of horror that has hung over us all will be lifted." Jil could hardly supress her excitement as she joined them at the table.

Ted looked at the wall clock and gulped down his coffee. "I'd better leave now. It's a long drive and I'll be bucking the morning traffic part of the way." He leaned over and kissed Jil tenderly. "Have I told you lately that I love you."

"No, as a matter of fact, you haven't. Not since about seven hours ago." She perked her nose and shot a quick kiss to his chin. "Get going, Mr. Scott."

"If you two would prefer, I could leave the room," Reynolds offered half mockingly.

Ted rose from the chair. "Sit still, old man, and when our intrepid secret agent returns tell him to sit tight until I return."

He had a snap in his step as he left the room and Reynolds thought it was the happiest he had seen Ted and Jil in several weeks.

Jil picked up the morning paper and poured herself another cup of tea.

Reynolds watched Ted walk around to the back of the house and approach the two remaining cars. Ted began to climb into his red Corvette.

"Hey," Reynolds called from the window, "no need to advertise to everybody that you're back in Washington. That thing sticks out like a sore thumb."

Ted looked up at him and thought for a moment. Reluctantly, he nodded in agreement and went to the rented Cutlas Supreme. As a precaution in the event it became necessary to leave the house quickly the keys remained in the vehicles at all times, even Ted's car which they seldom used and had only picked up from the garage upon returning from Paris.

Reynolds remained at the window and watched Ted drive away.

"Dick, look at this! Somebody found a journal written in German on the banks of a river not far from the other house. It must be Bauman's journal!"

Reynolds came over to the table and Jil pointed to a small item in a section under the heading *It Happens*.

NO BUCKS FOR BOOK

Two area youths, Donald Finley, 15, and Christopher MacDonald, 14, both of Alexandria, Va., found a handwritten diary in German earlier this week while on a fishing expedition that took them along the banks of Collier Stream. Convinced they had recovered a valuable book several hundred years old the boys took it to the police and asked for a reward. Amused police offers examined the diary and advised

the youths that it was in fact a personal recording
made by someone over the last few years. The boys
then tried unsuccessfully to sell the book to their local
library but were turned down again. Commenting on
the lack of interest adults showed in their find Finley
is quoted as saying: "I'll bet people would have been
interested if it was written by George Washington."

"It has to be the journal. The first safe house was only a
few miles from that stream. I'm going to Alexandria and
find those boys." Jil bolted from the table and headed
for the door.

"Jil, wait, I'm going with you," Reynolds yelled.

"No. Stay here and wait for Uri or in case we get a
phone call from Ted. I shouldn't be long." She paused
at the door and looked back at Reynolds, "I'll call you as
soon as I get it and then I'm calling Ted at The White
House. He could use it if President Chandler has any
reservations about the story." She thought for an instant
and added. "I'll call Ted *first*, then you. Bye!"

"But it's in German . . ." Reynolds voice followed her
and trailed off. Jil jogged around the house and came to
the Corvette. Both Ted and Uri had the other cars and
as much as she didn't like driving the Corvette, she slid
behind the wheel and drove off.

***

"Mr. President." Ted nodded and extended his hand.

"Ted, it's so good to see you after all this while.
David has kept me informed about your absence and I
must say we miss you around here. How's your mother
doing?"

For a moment Ted was caught off guard; then he
reacted quickly.

"Fine, sir. Just fine."

"Good, I'm glad to hear that. Now sit down both of

you and tell me what is so important that David asked me to clear my morning schedule to fit you two in."

The President came around from his desk in the Oval Office and led them to the comfortable couches that formed a pit for an informal atmosphere. He seated himself and relaxed in the deep cushions on the largest of the three sofas. Ted and David Holland each occupied a different couch. When they were all seated Holland began.

"Mr. President, I have reason to believe Susan Benedict was murdered."

***

Several miles away, as the mid-morning sun filtered through generously leafed trees, the black Mercedes began to move closer to the Corvette.

Jil Baker had called the police once she was in Alexandria and received the address of one of the boys who had found the journal. She stopped at a traffic light less than two blocks from the house she was looking for.

"Miss Baker?"

Jil turned to see a solidly built man wearing sun glasses standing alongside her car. "Yes?"

"I'm special agent Arnold Klein." He flashed credentials but retrieved them too quickly for her to recognize anything but the blur of a gold badge. "If you'll park your car around the corner we'd like to have a word with you."

"Is something wrong? Has something happened to Ted?" The concern in her voice was genuine.

"Not exactly." He smiled. "But the reason we want to talk to you concerns him."

Jil looked back and saw the black Mercedes limousine dwarfing the sportscar.

"Who else is with you?"

"Associate Director Mitchell, m'am."

***

Ted Scott was fidgeting on the couch. The President had looked at his watch twice in the last several minutes.

After David had unfolded his tale of being a cover for Elliott Benedict and Sharon Franklin's love affair, including her suggestions to do away with Susan and his own unwitting role in permitting someone to enter the compound and tinker with the speedboat, Ted told the President about Aaron Bauman's journal and the violent events that had taken place because of it.

The President seemed interested in the story but remained noncommittal. Ted noticed that he had hardly moved a muscle all the time he had been listening. Now Holland was talking again, rehashing details he had said previously. It sounded to Ted as if David were almost begging for some kind of support or reassurance from the President.

None came.

William Chandler rose from the couch and walked silently over to one of the massive windows as soon as Holland paused, apparently finished. He stood there looking out for a long time without saying anything.

Finally, without turning he addressed them.

"Thank you both for sharing your concerns with me. Now if you don't mind, gentlemen, I have a busy schedule I must resume."

The meeting was over. Ted waited an instant before moving, hoping silently that Chandler would add some words of encouragment. There were none.

The President moved away from the window and resumed his position behind his desk, immediately shuffling some papers and taking care not to look directly at Ted or David.

Ted rose first. He simply stood looking at the President, still hoping Chandler would say something else. Holland had also risen and gently touched Ted's arm and nodded his head toward the door.

The two of them walked silently down the white corridors of the Executive Mansion, each a prisoner of his own thoughts.

They exited the building and stood in the sunlight a few steps out of earshot of the Marine Corps guard.

"Did it do any good, David?"

"I don't know. He listened, but I don't know."

"Shouldn't we have asked him if he planned to do anything? Shouldn't we have asked him if he believed us?"

"It's all academic now, Ted. We didn't. He will do what he feels is necessary if he believed us."

"But that's not good enough! Suppose he didn't believe us, what then? Do we just sit by and do nothing?"

"Ted, I didn't know what to do last night when we spoke and now I'm not sure what we did was the right thing. Maybe . . . maybe I blew things out of proportion. It's possible Sharon's remarks and Susan's death were a coincidence. I hope I haven't made a serious mis . . ."

"Maybe? Maybe it was a coincidence? What about me and Jil and the things that have happened to us? No, David, it's not that easy to dismiss. You feel expunged now because you've had your little confession with the Great White Father but it's not that easy for me. I've been living a hell on earth these past months and it has been caused by one woman."

Holland looked at him and there was a challenge in his voice. "You had three suspects Ted, remember? Susan's dead but suppose Sharon isn't involved in this anymore than she was. That leaves Leona Crawford Gordon. Why aren't you considering her as a suspect in your gothic horror?"

"Because the circumstances just don't support it, that's why. Susan was an obvious suspect after we gathered some facts. Maybe too obvious. But now that all the cards are on the table and the race is nearing the finish line Sharon Franklin has played her hand.

"No David, Leona Gordon had nothing to gain by killing Susan Benedict. If she were the Phoenix she would have arranged an accident for Elliott Benedict and then hoped to win the election while the opposition party cut itself to pieces frantically looking for a stand-in candidate. She had nothing to gain but now she may turn out to be my strongest ally."

"What do you mean? You're not considering telling her about all this are you?"

"I am. If Chandler is going to sit on his hands and do nothing to stop Elliott and Sharon maybe there are some people on the Rutledge-Gordon ticket who will know what to do."

Ted turned on his heels and walked rapidly away from David. He never bothered to look back. When he got to his car he had already decided to go directly to Leona Gordon and tell her the whole story.

In the White House, President Chandler pushed a button on his phone console. "Get the Vice President on the phone as soon as possible. . . . I know he is mourning his wife, damn it, I said get him!"

***

Leona Crawford Gordon looked stunning in the high-necked, lightweight dress she wore, Ted thought. She was a remarkably beautiful woman who frequently underdressed in an attempt to turn attention away from her physical appearance and hold it instead by her brilliant mind. She was placing ice in her drink while she stood behind the built-in bar that fitted nicely into one corner of her spacious apartment. She had already prepared Ted's drink and was now returning to the comfortable armchair across from the leather rocker Ted was seated in.

"Forgive me for being so quiet, Ted. That is the most incredible story I've ever heard." She handed him his drink and gracefully seated herself. She touched an open hand to her chest. "Especially the part of me being a suspect too!"

Ted started to speak but she stopped him.

"Please, don't be offended. I'm not saying I don't believe you. After all you've told me that would mean I think you are either a crazy man or a pathetic liar. And neither is true.

"It's just . . . well, I'll say it again, incredible!" She shook her head in disbelief and continued.

"I think it is absolutely unforgivable that the FBI hardly lifted a finger to investigate these events with vigor."

"They did have Dick Reynolds and three other agents on it at different times, Leona . . ."

"Yes but be serious. That was Mitchell's way of handling a nuisance. He did it more out of regard for your friend Reynolds, I'm sure, than any real conviction that there was a real threat."

She rose from the chair and began pacing on the far side of the room.

"Ted, as much as I am convinced that you may have actually stumbled onto something involving subversive groups—quite possibly even the rebirth of Nazism—I simply don't know where to begin to make this information public. If anything about all this came out from our camp so close to the election, especially the part suggesting that Sharon Franklin is the power behind it all and tying her romantically with Elliott, I think we'd be laughed out of the country.

"However, I have some very good connections and I assure you what you've told me about Sharon and Elliott possibly having killed Susan will be followed up

. . . and quickly. If David Holland is correct and even a shred of evidence can be found to suggest that Susan's death was foul play, then believe me we'll make sure they pay for it."

She paused and sipped her drink. Then, looking at Ted over the rim of her glass, added:

"You must realize that if there is the slightest chance that Holland is wrong nothing will come of this. The ticket of Rutledge and Gordon may go down to inglorious defeat in this election but I intend to be back again and I'll do nothing that will in any way damage my chances. I'll not be made a laughing stock . . ."

"Leona, I don't know what else to say. I've told you the facts just the way they happened. I've told you what David said. What else can I offer? I know it all adds up to a wild story but those are the facts!" Ted had jumped to his feet.

She moved across the room closer to him and placed a gentle hand on his arm. "Okay, calm down, I believe you. Now we just have to uncover something concrete to convince others."

She slowly began moving Ted to the front door. "There's a lot to be done in a short time. I've got the address of the house you and the others are at but I do wish you remembered the phone number."

"I don't, I'm sorry. And it's unlisted, obviously."

"Then call me from there tonight. I have to have some quick way of reaching you. You know how to get through to me, I'm sure."

Ted nodded. They had reached the door. As Leona opened it she paused and looked directly into Ted's eyes.

"I guess you don't know this, but I was there also . . . at the first boat accident in Florida. I guess you could say I was a spy in the enemy camp.

"Now that I've told you that does it occur to you that Dr. Lupo could have gotten there with me?"

Ted was surprised at the admission but it changed nothing in his mind. "No, I didn't know but it means nothing. If I thought for a moment there was a chance you were the Phoenix I wouldn't have come to you."

She gave him a weak smile. "Well, if I were the Phoenix and responsible for even half of the things you've told me, you wouldn't be leaving here alive."

Ted sighed, "That's for sure."

As he walked down the hallway toward the elevator she called after him. "Remember, call me this evening."

***

The late afternoon drive back to the safe house was uneventful. In his mind Ted played back the two important conversations he had had this day. If the President failed to do anything at least he had made some headway with Leona. He was sure she would take positive action of some sort and one way or the other they would stop Sharon Franklin.

When he arrived at the house Reynolds and Uri were together in the living room. They had somber expressions on their faces.

"Where's Jil?" Ted asked.

Neither of them spoke as Ted crossed the room and headed for the kitchen. As he neared the door he stopped and turned to face them. "I said where's Jil?"

"We don't know, Ted." Reynolds offered. When she didn't get back in a reasonable amount of time I waited for Uri to return and we went looking around for her.

"The police in Alexandria told us she got an address from them—she found a lead about Bauman's journal in the morning paper—and we went there. She never got to the address."

Ted stood in the doorway in stunned silence. Then Uri added:

"She was driving your car. We found it parked a few blocks away from the house but there is no sign of her."

Chapter 23

Tuesday, October 30 (one week before the election)

"Congresswoman Gordon is here, Mr. President."

"Thank you, Wickes. Show her in but remember to bring me a message in fifteen minutes . . . you understand?"

"Certainly sir." Wickes smiled at the President and retreated to usher in Leona Gordon. Only a few seconds passed before he again opened the door to the private study as Leona swept by.

"Good evening, Leona." The President seemed unusually bright and bubbly considering the hour.

"Hello, Bill." She came up close to him and his nostrils filled with the pleasant aroma of her perfume. He leaned forward and planted a kiss on her cheek.

She gave him a weak smile and immediately began looking around at the various chairs in the room, seeking one that would be comfortable. She picked one that would be directly across from the chair she knew Chandler always sat in when he met with people in this masculine but casual room. They both sat and immediately Wickes came over and nodded.

"Leona, will you join me in a relaxing drink? Some bourbon and branchwater perhaps?"

"I'd prefer a little white wine."

"Then white wine it is." He turned to Wickes, "And you can refresh this while you're at it."

As Wickes again departed the President leaned forward and rested his elbows on his knees.

"What brings the first woman ever nominated for the vice presidency of the Republic to a meeting with the outgoing President of the opposition party exactly one week before the election?" He again smiled warmly and Leona could now tell that Chandler had apparently consumed a few drinks prior to her arrival, though he was not drunk.

"I've received some very disturbing information concerning Susan Benedict's death and though it may be hard to conceive, we must discuss it."

"Really? What sort of information? And why should we be discussing it?" Chandler pulled himself back and let his body sink into the generous tufting on the overstuffed chair.

"Bill, you had a meeting with David Holland and young Scott yesterday. I'm sure they told you the same incredible stories Ted later told me."

"Incredible is the right word."

"Those are my sentiments exactly. However, for some strange reason—and don't ask me why—I couldn't help but believe that there was a ring of truth in it all. Didn't you believe them, Bill?"

Wickes entered the study with a silver tray. He gave Leona a large crystal wine glass that had been lightly chilled. She quickly took a sip while he handed the President the bourbon.

Once Wickes had left the room Chandler answered her.

"I'm not quite sure what to make of it, Leona. I mean, I have nothing but the highest regard for David . . . and Scott always struck me as an intelligent, able man . . .

but all that hokum about Hitler having a daughter who is trying to take over our country, I mean . . ."

"Bill forget that part completely if you wish but concentrate on the murder." She paused to let her words sink in.

"Sharon and Elliott killed Susan, I'm sure of it now."

"What do you mean you're sure, Leona?"

"Just that. After Ted left me yesterday I had some people do a little digging. Oh, the lovers made an effort to cover their trail but there is enough evidence to raise a serious question about the accident."

Chandler was pensive. "What kind of evidence?"

Leona took a large gulp and finished off her wine. She placed the glass on the handsomely carved end table next to her chair.

"The Secret Service agent who let the boat shop van in and the agent who watched it stop near the dock while the man worked on the boat both remember and describe the van as a white Dodge with blue lettering "Este Marine Basin" on its side.

"Bill, there is no Este Marine, Este Marine Basin, or Este anything else listed in the local phone book. In addition, none of the area people with boats that were asked ever heard of Este Marine."

"Maybe it came from a neighboring community," Chandler offered.

"My people spoke with the local marina and boat shop, incidently it is McIntyre's Boat Works, and they never heard of Este. There simply isn't a business in the area with that name."

Chandler reflected for a moment, "I'm sure that is the name David mentioned to me also when he related the story."

"It is, and Scott used it when he told me about Holland's conversation with Sharon. Look at the implication.

"Sharon calls David and says she wants to get onto the compound to see Elliott . . . privately, no one is to know. She even tells Holland not to mention this to Elliott, that way Elliott can honestly say he wasn't aware of the planned visit or anybody playing with the boat. She tells David she will be with a boatman from Este Marine Basin. Loyal David alerts the Secret Service to let the vehicle onto the grounds. A few hours later Susan is dead."

The President took a sip of his drink, emptying it. Instead of putting the glass down he continued to hold it and moved his wrist in a slight back-and-forth motion, causing the ice cubes to rotate and chatter in the glass. His brow was wrinkled and Leona patiently waited while he thought. Finally he looked up at her.

"That's still mighty slim evidence for a charge of murder."

"There's more, Bill. Do you want me to get the county coroner's sworn statement that the impact that killed Susan struck her from the front? If the engine exploded, which is what the official report says, the impact would have been to her back."

"Was there any trace of foreign matter, anything that could positively be said to have caused the explosion? Something, oh, I don't know, an explosive of some sort, dynamite or whatever?"

"They're checking for that now. My people tell me Elliott almost went into rage when he heard that the county coroner was doing an autopsy. He had it stopped."

"Whaaat???"

"That's right, he had it stopped. The Vice President had the Secret Service remove the body and fly it back to Washington within minutes after she was pronounced dead."

Chandler was shaken. "I didn't know that. I thought . . . . wait a minute. I *saw* the news of her body, her coffin, being loaded onto the plane and Elliott standing solemnly by. That was Monday morning."

"It was an empty box. By the time you and millions of people saw that scene Susan's body had already been delivered to a funeral director Elliott had personally chosen the night before, only an hour after the accident." Leona got out of the chair and walked over to the high sash window that overlooked the rear White House lawn. She gazed out of it for a brief period, then continued.

"By now they've had all the opportunity they need to prepare the body any way they want but I have someone who will let me know if the slightest irregularity is found."

"The funeral is tomorrow morning," Chandler added.

Leona spun from the window and faced him. "And the election is one week away. Are you going to continue to sit here and drink bourbon while the man who everybody believes will succeed you gets away with murder? Is that the kind of man who should live in this house and lead our country."

Chandler looked directly into her eyes. He looked much more tired now than when she had entered the room several minutes ago.

There was a soft knock on the door, followed by the entrance of Wickes carrying a folded piece of paper, as ordered.

"Not now, please, leave us. I don't want to be disturbed."

As quickly as he entered Wickes was gone. Chandler again turned his attention to Leona. His voice was almost pleading: "What can I possibly do?"

She walked back from the window and stood behind her chair.

"You have to confront Elliott with what you suspect

and then gauge his reaction. I'll arrange for an interview with Sharon and do the same."

Wednesday, October 31

Ted had been out of the house all day trying to locate some clue that would lead him to Jil. Dick Reynolds, who had been with him most of the time, was now driving back to the safe house. It was late afternoon and the sun was casting a red and gold tint along the tops of the trees. Reynolds was still thinking about the several dead-end leads he and Ted had followed that day when he suddenly became aware of the news on the car's radio.

". . . was laid to rest today less than one week before her husband faces the nation in the Presidential election. Immediately after the services the Vice President and the President were seen huddling and according to informed White House sources they held an extraordinary one-hour meeting at the Executive Mansion before Benedict left Washington for seclusion.

"Just a half hour ago the White House confirmed what everyone had suspected: Elliott Benedict would do no further campaigning before election day. This announcement comes on the heels of news that Virgil Rutledge and Leona Crawford Gordon have also suspended their campaigns in respect for the Vice President's wife.

"In local news, the body of an attractive young woman identified as Jil Baker was taken out of the Tidal Basin near the Jefferson Memorial earlier today. The victim had apparently been beaten and raped. Police declined to say whether they had any suspects in the crime.

"Some good news for Washington Senator fans in a moment, but first this word about. . . ."

Dick Reynolds pressed his foot to the floor harder

than he realized. The car fishtailed slightly as it screeched to a halt.

There had to be a mistake, he thought. Not Jil. It couldn't be Jil. He could feel tears swell in his eyes and his facial muscles were twitching as he fought back the emotion that was overpowering him.

He sat there on the side of the road for several minutes, tears rushing down his cheeks, telling himself it was a mistake.

Then he remembered walking away from his front door and hearing the explosion. . . . he was running around the side of his house. . . . the bent and twisted remains of his car and his neighbor's son were scattered in his driveway. It wasn't a mistake.

He saw Mrs. Flynn sitting by her bedroom window and giving him a friendly wave each morning. And then hearing the news that she was found dead at the bottom of the stairs. It wasn't a mistake.

He saw Ari toppling backwards down the steps of the boat, a bullethole in his forehead. It wasn't a mistake.

***

The Assistant Coroner's heel's clicked as he led Ted down the dimly lit passageway to the morgue. As he fumbled with the keys so they could enter the refrigerated room with its several rows of two-foot-square drawers, Ted could again feel the pain in his chest and felt a slight trembling sensation.

As they entered the room the man switched on a light and the extreme brightness made them both move to cover their eyes briefly. Ted stood at the doorway while the man moved along the rows of drawers, finally stopping and confirming the name on the insert tab with the paper in his hand.

He turned to Ted with a look of near-satisfaction on his face. "Mr. Scott?" He pulled the drawer open with one hand and the slab responded with a muffled sound as it glided over the ball bearings.

Ted slowly made his way forward. He couldn't take his eyes off the prostrate figure outlined under the white sheet. The man quickly checked the tag hanging from the large toe on the right foot and again had a look of accomplishment on his face. But Ted didn't see it. His eyes were locked on the figure before him.

He stood directly across from the man, close to the side of the slab. Ted let his fingertips touch the cold, shinny steel ridge and a chill vibrated through his body.

The man reached for the sheet to uncover the face for identification.

"Wait! Not yet, please give me a few seconds." Ted tried to calm his body. He shut his eyes tightly and sucked in two deep breaths. Simultaneously he could feel tears building up in his eyes. The cold steel of the slab was creating a tingling sensation in his fingers but he did not remove them.

He slowly nodded and mouthed "Okay" but no words came out.

The man again reached for the top of the sheet and in a gentle but swift move pulled it away, revealing the battered and swollen face.

Ted was unable to move. He stood immobile, staring down at the figure before him.

***

"Congresswoman Gordon, it's a pleasure to see you." Sharon Franklin extended her hand as Leona crossed the deep-ply carpeting in Sharon's Washington office.

The room was decorated in rich earth tones and seemed more masculine than feminine. Large French windows looked out over Pennsylvania Avenue and the floodlit Washington Monument towered over the skyline some distance away.

"It was good of you to see me this evening, Miss Franklin."

"Please be seated." Sharon indicated a comfortable chair directly across from her desk and added, ". . . and do call me Sharon. 'Miss Franklin' sounds so formal."

"As you wish . . . Sharon." Leona didn't reciprocate and suggest a similar informality, something Sharon immediately noticed.

Sharon reclined slightly and locked her eyes on Leona's. "Exactly what is it I can do for you? I'm sorry I had to say no to your suggestion for an interview, but with the tragedy this weekend the network has decided to honor the wishes of the Vice President—and, I might add, your ticket—and refrain from broadcasting anything that even hints at campaigning."

"I understand exactly. My request for an interview was out of order and I apologize."

Sharon opened a gold-leafed box on the desk and removed a cigarette. "Then what is it?" She was feeling uncomfortable under the penetrating stare Leona had fixed on her since entering the room.

Leona let a slight smile curl the corners of her lips. "I want to talk about your cancelled plans to visit the Vice President's compound in a white van marked with the phoney name 'Este Marine Basin.' That's what this is all about."

The cigarette fell from Sharon's lips as her mouth snapped open. "How could you . . . what are you talking about? What is that supposed to mean?" There was a fire in her eyes as she lurched forward in her chair and slammed her hands down flat on the desk top.

Leona remained calm but the smile was now a bit larger. "You should be careful with cigarettes. They can cause fires."

"The hell with the cigarette! What did you mean . . .

what was that nonsense about me trying to visit the compound?"

"Exactly what I said. David Holland says you called him . . ."

"David Holland is a twerp! He doesn't know what he is talking about. Furthermore he is a liar. I was in a private meeting with the network brass when he got that call."

"I didn't say *when* he got a call, Sharon. My, my, that was a careless mistake."

Blood rushed into Sharon's face as the full impact of her slip registered. She rose from her chair and Leona did likewise.

"Look, you bitch, get out of here! Don't come to my office with trumped up charges and try to save your own ass in this election by smearing the Vice President . . ."

"Wait just one minute, madam." Now Leona was angry and she was no better at containing it than Sharon. "I came here to talk to you about suspicions and rumor, not charges, but you seem to have confirmed them through your own stupidity." Leona swung around and headed for the door. She pulled it open with force and turned to yell back one final outburst at Sharon.

"I'm not through with you, darling, not yet. Before this week is up you'll have a chance to tell the American public why it was so important for you to lie about seeing the Vice President on the same weekend his wife was murdered. You'll have a chance to explain that David Holland couldn't have received a call from you because you were in a meeting.

"And then we'll hear from Holland and Secretary of State Chester Manning who has been your 'official' escort while you and Elliott Benedict were lovers. And one more thing. There is a Secret Service agent who has a remarkable memory about dates and places where you lovers had rendezvous. He'll have quite a bit to say also."

She slammed the door and stormed through the executive offices. By the time she reached the ground floor the two men in the black Mercedes had turned off the recording device and waited for her to emerge from the front of the building.

Upstairs in her office, Sharon Franklin frantically dialed a private phone number.

"Hello? It's me. We have a serious problem."

Thursday, November 1

"I wish Uri hadn't gone back to Israel," Reynolds said as he finished washing out the dishes from the light breakfast he just had. He looked into the living room but there was no reaction from Ted, who was sitting before the television—galvanized—as the cheery faces on *Good Morning America* told citizens throughout the land of the world news. But Ted was unaware of their presence. He seemed comatose since the shock of Jil's death had sunk in last evening. He had returned to the safe house from the morgue and after briefly telling Dick that he had identified the body, Ted had lapsed into silence.

The phone rang. It was less than three feet away from Ted but he ignored it. Dick grabbed a dish towel and rapidly wiped his hands as he went over and picked it up.

"Hello? Uri?" Reynolds wanted it to be him.

"No . . . this is Leona Gordon. Whom am I speaking to?"

"Oh, Congresswoman Gordon, good morning. I'm Dick Reynolds, a friend . . ."

"Oh yes, the F.B.I. man. Is Ted there?"

"Yes he is, just a few feet away from me in fact. I'll

put him on." Reynolds covered the mouthpiece with his left hand and leaned toward Scott.

"Teddy, it's your new lady-friend from The Hill." He held his arms out, extending the phone to Ted.

Ted didn't bother to face Reynolds as he spoke. "I don't want to talk to anybody."

"C'mon, it could be something important!"

"Nothing is important anymore. Jil is dead. I don't give a shit about Gordon, Benedict, Franklin, Chandler, any of them. Leave me alone." He spoke in a monotone that sounded artificial.

Reynolds thought for an instant and finally removed his hand from the mouthpiece. He picked up the phone's cradle and took advantage of the long extension cord by walking back into the kitchen with it.

"Congresswoman . . . I'm afraid Ted is in no shape to come to the phone yet. He took Jil's death pretty hard."

"What?" There was surprise in Leona's voice.

"The police fished her body out of the Tidal Basin yesterday and Ted went down to the morgue last night to identify it."

"Oh my God. I didn't know. I simply ignored the local news in the papers this morning and last night I was so busy I missed the evening news. Oh, this is dreadful."

"Yea, he's really down. They were very much in love."

"I'm so sorry. I didn't know the girl but I gathered that, from what Ted told me. This whole thing began when someone tried to kill her in their apartment, didn't it?"

"Yes. That almost seems like a lifetime ago now." There was an awkward silence that was broken when Reynolds asked. "Is there something I can help you with?"

"Thank you. I just wanted to alert Ted that I paid a

visit to Miss Television America last evening and confronted her with the facts we had discussed."

"You took quite a chance, Congresswoman. Those people play for keeps."

"Don't forget, Mr. Reynolds, I now have Secret Service protection. Two agents waited outside her office all the time I was with her."

"What did she say? How did she react?"

"She crumbled totally. I was amazed at how easily she lost her composure. There is no doubt in my mind now that Sharon Franklin did exactly what David Holland suggested and murdered Susan Benedict."

"That's great, now we can go to the police and . . ."

"No! Not the police. I have an appointment with the President in less than an hour. I spoke with him last evening after seeing Sharon and as you would expect he was quite disturbed. He had a long meeting with Elliott yesterday after the funeral and I gather from our conversation last night the President satisfied his own doubts as a result of it."

"What will he do? Is he going to help?"

"He can help us by doing nothing."

"What do you mean? We need him to make a statement or have the attorney general . . ."

"Listen to me, please. William Chandler can be the greatest help in pointing a finger by being absolutely silent. When I see him I'm going to tell him I've already begun having some details of Susan's death leaked to the press—naturally they won't be traced back to me or my people, but they will come from very good sources—the media will *have* to follow up and before nightfall the bombshell will drop. All Chandler has to do is take a 'no comment' position. Once he does that everything else will fall into place."

Reynolds was quiet for a few seconds, then excitedly said, "That'll do it! If the President of The United

States fails to publicly come out and say he is standing behind his Vice President the press will have a field day."

"Exactly what I'm counting on. Elliott will probably not make any statement one way or another—because he is in mourning—but I think Sharon will be quite vocal. If she says *one* word about this we can then turn the media loose on Chester Manning, David Holland and a Secret Service agent named Brock. What he knows is enough to establish the long romantic link and further create the cloud about Susan's death."

Reynolds was excited and turned toward the living room to tell Ted what was happening.

Ted was no longer in the room.

"Excuse me, Congresswoman, I think Ted just slipped out of the house. I want to find him and let him know what you've just told me. Thank you very much for what you've done. I think we are finally doing something to stop her."

"No thanks necessary, Mr. Reynolds. Now go find Ted. . . . Oh, there is one more thing."

Reynolds had taken the phone away from his ear and faintly heard her still talking. He impatiently listened again.

"The doctor Ted spoke about, the one who was in the SS, Lupo?"

"Yes, Harold Lupo, formerly Standartenfuehrer Helmut Wolf, what about him?"

"The reason you've been unable to locate him is because he isn't licensed to practice in this country. He is calling himself a PhD, not a medical doctor."

"We never thought of that. We searched the medical directories for him but came up with zeros."

"Well, if you want him try the Institute for Social Behavior on Connecticut Avenue. I believe it is the same man."

***

"I want to talk to the police officer in charge of the Baker case." Ted stood before the high bench in the precinct and spoke to a middle-aged sergeant.

"The what case?" The officer looked at him without any hint of what Ted was talking about.

"Baker . . . the girl, woman, who's body was removed from the Tidal Basin yesterday. I want to talk to the officers who are working on that case."

The sergeant looked Ted over and slowly stood up. "Are you a relative or are you here to confess?" He made a slight motion with his hand and another officer standing alongside the bench slowly moved a bit closer to Ted.

"A relative, sort of . . . we were going to be married." Ted was aware that the other officer had moved closer but this didn't disturb him.

"What's your name, buddy?"

"Ted Scott." At once Ted realized the tone of the sergeant's voice was official rather than helpful. He added, "I work at The White House." He still had his credentials to prove it.

The sergeant looked to the other officer and for a moment they were caught off guard.

"What do you do at The White House, Mr. Scott?"

"I'm on the President's press staff. I work for David Holland, the press secretary and communications director."

Again the two police officers looked at one another. The man standing next to Ted shrugged his shoulders. Ted produced his White House credentials and after briefly inspecting them the police officer passed them to the sergeant who also gave them a fast look.

"What exactly is it you want to talk about concerning that murder, Mr. Scott?"

"I know who did it and I want to see them caught."

The sergeant pushed a buzzer and continued to size up Ted.

"Detective Boyle will be out here in a moment. You'll be going into that room over there to give him a statement. If he feels it is important enough we'll have a stenographer join you and you can do it over again. Now why don't you take a seat along the wall. Boyle will be with you in a few minutes. Officer Drekel will stay with you until he arrives."

***

"Good afternoon. Your name please?" The receptionist struck Dick as being almost as antiseptic as the outer office. A gray fabric wall covering closed the small area in totally and made it seem very confining. It was also on the ceiling, which included a large triangular florescent light fixture. Besides the receptionist's desk there were only two hard-back chairs for patients or guests. A modern realistic painting was the only decoration on the otherwise bare walls and it was directly across from the room's only window.

"Reynolds, Richard Reynolds, Special Agent, the Federal Bureau of Investigation."

The receptionist was not impressed. Her plastic smile remained fixed. "Do you have an appointment, Mr. Reynolds?"

"Is Dr. Lupo in?" He ignored her question.

"Yes, he is, but unless you have an ap. . . . wait one moment! You can't go in there."

Dick had walked past her and to the door that obviously led to Lupo's inner office. He grabbed the doornob and pushed the door open with force. The receptionist frantically followed him.

"Doctor, I'm sorry, this man just . . ."

"That's all right, Miss Warwick. I understand. You can leave us now."

Reynolds stood approximately five feet in front of the

desk that Lupo was behind. The door behind Dick closed and he and Lupo were alone in the room.

Dick looked around at the furnishings. In contrast to the outer office this room was lavishly decorated. Several signed lithographs were clustered at various points on the walls. The carpet was much deeper than anything Dick had been on in recent memory. The desk Lupo was behind was a beautifully, hand-carved wooden antique. Overall the room signified power and success.

"What can I do for you, Mr. Reynolds?" As he spoke Lupo opened the top drawer of his desk and produced a gun which he was now aiming directly at Dick. "These walls are soundproof, I assure you. If you do anything foolish not even Miss Warwick will hear the shots."

Dick hadn't expected the suddenness of the confrontation and he cursed himself for not having drawn his own gun as he entered. He looked directly at Lupo and clenched his teeth.

"I'm impressed that you were prepared for my visit, Doctor."

"One must always be prepared. But I'll admit I had a warning that you might come snooping around. I've been trying to locate you and your friends for some time when all the while we should have simply let you find us. It would have been so much easier and less messy that way."

"You murdering bastard! Messy? Is that how you describe killing so many people?" Dick took a step forward but Lupo cocked the hammer of the gun.

"Easy, Mr. Reynolds, or your visit will have been in vain."

Dick controlled the urge to lunge for Lupo. He knew he would be dead if he did. "What is that supposed to mean?"

"Well, I just thought you were coming here to get the 'truth' from me. Any good police officer would want to get a confession from his suspect . . . even if he knew he wouldn't live to make use of it. And, Mr. Reynolds, you will not live to use it. That is a promise.

"So, FBI man, ask your questions. I'm your witness!" Lupo let himself grin broadly while all the time keeping his gun on Dick. "I'd ask you to take a seat but frankly I prefer having you standing right where you are. It will afford me a cleaner shot, you understand."

Dick seethed inside. Lupo was enjoying the game he was playing. At least I'm buying time, Dick thought, and maybe I can rattle him enough to do something careless. He decided to accommodate Lupo.

"Alright, Standartenfuehrer, we'll go to the beginning . . ."

"Please, Mr. Reynolds. I haven't used that rank in years. I am now Dr. Harold Lupo, not Helmut Wolf."

"Call yourself what you like, you scum. You're still the butcher who ordered your loyal SS troops slaughtered on the quay at St. Nazaire the night you brought Hitler's mistress to that U-boat and then murdered her in that Boston fire. You've had people killed over the years, I'm sure, but the ones I know about these past several months are the ones that interest me."

"Let's back up a bit, shall we?" Lupo interrupted. "First off I'm going to tell you something no other living person in the world knows. It is something I have wanted to tell somebody for years, especially this year with our dream actually happening, but I couldn't, and you can understand why for obvious reasons."

"What's your 'big' secret . . . Hitler was really a nice guy?"

"Don't be flip with me Mr. Reynolds, I'm not impressed with your cleverness. . . ."

"I thought we kept you at bay for quite a while. I mean, Nazi supermen and all that, yet you couldn't manage to corner a handful of civilians. How do you expect to deal with the rest of the world if your plans actually come off?" Dick was frantically trying to keep Lupo busy while his mind raced for some way out of this predicament.

"We won't have to lift a finger. As I noted earlier, you came. So did your Miss Baker . . ."

"Jil?" Reynolds could feel the anger swell inside him and again he had to restrain himself from lunging at Lupo. "What do you mean she came also?"

Lupo smiled. He was obviously enjoying this very much. "Let me use an American expression I'm becoming quite fond of: we chased you until you caught us. You and your friends did remarkably well managing to keep just enough ahead of us to remain alive.

"Then we did the obvious. We let you find us! First the Baker girl responded beautifully to the newspaper story about the boys finding the journal . . ."

"You mean that was a fake, you arranged it?"

"Naturally. And it worked perfectly."

"Then you have the journal."

"No, unfortunately." Lupo became sullen. "But we are also sure that you don't have it either. It will turn up." He ran the back of his hand across his chin. He was getting nervous.

"So what's the secret you were going to tell me, Doctor. I'm waiting."

Lupo looked at him coldly. There was a long silence but finally he spoke.

"Hitler never knew he had fathered this child. I kept it from him. She was to be my passport to freedom. I arranged the entire journey right under his nose and he never knew. It was easy, actually. Everyone of importance was familiar with the regularity of my visits and requests that would sometimes be the result of those visits.

"When I discovered that the woman was pregnant

during a routine checkup I decided to keep that information to myself. The end for National Socialism as we knew it in Germany was at hand. It was time to plan for its rebirth elsewhere.

"This child, fathered by Adolf Hitler, would be my means of escape and the genesis of the rebuilding of a new Nazi party.

"Mr. Reynolds, that has all come to pass. I've built the Organization and because I had been 'chosen' to raise Hitler's daughter I have had the position of leadership and power to pull together all the splinter groups that dream of the day Nazism will again rise. We now have more power, more authority in world capitals than the Third Reich ever had! And soon the Phoenix will be in the center of power, in the White House."

"Why did you have to do this without Hitler knowing it?"

"It wasn't a matter of him knowing or not. He was too busy, too occupied with trying to run the war to be bothered by this. He never would have approved of such progressive thinking. For him the war was not lost until that very last day. For anyone to suggest leaving to lay the groundwork for the future would have been treason. Not until he himself began to tell people they should leave was I able to arrange for the departure. There was chaos in the bunker.

"He ordered me to leave and unlike many others who foolishly stayed to die there with him I followed his orders. I asked him for a safe conduct letter in order to get through our own lines. They were shooting deserters on the spot, it made no difference what your rank was . . . even generals weren't immune, unless you had the personal authority of Hitler.

"I simply put other papers I had prepared with the letter and kept talking to him. He signed them all without reading any. He just kept nodding his head as I spoke."

"Tell me something, Lupo. Did Hitler have any other children? Bauman seemed to think he did. Was the Phoenix the only one?"

Lupo's eyes narrowed and he looked menacingly at Reynolds. "The Phoenix is the rightful heir to the Fuehrer, no one else! There were stories about other children, a boy and a girl . . . some say two boys and a girl, but I knew nothing about this. I only know the Phoenix is his daughter and I managed to get her out of Europe before the end."

"And you killed her mother in a Boston fire."

"The woman was nothing to me. The child was important. It was a marvelously simple plan that worked without the slightest flaw because of its boldness."

"You missed one thing, Lupo. The ambulance driver and the man on the quay who saw the slaughter."

"They were nobodys. Who would believe them? Europe and the rest of the world were full of rumors that Hitler had escaped, Bormann was at large, others had gotten away. Those kind of stories were part of the hysteria. No one would have believed them."

"No one except Aaron Bauman."

"That lousy Jew and his wild guesses . . ."

"They weren't too wild Lupo. I'm here."

"Yes, but you'll never live to tell about it."

"But Ted Scott will. He has already told the President and Congresswoman Gordon, plus David Holland and Associate Director Mitchell all know . . ."

"Nothing!" Lupo shouted. "They all know nothing except the stories you and Scott have told them. Mr. Scott will be joining you in the grave very shortly also. The others will not dare to challenge the Phoenix. It will all end with your deaths."

Lupo's eyes seemed distant for an instant as he lost

himself in reverie. Reynolds seized the moment and threw himself to the floor, rolling quickly to the front of the desk. He grabbed the base of the full front panel and with all of his strength lifted it causing it to topple onto Lupo.

A shot rang out. Reynolds lunged to the right side of the desk and lifted the corner, again forcing the heavy wooden antique to come crashing down on Lupo, who was trapped behind it against the wall.

"You bastard!" Lupo screamed. He caught a glimpse of Reynolds' torso and squeezed off two rapid shots just as the heavy brass floor lamp that had been alongside the desk on the left side struck him with the force of an axe.

Lupo tried to let out a scream as the crystal globe from atop the lamp shattered against the side of his head, a jaggered, sharp piece slicing through an artery in his neck.

Reynolds' eyes were getting foggy as he looked at the two large patches of blood spreading across the front of his shirt and jacket. There was a strange throbbing pain moving through his body but instead of increasing it hurt less with each pump of his heart.

The ornate, gold-topped cane Lupo had depended on throughout life was several inches ahead of Dick on the floor. He managed to prop himself up on one elbow and move closer to it. With some effort he lifted it. There was a gurgling sound in his chest and he could taste the warm, sticky feeling of blood in his mouth.

With the cane as a weapon he tried to focus his eyes on Lupo and crawl toward him but he couldn't muster the strength. His legs and lower body did not respond. He dragged himself another few inches and now he could see around the corner of the overturned desk.

Lupo's eyes were staring at the ceiling and his mouth hung open, frozen in anger. There was a slight twitch in his pinky finger but otherwise there was no sign of life. Blood from the savage cut in his neck was now trickling out yet high splash marks on the wall indicated it had only pumped out furiously seconds before.

Reynolds felt his hand slipping down the polished shaft of the cane and the carpet rising to meet his face rapidly. He was happy that he felt no pain as his head struck the covered floor. There was another, violent gurgle in his chest and all at once he felt a coldness rise from his body into his neck. The cold was more than a chill, it was all encompassing and it rose past his lips, nose and ears.

Now he could feel it in the back of his head as it came around over the top. Funny, he thought, my eyes don't feel it. There was a loud hum in his head and it grew in intensity. Now the cold was rushing into his eyes. Dick tried to move his lips but it was the last function his brain ever had.

There was a soft rap on the office door. After a brief pause Miss Warwick entered. She immediately saw Reynolds and the crimson stain his blood created as life ebbed from him.

"Dr. Lupo!" She looked around the room before moving closer to the desk. As she did she saw one of Lupo's legs motionless on the floor and partially under the desk. Without going any closer she retreated to the outer office and closed the door.

She lifted the phone off the cradle and quickly dialed a number she knew by memory. She recognized the voice on the other end and was relieved it was she who answered.

"It's over. Reynolds is dead . . . but I have some bad news."

"What bad news?"

"He somehow managed to kill the Doctor also.".

Miss Warwick had to hold the phone away from her ear as the anguished cry of the Phoenix came over the line.

***

President Chandler walked briskly across The White House lawn to the helicopter pad where Marine One waited to take him to Camp David for the long weekend. The sun was hanging lazily to the west of the Washington Monument and in several minutes would be setting.

"Mr. President, Mr. President!"

William Chandler turned to see a familiar White House reporter trotting toward him. "No questions, Skip. Wait until I get back Sunday night."

"But sir, something urgent just came over the AP wire. Secret Service agent Brock Davis reportedly just told the *Washington Post* that Mrs. Benedict's death may have been murder. He also says he personally knows about several clandestine affairs the Vice President had with Sharon Franklin. Do you have any comment, sir?"

William Chandler looked at the reporter and then around at the shocked reactions on the faces of those traveling with him. He let out an audible sigh of relief but quickly regained his composure.

"I have no comment." He replied bruskly, then added. "Off the record, see Dave Holland and he'll give you a private number where you can reach the Vice President." The President turned and continued walking toward Marine One.

The others, including the reporter, just stood there in dumbfounded silence.

Friday, November 2

"You see, captain, Mr. Scott has been under great strain for some time now," Holland was telling the precinct commander. "That's why we placed him on permanent leave from his duties at The White House. I'm sure he and Agent Brock Davis had discussed what was going on between the Vice President and Miss Franklin and then when Mr. Scott learned of the horrible murder of Miss Baker his mind snapped." Holland was very convincing, using every trick he knew of persuasion.

"I'll have to grant you that, Mr. Holland. He certainly told us one tall tale about Nazis, Hitler having a child, other murders here in the Caribbean and France. I got to tell you he is one sick man."

"Yes, and I'm sorry he managed to create such a ruckus here for you. We've had him under treatment. Quietly of course."

"Of course." The captain was eager to agree with Holland. You could never tell when such an important contact could be useful.

". . . But he gave us the slip. Thank you again for calling me directly."

"Well, we weren't. After he acted up and began raving about Nazi plots to kill him and somebody called the Phoenix we just kept him isolated and under surveillance. I was planning to call for a medical opinion and have him committed . . . then we heard the news on TV about the Vice President and that newswoman and the Secret Service guy saying somebody should look into the possibility that Mrs. Benedict was murdered."

Holland permitted a quiet chuckle, "I assure you that's more nonsense. Naturally the proper authorities are checking every possible clue but it is extremely unlikely that anything will be found to substantiate such a preposterous charge.

"Frankly, I'm told Agent Davis is a bit of a womanizer himself and he was afraid Miss Franklin had told the Vice President that he tried to force his advances on her more than once. He must have concluded that his career with the Service was finished should Elliott Benedict win and this was his way of trying to discredit any such effort."

"But confidentially, Mr. Holland, was anything going on between them . . . I mean Benedict and the woman?" There was a trace of lechery in captain's voice and Holland knew he had passed the critical point.

"Captain!" He responded in mock horror, "A gentleman doesn't discuss such things . . . especially about his employer. Let's just say the Vice President has an extremely active libido."

The captain let out a raucous belly laugh and Holland awkwardly tried to immitate it. It lasted several uncomfortable seconds. Then Holland gave the captain a sympathetic look.

"I would like to take Mr. Scott home now, captain. And I trust we won't be reading about this unfortunate incident in the papers?"

"Certainly, Mr. Holland, he's in your care and don't you worry one bit about anything leaking out of here. We understand the sensitive nature of these things. Hell, we pick up senators and congressmen drunk or in the wrong place at the right time on a regular basis . . . but it goes no further then here."

Saturday, November 3

". . . And now stay tuned for the award-winning *Washington Report*, America's most comprehensive television network news program originating in the nation's capital. Tonight the news will be brought to you by Dwight Sandler, substituting for Sharon Franklin. Ladies and gentlemen, Dwight Sandler."

"Good evening. The story that has held the attention of the nation and began last weekend with the tragic death of Susan Benedict has taken yet another unusual turn today.

"Secret Service Agent Brock Davis, the man who on Thursday made the startling announcement that the Vice President of The United States and this network's top-rated broadcast anchorwoman, Sharon Franklin, had been lovers for more than three years, died today of what police are calling a 'self-inflicted' gunshot wound.

"Davis, who was separated from his wife of nine years and living in a furnished apartment on E Street, apparently left a note that informed sources say denies his earlier claim that Elliott Benedict and Sharon Franklin had any involvment in Mrs. Benedict's murder.

"The source also says that the note, which is reported to be several pages long, does, however, continue to maintain that the pair were lovers. A spokesman for the district attorney's office earlier this evening issued a statement saying the full text of the note would be made public as soon as the authorities were satisfied that no foul play was involved in Davis' death.

"Meanwhile, federal investigators who had begun an immediate inquiry into Mrs. Benedict's death today released a preliminary finding that they say, and I'm quoting, 'unequivocably rules out any possibility of murder in her death.' The investigators say their findings substantiate the initial report attributing the cause of death to a fuel tank explosion aboard the speedboat she was driving. They point out, however, that a second series of tests are being conducted simply to confirm both of the earlier reports.

"The Vice President has continued to be unavailable for comment, having gone into seclusion immediately after having a private meeting with President Chandler after Mrs. Benedict's funeral.

"Meanwhile, the management of this network has repeatedly tried to reach Miss Franklin for her answer to the charges that she and Mr. Benedict had been intimate over an extended period of time. At this hour we regret to say we have still been unable to elicit a response from her.

"In a related development, the Associated Press reports that there is a move underway among a small group of congressmen to introduce legislation Monday morning that would postpone the Presidential election for ninety days. One supporter of the move is Rep. Edward LeClerc of New Jersey who has also publicly called for Elliott Benedict to resign from his party's ticket.

"Such legislation would have to pass both houses as the first order of business Monday morning and immediately be sent to President Chandler for his signature.

"According to Administration spokesmen, passage is unlikely and even if it succeeded insiders believe President Chandler would veto it.

"So as the strangest election in U.S. history nears, Americans across the country find themselves perplexed and confused: first by sympathy for the Vice President and the terrible tragedy he suffered last weekend and second by the persistent rumor neither he nor Sharon Franklin has yet denied—that they had been lovers and that the image of the Vice President and his lovely wife as the modern-day heirs to Camelot was nothing more than a myth."

Sunday, November 4

Ellen Holland slowly opened the door to the guest bedroom and looked in on Ted. He immediately opened his eyes and gave her a weak smile.

"Hi, Ellen."

Her eyes brightened and she could hardly conceal her delight. "Hello, Ted. How do you feel?" She said something to the man who had been stationed outside the room by her husband and quickly closed the door behind her as she entered.

"Still a little groggy, but otherwise okay, I guess."

"You should be groggy," she admonished, "After David brought you here Thursday night you became difficult for a while . . . yelling and cursing about killing people. Tish, tish, I'm surprised at the language I heard from your mouth. We had to call Dr. Friberg to give you a sedative."

"I'm sorry . . ."

"Then again yesterday, after you heard the news . . . you were almost violent with David. It's a good thing I was a nurse and Dr. Friberg left that injection. I don't think we could have contained you otherwise.

"I really am sorry. I've been acting like a fool. Where's David?"

"Downstairs on the phone. I'll have him come up."

"No don't bother. I could use a little exercise, I'll just go down to him."

"No funny business?"

"I don't have the strength even if I had the inclination.'

***

Ted found David sitting on a couch in the spacious living room. He had a grim expression on his face as he listened to Elliott Benedict's campaign manager explain that both the Harris and Gallup polls were now calling the election a tossup. Ted lowered himself into an overstuffed chair next to the couch. Holland gave him a big smile and a bright wave, then immediately set his face somberly again.

"You have to expect that, John. The news since Thursday hasn't been good for the campaign. . . . yes, yes, it doesn't look as if there is enough support for the postponement motion . . . LeClerc is a bag of wind. I haven't spoken to Elliott since before the funeral but I doubt he will resign . . . well, whatever happens, happens. . . . me? No matter what the outcome I'm leaving government service. I'll probably do what Pierre Salinger did and go over to the other side, become a high-paid commentator for one of the networks. Listen, John, I really have to go now, thanks for calling, and keep in touch." He replaced the phone and turned to face Scott.

"Well, you certainly look well rested. You gave us a bit of a scare these past two days. I hope you have all the hostility out of your system now."

Ted lowered his head a bit, "Yes, David. Thank you for everything. The . . . my memory of these last few days is a jumbled mess . . . ever since I saw Jil on that slab in the morgue."

"Ted, I wish there was something comforting I could say, but no matter how hard people try at times like these there never is."

"I know . . . I understand."

Holland looked across the room at his wife who was still standing at the foot of the stairs. "Ellen, would you make me a double Scotch?" He turned to Ted. "I don't think you should have anything stronger than soda until the effects of the injection fully wear off."

"No, nothing, thank you. Maybe a cold glass of water."

Ellen departed to get the drinks and David looked at Ted.

"Do you feel up to hearing what's been going on?"

"Yes, I'd like that very much."

"Well for openers both Harris and Gallup now think it's anybody's race. . . ."

Monday, November 5

Public indignation about Elliott Benedict's affair with Sharon Franklin took several unusual forms around the country.

In Chicago church leaders called for his resignation from the race and staged prayer vigils for the well-being of the nation . . . San Francisco was the site of protest marches involving various groups who tied up traffic on the Golden Gate Bridge for nearly three hours . . . Sharon Franklin's network received several bomb threats at its New York offices . . . a former congressman from Georgia urged people to write-in the name of William Chandler as a hold-over president . . . and these actions were multiplied a thousand times over by letters to the editor and protests by individuals. A woman in Kansas was interviewed on the *Today Show* explaining that she was wearing a black armband to signify her disgust with politicians in general. By nightfall Monday there was hardly a piece of black cloth left anywhere in the country that hadn't been fashioned into a sign of protest.

Ted Scott was having dinner with David and Ellen Holland when the doorbell rang. It was Leona Crawford Gordon. As always she was particularly stunning yet underdressed. She moved across the room and greeted Ellen and Ted. David was a few paces behind her after having opened the door.

"How do you feel?" she asked Ted directly.

"A lot better, thank you."

"Leona, won't you join us? I can arrange another setting . . ."

She cut David short, "No, please, continue. Don't let me interrupt your dinner." She seated herself at an empty chair around the table. "I just wanted to come by and say a few things before I catch my plane for Boston. I've been trying to reach you at the number you gave me, the safe house, but . . ."

"Ted's been here with us these last few days," Ellen offered.

"Did you talk to Dick?" Ted asked her then turned to Holland, "David, have you heard from him?"

"No, Ted, I haven't heard nor seen him all week."

"Leona?" Ted turned back to her.

"That's what I was starting to say. There was no answer at the number. I had one of my people go out there on Sunday but the house was empty. There was nobody there."

Ted buried his head in his hands, his elbows resting on the table. "Oh my God, they got him too!"

"Now Ted, don't get all excited. We don't know that." Holland was afraid Ted would lose control again.

"No, please!" There was alarm in Leona's voice. "All I said is that there was no one there. I didn't mean to alarm any of you. I'm sorry." She paused and added, "I may have just called, and my assistant arrived when he was out, that's all."

Ted silently shook his head and slowly began picking at his food.

"Can we change the subject?" Holland suggested. He looked directly at Leona. "Well, Madam Congresswoman, there is a very good chance that by this time tomorrow night you will be the Vice President-elect of these United States." He offered a weak smile.

"It will be something of a hollow victory if it happens at all," Leona responded quietly. "Not this way, not with such a tragedy." Her voice broke on the last word.

David, Ted and Ellen looked at her. Her face was twisting in pain and tears were running down her cheeks.

The Holland's cook entered the room. "Excuse me, sir, but there is something on the radio about Sharon Franklin resigning from her television job."

David Holland sprang from his chair and quickly turned on the television.

He switched from one station to another, passing commercials, a movie, and a situation comedy until the screen filled with the somber face of Dwight Sandler.

". . . today from Aspen, Colorado. A video tape of

her remarks, made to our network affiliate there less than a half hour ago, has just arrived. Here, then is the first word this network, or the American people, have had concerning her relationship with the Vice President and future with the network."

Leona, Ted, and Ellen had been joined by the cook as they all huddled behind David watching the screen go blank for an instant then filling with the familiar face of Sharon Franklin. Despite the obvious stress she was under she managed to look poised and still beautiful.

"Since the unfortunate disclosure earlier this week that Elliott Benedict and I had been more than acquaintances and friends . . ."

"My God, she's admitting it!" Holland gulped.

". . . I have avoided making a public statement lest anything I say be used against him in the campaign. However, the demonstrations which began last evening and may have hit their zenith today, leave me no choice but to explain in all truthfulness how two mature adults were attracted to each other without regard to their positions or obligations to the public which they both served.

"For anyone to imply that there was anything sordid between me and Elliott is grossly unfair. We shared a mutual respect and admiration for each other and managed for an unbelievably long time to keep our feelings nothing more than a warm and strong friendship.

"I was extremely distraught when the news of Susan Benedict's death was given to me last week. We were not close friends but I admired her and had only the warmest feelings for her. I also felt a pain that she was unable to reconcile her marital differences with Elliott.

"These differences, and I can't emphasize this too strongly, existed in their marriage long before I entered the picture.

"That Elliott was able to find comfort and solace in

his relationship with me has been one of my life's great joys.

"As to why some people felt obliged to make our private lives public, and to do it when they knew it would have a devastating effect on the election, I can only suggest that jealousy, political ambition and other equally unsavory motives guided them.

"Brock Davis had been assigned to guard the Vice President ever since Elliott was elected to that office. On more than one occasion he thought he could compromise my position with Elliott by making improper advances, which I flatly rejected. For some reason, known only to himself, he believed I had told Elliott about it and as a result he would be asked to leave the Service. I had never mentioned anything that happened to the Vice President.

"His unbelievable statement that we might have had something to do with Susan Benedict's death doesn't deserve the dignity of a reply. The findings of the special inquiry that was conducted these past few days underscores that dramatically."

Sharon Franklin paused and looked down for a moment as if to collect her thoughts. No one in the Holland estate spoke.

"I hope in all earnestness that the American people will not let their private prejudices and personal moralities cloud their thought process when they cast their votes tomorrow.

"I firmly believe Elliott Benedict is capable of leading this great country and feel it would be a disastrous mistake for the voters to reject his candidacy because of the personal conflicts that caused two people to cling to each other in misbegotten love.

"As for my future plans, whatever the outcome of the election, I will be leaving the network and living abroad.

It is unlikely that the dreams and aspirations I once held so close to my heart can now ever be fulfilled.

"I have kept a daily diary these past several years and it will serve as the basis of a book I will write, but publish posthumously."

Her face remained frozen for a few seconds and then the screen faded to black again.

"Wow!" was the only thing anyone in the room said. It was uttered by the cook who immediately felt uncomfortable and left.

David Holland got up from the stooped position he had been in and faced the others.

"I think that does it, ladies and gentlemen. If there was any doubt left on the possibility of Elliott winning the election she just shot it down."

"I disagree," Ellen responded with a trace of indignation in her voice. "That took an extraordinary amount of courage. David, did you know the Benedicts had marriage problems?"

Holland looked sympathetically at his wife and realized that his efforts to protect their private life over the years and not disclose the confidences he was privy to had left her much more uninformed than people thought. She was totally unaware of the real reason Ted Scott was living with them or anything factual about the situation involving Jil's death.

"Ellen." He took her hand and began walking back to the table. "Let's just say that I knew more about Elliott's unfaithfulness than could be printed in a family newspaper."

"My goodness, David! Well, at least *you* worked for the President, not that man." She paused as he assisted her reseating at the table. Ted and Leona followed.

"David," Ellen again pressed, but she looked at Leona almost apologetically, "if the Benedicts were having . . .

problems, do you know if they shared the same bed-room?"

Her question caused Holland to catch his breath. Ted looked at David then at Leona who quickly shot a glance at both of them.

"No, dearest, they did not share the same bedroom . . . for quite some time."

"Well then," she continued, "I think the voters will just have to come to grips with what was a foregone conclusion: their future President was an active male who needed the companionship and affection he could only get from a woman who apparently loved him dearly."

"Ellen! How can you say that. . . . I never thought I'd hear you advocate philandering. I'm shocked!"

"It's not philandering, David. That's when people take advantage of the emotions of their partner. I think there may have been love between these two. I hope you don't mind my saying so, Congresswoman Gordon, but I don't think many people will hold this against Elliott at the polls tomorrow."

Leona Gordon was taken aback by Ellen's remarks. "I . . . I . . . don't know what to say. My upbringing taught me to frown on extra-marital sexual activity . . . I . . ."

Ted came to her rescue. "No, Mrs. Holland, I don't agree with you. Sharon's little talk tonight only confirms what has been said throughout America all week . . . that Elliott and Sharon have been carrying on at the expense of his wife for the last few years. If he wins the election you can bet she will make a hasty retreat from Europe or wherever she is going and be back here post-haste. BUT SHE'LL NEVER GET TO MARRY HIM! I'll see to that!" Ted slammed his fist on the table and rattled the fine crystal.

"Take it easy, Ted." David grabbed his arm.

"Calm down, everybody." Leona took control. "Mrs. Holland, I don't the American public will be as sympathetic as you are . . ."

Ellen interrupted, "But what about Franklin Roosevelt? He carried on, they say. And young John Kennedy? You've heard the stories about him. . . . and Eisenhower, they say he and his female chauffeur . . ."

"But those facts came out after they served in office, Ellen," Holland noted. "Elliott can't survive this kind of disgrace before the election."

Ellen thought for a moment then decided not to continue the argument. She had made her point and tomorrow would prove if she was right or wrong.

Tuesday, November 6 (Election Day)

Ted had just returned to the Holland estate after taking a morning drive to the safe house, in the company of two armed guards that David had provided.

The house was just as he had last seen it. There was no trace of Dick Reynolds.

As he entered the foyer Ellen Holland called to him from upstairs.

"Ted? Is that you? Congresswoman Gordon is on the phone from Boston. You can pick it up in the living room."

He walked through the marble arch and entered the smartly done room. The phone was on a gold-leafed desk behind a comfortable couch facing a fireplace.

"Hello, Leona, how's it going?"

"I don't know. The voters are turning out all over the country in record numbers. This election will probably set a new record. I tried to reach you earlier but you weren't home."

"I dropped by the house. Still no sign of Reynolds. I fear they got him. Christ, will this insanity ever end?"

"Look, don't worry about that." There was noise in the background and she covered the phone and apparently asked for some consideration. When she came back on it was much quieter.

"I want to ask you something important, Ted, but don't give me a quick answer. Think about it. This is a serious thing I'm about to say so listen good. Do you hear?"

"Yes Leona I hear you."

"Good. If things work out the way I think they are going to I'd like you to join my staff. Jim Hanlon will be the press secretary or special aide to the veep, whichever he chooses. I want you there to do the actual speach writing and handle the press when Jim isn't around. Will you at least consider it?"

There was a long silence while Ted collected his thoughts. He remembered his conversation with Jil when he told her he was getting out of government service, but things had changed now. He no longer thought about buying a small weekly paper and having a home in the suburbs somewhere. He could no longer fantasize about pulling into the driveway and seeing Jil at the doorway. He didn't see visions of children playing in the backyard on a swing set he hoped to build.

"I . . . I . . . it's not what I had in mind, Leona, it's . . ."

"I said don't give me an instant answer. This country is going to have to pull itself up by its bootstraps and recover from the most damaging political disaster it ever faced. It makes Watergate insignificant in its wake. We'll need you, Ted. You've been privileged to be close to the throne. You know what clicks and what doesn't with the media. Hanlon is good, otherwise he wouldn't be on my staff, but we need your inside experience. I realize this is an extraordinary request. No former press aide to an outgoing administration ever landed so high a job in the new administration of the opposition party but this isn't the time for party politics. If we win, and I think it looks pretty good up here in Boston, Virgil is going to name members of both parties to the Cabinet. I hate to use clichés but we've all got to pull together if the Republic is to survive this catastrophe. Please think about it, will you. I *need* you."

After some brief remarks that avoided any direct answer to her question Ted said goodbye and hung up the phone.

He walked around the Holland house for a few minutes lost in his thoughts then finally he went outside, into the shaded grounds that covered more than two acres behind the house.

As he walked among the trees and the rich earthy smell of growth filled his nostrils he thought about Leona's offer. It wasn't the way he had hoped his life would go but Jil was gone now and maybe it was time for a new beginning.

He walked deeper into the trees and came upon a stream he didn't know was there. Ted squatted down and let the cool water wash over his hands. He cupped them and lifted the refreshing liquid to his face, splashing it on.

Through the trees he could see the bright midday sun fighting to penetrate the protection of the leaves and smother the earth with its life-generating warmth. He stood up and watched its light flicker for several minutes then turned and headed back to the house.

He would accept Leona's offer, if she was elected.

That night after the polls closed the three networks, which in past elections accurately predicted the winner before all the tallies were in, found themselves unable to do it this time.

Millions of Americans sat transfixed before television sets across the country as the vote counting confirmed what Harris and Gallup had already known: it was anybody's race.

The first returns, from New York and Pennsylvania, gave Rutledge a slight lead. Then the numbers came in from Ohio, followed by a sprinkling of Southern states and something happened that had never previously occurred in a Presidential Election.

With more than two million votes counted Rutledge and Benedict were separated by less than one thousand. For the next three hours they remained neck and neck. Benedict would pull ahead, opening the lead to nearly twenty thousand but Rutledge would pass him and himself take a three thousand vote lead.

And so it went, all night and into the next morning. At three separate times the margin between them was less than one thousand votes.

More people had voted than in any other election in American history, an unbelievable 86 percent of those eligible, but it wasn't until fourteen hours after the polls closed that the nation learned who would be its chief executive for the next four years.

Benedict's lead had widened to a relatively comfortable thirteen thousand and had been holding that lead for the last hour. Then the last numbers from California came in. The Computer Control Center in Sacramento had malfunctioned early the previous evening so despite sporadic returns from the state the complete official tally was only now being recorded.

The digital readouts on the large monitors held the attention of all who had the fortitude to remain with the counting overnight. Numbers flashed, stopped. Benedict led Rutledge by barely nine thousand votes. Numbers flashed again, stopped. Rutledge was now ahead of Benedict by sixty-three hundred votes. Still another time flashing, the low hum of the giant machine and the kaleidoscope of light continued longer this time than previously.

The tension was building almost to a breaking point. The numbers were flashing so rapidly that they created a blur. Everyone knew that this time when they stopped they would indicate who the next President would be.

"Elliott, wake up." his campaign manager nudged the bottom of his shoe with an empty beer bottle. The hotel room was thick with smoke. Elliott Benedict pulled himself to an upright position on the couch and looked around the debris that was strewn about the place. He touched his face and felt the stubble of growth. He couldn't avoid the sour smell that his nostrils picked up no matter which way he turned his head. Finally he realized it was the total scent of smoke, hours-old food and stale beer.

He focussed his eyes on the television screen and saw the rapidly moving digits.

"Hey, you clowns! This is it. Get your asses over here. The campaign manager called to other staffers who were sprawled in various parts of the room in semi-conscious states. Just over a half dozen responded and huddled around the couch that Benedict was seated on.

The numbers didn't slow down, they simply came to an abrupt halt. There was total silence in the room as tired eyes and minds read the totals for Benedict and Rutledge.

"Holly shit!" someone behind the couch said.

More than one thousand miles away the same hypnotic spell kept Virgil Rutledge, his wife and some fifteen close friends and staffers glued to the large screen TV set especially set up in the home's finished recreation room.

In contrast to the hotel room where Elliott Benedict

received the news Virgil Rutledge was in the comfort of
his own home, surrounded by genuine friends and family.
Though tired, he had remained awake throughout the
long counting process.

He now stood before the screen with his hands planted
firmly on his hips. He had removed his jacket and tie
many hours ago. Virgil Rutledge watched the numbers
stop suddenly and here, as in the hotel room where
Benedict was, there was an uneasy silence.

Eyes quickly registered the Rutledge figures and then
took in the total for Benedict.

The difference was under twenty thousand votes.

There was an audible sigh from several people in the
room. It was a collective expression of relief that the
long and painful campaign was now really over.

Virgil Rutledge turned around and faced the group that
had gathered around him. His lips trembled and his eyes
filled. Slowly a tear began to run down his face.

Someone reached for a handkerchief and handed it to
him:

"Here, Mr. President."

EPILOGUE

The captain, sergeant, detective and police officers involved in the case surrounding Jil Baker's death all died in the line of duty within the first year after the incident. An extraordinary death toll for one precinct anywhere in the United States.

The bodies of two men were found in the remains of a plane crash in the Virginia hills nearly six weeks after the new administration took office. They were identified as Dr. Harold Lupo and F.B.I Agent Dick Reynolds.

On an overcast May morning, less than four months after she had taken the oath of office as the first woman Vice President of The United States, Leona Crawford Gordon learned that President Virgil Rutledge and his entire staff had been killed in the crash of Air Force One as it failed to make a landing at Patrick Air Force Base in Florida.

The new President took the oath of office aboard the yacht of recently appointed FBI Director Lucien Mitchell on which she was a weekend guest.

After some brief words concerning the great national tragedy that now engulfed the nation she added some personal comments about the staffers who perished with the President, including her recently appointed press aide Ted Scott and network news correspondent David Holland.

The boat she took the oath of office on was named Phoenix II.

Author's Afterword

The French port of St. Nazaire mentioned as the departure point for the fictional U-boat in this story is real. It *was* one of two French ports that remained in German hands until the end of the war. After the Allied landings at Normandy on 6 June 1944 and the subsequent breakout via St. Lo which followed, the Allies bypassed pockets of German resistance in their drive toward Paris and eventually the Rhine. St. Nazaire, and the other port, Lorient, served as havens for U-boats.

These two U-boat bases were the target of an American and English bomber raid in May 1943. More than 9,000 tons of bombs failed to destroy the U-boat pens' 22-foot roofs but did, however, cause considerable damage to the towns.

As noted in this novel, St. Nazaire remained in German hands and was capable of functioning as a hostile base until the capitulation of Nazi Germany in May, 1945.

U-boat 977's unbelievable journey, including sixty-six days under the sea, is also historical fact. Under the command of Captain Heinz Schaeffer, U-977 was the only unit of the former German Navy that was still at large long after the war ended.

Hostilities between the Allies and Axis powers ended

on 8 May, 1945. U-977 did not surrender until 17 August, more than three months later, at Buenos Aires, Argentina. Newspapers around the world immediately speculated that U-977 had carried Hitler and other high ranking Nazis to safety.

Captain Schaeffer was turned over to the Americans who put him in a prisoner of war camp in Washington where he was among important and high-ranking German officers. During a series of interrogations he was continually asked who, besides Hitler, he carried on U-977.

Eventually the U.S. Supreme Command decided to ship Schaeffer back to Germany to be repatriated. Upon arriving in Antwerp, Belgium, he was, however, held prisoner by the British. They also quizzed him about being Hitler's escape ship. Scheaffer continued to deny having carried anyone other than his normal ship's crew. Unable to break him, the British permitted Schaeffer to return to Germany.

He left to return to Argentina and make his home there after a book by Ladislas Szabo, *Hitler Is Alive*, was published and included photographs of the U-977, Hitler and Eva Braun and a girl with two children who "looked very like Hitler." The book charged that the U-977 was their escape ship.

Schaeffer wrote his own account of the journey of U-977, which was published in the U.S. by W. W. Norton & Co. in 1953.

In November, 1981 the British Medical Association published the findings of a ten-year study on the World War II records of Adolf Hitler and Eva Braun, including dental evidence by a California research team that casts doubt on her death.

According to the report, Hitler's dental records match those of one of the thirteen bodies found near the bunker in Berlin on 26 points, including a unique window crown.

However, the odontological data for the female body

presumed to be Eva Braun's does not agree with her personal records. The report points to the possibility that she may have escaped.

In 1945, the U.S. Army released a photo of Hitler and Eva Braun with a child named Uschi who was thought to have been Hitler's daughter.

It was this assortment of facts that led me to write this novel.

Timothy B. Benford